CHAMELEON
GIRL

LIZ FERRO

LIBRARY TALES PUBLISHING
www.LibraryTalesPublishing.com
www.Facebook.com/LibraryTalesPublishing

Copyright © 2021 by Liz Ferro
All Rights Reserved
ISBN:978-1736241837
Published in New York, New York.

No part of this publication may be reproduced, stored in a retrieval system, or transmitted in any form or by any means, electronic, mechanical, photocopying, recording, scanning, or otherwise, except as permitted under Sections 107 or 108 of the 1976 United States Copyright Act, without the prior written permission of the Publisher. Requests to the Publisher for permission should be addressed to the Legal Department: Legal@LibraryTales.com

Trademarks: Library Tales Publishing, Library Tales, the Library Tales Publishing logo, and related trade dress are trademarks or registered trademarks of Library Tales Publishing and/or its affiliates in the United States and other countries, and may not be used without written permission. All other trademarks are the property of their respective owners.

For general information on our other products and services, please contact our Customer Care Department at 1-800-754-5016, or fax 917-463-0892. For technical support, please visit www.LibraryTalesPublishing.com

Library Tales Publishing also publishes its books in a variety of electronic formats. Every content that appears in print is available in electronic books.

PRINTED IN THE UNITED STATES OF AMERICA

For Jake, Morgan, and Frank

1

If you could look at someone and see exactly who they really were, would that be a good thing or a bad thing? Would the world be a better place if you couldn't hide the real you? I'm not talking about using a filter on Snapchat, or making your life seem more exciting than it really is on Facebook or Instagram. I'm talking about honest to God transparency. I look at people and wonder how they would act if everyone could see the real, unedited, unadulterated versions of themselves. I wonder if my shit excuse for a mother would have done what she did. And I wonder how people would react to me if they could see through my carefully crafted shell.

Nathan's sharp nibble on my nipple brings me back to his sweaty sheets. For once, I'm spending the night, but I'm not sure the second act is worth cutting into my morning routine. His fucking sincerity sometimes messes with my head, and I toy with returning his gaze and letting him see who I really am. Instead, I stare at the ceiling and try to bring my body into the present for a moment or two.

I can't help but think that when I'm walking down the street on a beautiful fall day, and a squirrel stops dead in its tracks on a fat tree trunk to lock eyes with me, that he can in fact see right through me. It's his condescending tilt of the head and the way he chirps at me that makes me feel like he sees the real me, and that I'm not fooling anyone with my façade.

What is it about the way a squirrel looks at me that makes me feel guilty of something horrible and dirty?

I have the answer to my own question but shake it off, as I shouldn't be thinking about any of this right now, not while poor Nathan is trying his absolute best to satisfy me—and yet here I am thinking about the realness of squirrels and the fakeness of humans. A squirrel's eyes boring into my soul, and a man boring me with his cock. The story of my life.

"Is that good? Do you like that?" he whispers. For a nanosecond, I consider telling him the truth. But I know this will be the last time I allow myself to do him, so why spoil it? So as not to lie, necessarily, but to also remain somewhat non-committal, I respond with a throaty, drawn-out "uhhhhh" as I look forward to heating up my leftover Chinese when I get home and try to decide what I'll watch on Netflix while I'm eating it.

He lets out a heavy moan and rolls off. We lay there and stare up at the ceiling, Nathan panting like he's just run a 5K race. I'm as silent as a crop duster fart.

"Are you okay, Nora?"

He props himself up on his elbow to look at me, but I don't meet his puppy dog eyes, and I thank God that I'm more of a cat person.

"Nathan, you are such a great guy. You deserve a real relationship, and frankly, hooking up with me is going to keep you from finding the person and the happiness you truly deserve."

He breathes out, slow and heavy. The inferred exasperation strengthens my resolve to break it off for good and makes me feel like I can't get out of there fast enough.

"That's a load of shit and you know it, Nora," he says. "You run so hot and cold. I try to understand the stop and go of our relationship, because I like you so much, but it's hard to keep up."

"Nathan, speaking of running, I have to get up in a few hours to do just that, so I don't think psychoanalyzing me or romanticizing what we have is a good use of our time right now. It is what it is," I say flatly.

I hate those stupid relationship clichés and feel angry at

myself for using one. God, I'm a real asshole sometimes.

"You never want to talk about anything. One minute you get pissed at me for wanting to know you, and the next you want to be as close to me as possible. I have honestly never met anyone like you," he said, "and that's, frankly, both good and bad."

I start to feel blood rush to my ears. That's never a good sign. I have to push back my frustration and anger when I say, "Just because I want to fuck the shit out of you doesn't mean I want you to know me. The two things aren't mutually inclusive, Nathan. Maybe I just want you to make me think I'm somebody else for a while or—at the very least—forget that I'm me."

He tells me that my warmth is like the orange and red swirls you see behind your eyelids when you shut your eyes and tilt your head towards the sun. It's like laying on the beach on a gorgeous day and feeling the heat of the sand lull you into paradise. He goes on to explain, in painstaking detail, that when I turn that warmth off, the shade I cast is colder than Siberia. He says it's a horrible place that he never thinks he'll survive or go back to...until the next time.

"Jesus, Nathan...seriously? Grow a sack," I spit. "Ya know how people and memes and all that stupid shit you see in self-help books always say, 'Do more of what makes your soul happy'?"

"Yeah?" he mutters.

"Well, that's one of the reasons why I'm not on any social media. I fucking hate Fakebook. Oh sorry...I mean, Facebook! And second of all—if I'm supposed to do more of what makes me happy, then why does society want to punish me when that's exactly what I'm trying to fucking do? Just because it doesn't fit into the stereotypical ways that a woman is supposed to find happiness?!"

I could feel that I was getting away from myself, but I kept on going anyway.

"If I want to be happy—or try to be—and I want to feel good once in a while, then *doing you* is what makes my soul sing, or however that flowery, vomit-inducing expression goes. If we aren't supposed to take those sayings to heart, or heed their life-changing advice, then why the fuck are they so trendy and popular and emblazoned on every knick-knack, Hallmark card, and wine glass for the female population's consumption?!"

I was almost out of breath as this barrage of lunacy tumbled from my lips, accompanied by plenty of my spittle that blended with the newly sweat-soaked sheets. If I didn't know better, I would have confused the angry, burning sensation behind my eyeballs with impending fat droplets of tears, but I don't cry.

I could hear genuine hurt in his voice when he said, "So I'm some kind of sex toy to you, that you take out whenever you're horny—and put me away when you're done?"

Guys do it all the time. Why can't a woman use a man as a tool?" was my quick retort.

"'A tool?' Fuck, Nora, that's cold, even for you."

"Oh, grow up, Nathan. We're all tools for something. If it makes you feel any better...I can be a tool too. Here...I'm a hoe for your secret garden." A glimpse of my little bag of tricks flashes in my mind, and then goes out just as quickly.

I try to go down on him, while laughing in my expertly smart-ass way, but he pushes me away.

"Cut it out, Nor. This isn't fuckin' funny." Then with more pain in his voice than I expect, or want, to hear, he says, "So, you don't want to see me anymore? Can we still talk?"

"Um, hello?! We're neighbors! I see you all the time, and I really do consider you to be a friend. I care about you, Nathan, I just don't think we should fuck anymore."

"Yikes. Okay. None of that makes any sense to me, but since you pride yourself on not being easy to figure out...I suppose this is all par for the course." He runs his hand through his gorgeous black hair and says sheepishly, "I thought women were always bitchin' that guys don't open up. I'm a fuckin' open book, and here you are getting pissed at me for it. I just don't get it."

"I rarely make sense to myself—so consider this as me doing you a huge favor. In the long run, I swear, you will be glad you didn't get any more tangled up in my shit."

"Well, of course I'll respect your decision, but I hope you

know how much I care about you, Nora, and that you can always count on me if you need me. Even if it's just for a shot of vitamin D." He flashes that megawatt grin of his that immediately shoots what feels like an electrical current straight to my clit.

"Hey—look at you trying to be funny! Good one!" is all I can come up with. My brain is otherwise occupied with thoughts of spending the rest of the night in bed with him, or maybe even shooting back to my apartment for my bag of tricks as a parting gift.

"But seriously, I'm here for you, even if I can't figure out what's going on in your head or your heart," he says earnestly.

I jump out of bed and yank on my clothes, then storm out the door yelling, a little too roughly, "Did it ever occur to you that it's not your job to figure me out?!" I use the slamming of the door behind me as my personal exclamation point, and immediately regret it.

About ten minutes after I get back to my own apartment, I receive a text from him saying, *Don't forget that I love Chaos...the cat. I still want to watch her when you're on OT at the house.*

I shoot back a smiley face and thumbs-up emoji. I almost send a heart as well, but delete it, not wanting to send the wrong message.

*   *   *

Ever since then—it's about three weeks after that last 'last time'—for me anyway—our relationship has been strained, but we will probably always be friends with benefits, at the very least. I don't know; it's so dumb to describe it this way, but it truly is complicated. I know, deep down, he loves me, but he knows I will never concede to a real relationship: whatever that really is. I just can't do it, and I can't tell him why. The reasons go far beyond my gypsy heart and bohemian soul. Sure, those parts of me are real, but there is much more behind the mask that I can't show anyone. I live with a malignant fear that one day I will come face to face with a person who will see me for who I really am—no matter how hard I try to hide it.

So instead of being my boyfriend or lover, Nate has sort of taken on the role as caregiver...providing whatever form of care might be needed at the time. He helps me with the cat when I'm working and thrives on giving me shit for any men (or women) who he sees come and go from my place. If he catches me rolling in at noon with racoon eyes, he hounds me about it for days. I like to pretend I don't like it and that he's a freaking weirdo who should mind his own business, but truth be told, he makes me feel calm, and that's a priceless thing in my world.

I'm sitting on the kitchen counter waiting for the kettle to let out its high-pitched whistle, letting me know it's time for tea, reminding me of the old *Flintstones* cartoon I watch sometimes on YouTube. The squawk of the boiling kettle brings to mind Fred Flintstone's quitting time at the Slate Rock and Gravel Company, where he works as a brontosaurus crane operator, and where a dude pulls a string attached to a pterodactyl's tail, causing it to let out a freight train scream, signaling the end of the work day. I love the joy and excitement Fred exudes as he slides down the tail of the dinosaur he's working on, so he can bolt out of there.

Sometimes, when guys at the firehouse practically run out the door at the end of their shift, we call them Fred Flintstone, or yell "Yabba Dabba Doo!" as they hightail it out the door. I get a big kick out of it and enjoy the camaraderie... even though the older guys give me shit for being too young to know the show when it was actually on regular TV.

As I rifle through my collection of teas, trying to both decide what I'm in the mood for and why on earth I even have so many different boxes of tea, I get a text from Nathan that simply says, *Hey*.

I look at it for a heartbeat longer than I need to and respond, *Hey* and then *What's up?*

Not much

What r u doing?

I tell him I'm good and that I was thinking of doing some painting.

He asks me, *What r u working on?*

I say, *Nothing, really*

Just putting paint on canvas because it makes me feel good

And then I add,

You can come up and hang out if you wanna

He answers, *What do you wanna do? Is this going to be PG or X?*

I sit back for a moment and watch my tea bag steep, then answer,

Don't be a dick

Just come up if you want

Nathan answers with,

K

U gonna freak like last time?

I shake my head with a smile as I type,

It's worth the risk

We always make up again

But I'm a freak

Can't help it

He responds,

I love that u r a freak

Lol

Be up in ten

I hop off the counter and throw the tea bag into the sink. It's still too hot to drink, so I just hold the mug close to my nose so I can simultaneously take in the lovely scent of hibiscus and give myself a 'poor man's facial' with the steam.

Chaos is curled up peacefully on the stool in front of my easel but is startled when she hears Nathan knock at the door. Her ears pin back, and her eyes become comically large and round, bringing to my mind, again, all the cartoons I watch. I make a mental note to try to crank up the sophistication level of the shows and movies I choose.

I swing the door open and Nathan is standing there in his usual worn-out Corrosion of Conformity concert T-shirt and low-riding, faded Indigo jeans. His hair is the perfect ratio of styled and bedhead, and his lopsided grin is, well, adorable. He's barefoot and has a bottle of Bulleit Bourbon in his hand.

He looks at my mug of tea and howls with laughter.

"Um, whatchya got there, Gladys?"

"Shut up," is my witty retort of choice as I step back and wave him in. "It's 4:00 on Tuesday, ya know."

"As if that has stopped you before," he says as he makes his way past me, hesitating briefly to peer into my mug. "You can put some in that tea, or dump it out and we can start over properly with the bourbon and some ice. Are you off tomorrow, or do I need to check in on the little monster for you?"

Chaos jumps from the stool as if she knows he's talking about her and runs to greet him by winding around his legs in a figure eight. He hands me the bottle and bends down to pick her up. She immediately starts to drum out a rhythmic purr that actually makes my heart skip a beat.

"No, I'm off the next twenty-four."

I watch the two of them for a few seconds and say, "It never ceases to amaze me how much she loves you."

"Of course she does. We're buds." He hooks his hands under her little arms and holds her up to his face and says, "Aren't we, Chaos?" She has always been excellent at comedic timing and responds as if on cue with a long, drawn-out meow.

"I think your mama is jealous or something," he jokes as he playfully rubs his face into the top of her head in-between her ears. She rubs her face on his chin and then tries to headbutt him.

"Do you two want to be alone?" I tease as I take the bottle into the kitchen.

He sets Chaos down and follows my lead. I dump my tea in the sink and watch it pool around the used tea bag that has somehow changed in appearance from comforting to pathetic, just lying there in a heap on the cold steel near the drain.

"Fuck it," I say as I look over my shoulder and eye Nathan like he's a gazelle and I'm a hungry lioness. "I'll get the glasses; you get the ice."

He immediately heads for the freezer with an, "Atta girl!"

2

My fifth-grade math teacher, Mr. Gibbons, stood in front of the class and droned on about how to use problem-solving strategies for real-world math problems. I tried to focus on what he was saying, but I had already mastered advanced algebra, rendering word problems a joke. Instead of listening to him, I argued with myself as to whether his horrible excuse for a button-down shirt looked more like a dollar-store tablecloth or a Hobbit's cloak. And really, not even Albert Einstein himself would have been able to come up with a theory to solve *my* real-world problems.

When I raised my hand to ask if I could go to the bathroom, he chose to ignore me for a good ten minutes, so I put it back down again. I hated the burning feeling that crept around my neck and chest when I thought the other kids were looking at me with my hand in the air, snickering at the fact that even the teacher thinks I'm a weirdo who should be overlooked.

Mr. Gibbons asked Lauren Kirk, one of the popular girls in the class, to get up and pass out the word problem worksheets, and he told everyone else to take out their pencils in preparation to work independently. He then, almost triumphantly, sat behind his desk and peeled an orange.

Everyone was handed a paper except for me. The smell of the orange peel brought a rush of one of Momzilla's punish 'til I puke sessions to my mind so vividly that I was able to taste the bitter rind in the back of my throat. I felt like I might barf and did everything I could to keep that from happening, putting my hands over my mouth and nose to block out the smell.

As Lauren approached my desk, and saw the repulsion on my face, she immediately thought I was feigning that *she* was making me sick, and her anger towards me flared ugly and red—like a baboon's ass. She rushed over to my desk at a speed that seemed inhuman, and just before she turned on her heel and huffed off, she hissed, "I don't know who you think you are, Nora Horvath, but you'd be lucky to look or smell like me, so cut the shit, douchebagette."

The rest of the class was working quietly as I raised my hand to let Mr. Gibbons know that I hadn't been given a worksheet. He came over to me, begrudgingly, but when I looked up at him, his face registered a look of concern, as opposed to his usual apathetic expression of a teacher who should have retired years ago. He reached for my face delicately and said, "Nora, you have something on your eye. Hold still."

I felt his fingers gently grasp my eyelashes, and in what seemed like a video using high-speed footage to condense a lengthy scene into superfast, bite-sized clips, my eyelashes were yanked from my face over and over again, and every single one became a nasty, wriggling centipede before it hit the floor. Mr. Gibbons continued to pull out my lashes out in large amounts, the residual orange peel stink still fresh on his fingertips.

The insects rained down like hailstones, completely covering my desk and lap. Jaw-like antennae, disgusting mouth parts, as well as tiny, venomous claws began to protrude from the corners of my eyes and wiggle their way out from under my upper and lower eyelids. I couldn't blink, and I froze in a horrified, pie-eyed expression as he ripped the nasty creatures from my eyes. I cried centipedes as I screamed and tried to stand up, but I couldn't use my legs. In a frenzied panic, my eyes darted around the room, and I saw that the classroom had become our basement playroom, but all the desks were now giant, white porcelain toilets. None of the other kids seemed to be afraid, and everyone was sitting on one, as if it wasn't unusual to have a toilet instead of a desk.

Mr. Gibbons was at the front of the class again, but this

time he called on me to come forward to solve the problem on the SMART Board. I looked around the room and noticed that somehow my desk, or throne or shitter, was now in the center of the class, and all the others were arranged in a half circle that faced me.

I looked down and saw that I was stone cold naked, yet everyone else in the room was fully clothed. A sense of dread and terror which kept me from standing overtook my body. Everyone's eyes were on me as my seat started to vibrate and rumble. The overhead fluorescent lights were unusually intense and bright, and they made the faces of all the kids look like white, waxen statues. Like creepy, perfectly assembled mannequins, each child sat frozen with the same expression of open-mouthed smiles and giant eyes.

I felt like I was going to pass out, and that's when the explosion happened. My toilet, and my toilet alone, erupted with a geyser of wretched vermin. In a matter of seconds, hundreds of dark brown, mucky, screeching rodents covered the floor and climbed the walls of the classroom. They were everywhere, feverishly scratching their way up pant legs and under skirts. The screams of the children were the only thing that could drown out the high-pitched squealing created by the infestation. They filled the room so quickly, we were drowning in a sea of mice and rats.

I bolted straight up in my bed, screaming and tearing at my face and chest from the reality of the nightmare. I was thoroughly drenched in sweat, and the sheet-free mattress I shared with Omzi looked like someone had just dumped a bucket of water on it. The commotion startled her out of her sleep with an ugly snort, angered that I woke her at 3:00 a.m. The look in her eyes was horrifying, and she was so riddled with rage she didn't even use an old-timey saying on me. I could almost see the yellow of her eyes glowing in the dark, like the monster's eyes do in every scary movie I've ever seen.

She yanked me by the arm and yelled at me while she dragged me out of bed in what can only be described as a hissy fit. I was pulled, sweaty, scared, and naked, down into the basement, where she beat me in the playroom with a hard-soled Dr. Scholl's clog. I wished like hell that I were back in my nightmare, because being locked in the playroom with the real mice and insects was way worse than anything Freddie Krueger could ever dish out.

I begged her to let me go back to bed, but that only made it worse.

It was early on Saturday morning, so she left me there for the weekend. I drank the dirty water in the laundry buckets and cried enough tears to fill them back up again. My legs, chest, and stomach were raw with bloody scratches made by the mice while I slept and made by me when I was awake.

When Omzi let me out, she unlocked the door, opened it, and simply turned and walked away without saying a word. I slowly got up and made my way up the stairs, to find all my stuffed animals hanging from their own homemade nooses. I should have expected it, really, but I just stood there, completely overcome with exhaustion and sadness. I didn't have any tears left to cry, which was a good thing, because it would have "gotten my mom's goat" if I had. She looked at me and said, "We are born crying, live complaining, and die disappointed. I don't know who originally said that one, Nora, but you best believe it's the truth."

It was exactly at that moment that I decided I would no longer live in a waking nightmare of fear and pain.

I was going to run.

3

Chameleons are known to change their colors depending on their mood, and so they can blend into any environment to protect themselves. When I was little, I used to think that maybe I was born a chameleon, straight out of an egg: a silly delusion that probably stemmed, in part, from a desire to feel better about—and understand—the actual way I was brought into this world, and the motivation behind it.

Over time, and out of necessity, I learned just how crucial blending into the scenery was, for a variety of reasons, the greatest of which was to stay off my mother's radar as much as possible. My mother may not have given me many things, but she was never short on dispensing her own unique brand of hard knocks knowledge. She told me over and over again that there is great power in remaining unseen. When you can remain invisible while in plain sight, you hold great power over those who stand out and demand attention. Camouflage is needed for survival, and not just in the wild. It's a skill that I have honed over the years and learned from the best: my mother—Ms. Eleanor Horvath. People who saw us around town usually called her Ellie.

Ellie looked like your typical mom for the area of Upstate New York in which we lived. To the naked eye, nothing stood out about her, and she wasn't too much of anything in par-ticular—which is exactly how she wanted it. From what I've heard, she looked very different before she had me. Ellie has always intentionally based her appearance on what she specifically wants or needs from the people or the environment around her. So, although this wasn't always the case, the Ellie I have always known is a straight-up soap and water, no-make-up kind of gal. And, if I'm being honest, she truly didn't need makeup of any kind. She wore baggy jeans and sweatshirts, or big boxy T-shirts—all from thrift shops. Ellie was notoriously cheap and absolutely refused to buy our clothes anywhere else.

She was medium height, with a decent mom bod that looked like she took walks at the mall and did housework and gardening, but certainly no one was going to mistake her for a gym rat. Her straight, dirty blonde hair was shoulder length and was often pulled back in a clip or low ponytail. Even though she had classically beautiful bone structure, big, deep green eyes, and almost alabaster skin, she was rarely looked at twice. The moms who I suppose were considered attractive in our town were a lot flashier, with big hair, super loud makeup and perfume that kind of made me want to puke. They flocked together in front of the school or library, and my mother always pointed out how they looked and sounded like loud, squawking birds. I thought they looked pretty, in an awkward sort of way, like a bunch of flamingos. When I saw them, I couldn't help but wonder what it would be like to have a flamingo as a mother instead of a monster.

Ellie was only monstrous to me and may as well have been invisible to everyone around us. After all, she was Queen of Chameleonland. If people did consider her at all, it was most likely as an eccentric, earthy, crunchy, granola type—and they probably assumed she took good care of her only daughter. That would be me, Nora Horvath, the evil spawn of Ellie dearest.

I mean, the way I see it, I must be evil, since I was created by design directly from it. Even her name was a disguise of sorts. I never felt like it suited her, because Ellie sounds like a name for a kind-hearted, happy person. And the title of Mother doesn't work either, because shouldn't it be earned by some of the most basic of motherly qualities or duties, like, oh, I don't know, love and care?

This woman needed—no, deserved—her own special name. And like some sort of sign from the Universe, around the time that I was trying to come up with the perfect name for her, I came across piles of old comic books amongst the mountains of trash that filled our house. The once brightly colored covers of each slim, flimsy book were now worn, torn, and faded, but the intrigue and excitement of them remained bold and bright in my eyes. I sat down and began voraciously reading them all. I tried to find a spot to sit while I read, and as I wriggled my butt down into a tight, empty spot against the wall, I accidentally knocked over a huge stack. Dust and comic books flowed around me, but one in particular stuck out. It had Godzilla vs. King Kong on the cover, and I picked it up and flipped through its worn, sticky pages. What was that anyway? Old banana peel? Spilled juice? Whatever the heck was on the slightly sketchy pages, it didn't keep me from laughing to myself as I noticed the strong resemblance between my mother and the giant, destructive lizard. (Who pissed in his Lizard Wheaties to make him so mad, anyway?)

I felt that if I had my own personal nickname for her, it would somehow make me feel better when I was feeling the brunt of her anger, and also help me feel like I had something of my own that no one could strip from me. I figured if I called her Godzilla in my head, it would help me get through a lot of painful times. But I couldn't quite stomach the thought of giving her a moniker with any inkling of a deity status—whether I believed in one or not. So, in my childish mind, Momzilla (Omzi for short) seemed perfectly appropriate, since her sole purpose for becoming a mom in the first place was literally to be the ultimate monster and queen of destruction, both which she lived up to with distinction.

Sadly, in many ways, the story of my childhood isn't all that unique, but the need to know why it happened in the first place tends to gnaw away at a person the way a mouse chews relentlessly at the corner of a box of rice in a cupboard. I guess if people feel like they understand the reasons behind crappy behavior and the ugly things in life, it makes those things slightly easier to stomach. As humans, we seem to possess the need to answer the heavy-hitting question—*why*?

I will do my best to help make Omzi's repulsive behavior as palatable as possible, but be advised, if you have a weak constitution, you may want to stop here. Believe me, I would completely understand if you turned around and never looked back, but if you continue on, please don't say I didn't warn you. A lot of the stuff I'm going to tell you will help you understand a *little,* but it will also wrench your heart and turn your stomach a *lot.* But my main objective in life is to break the cycle that has brought me here in the first place. So, if you can choke down some of the really bitter and unsavory parts, I think you might actually be inspired—or maybe just disgusted and petrified. That's up to you.

Ellie Horvath was raised in Utica, a city of 60,000 people in the middle of New York State, in a big, old, yellow house. Yellow is supposed to be a happy color that conjures thoughts of warm, sunny days, sickly-sweet, ice-cold lemonade, and pinwheels spinning in the breeze. It's the color of a soft, warm sweater, or the apron that a sweet, chubby grandma would wear while rolling out dough for cut-out cookies.

The color of my mother's house, and the seemingly toxic, hazy air around it, however, reminds me of the stages a healing bruise displays—funny shades of yellow and green, like gasoline mixed up in a puddle. It's the color of bile, or the nicotine stains on Omzi's fingers.

When she is angry and tired, which seemed to be most of the time, yellow is also the color of her eyes where the white parts are supposed to be. Like Omzi's eyes, some of my memories about her childhood (and my own, for that matter) are unclear and fuzzy. I am prone to terrifying nightmares that are so exceedingly vivid I often confuse them for reality.

However, because I was beyond my age intellectually, and was an expert at fading into the background, I learned snippets about myself and Omzi from counselors, court staff, lawyers, case workers, foster parents, and social workers at Children's Services. If you are a truly talented chameleon, adults tend to forget that you're there, and they spill all kinds of beans in your presence. The fact that Omzi herself was a bit of an over-sharer, especially when she was drunk or high, which was pretty much all the time, meant that she provided a running commentary about her life. But, like my nightmares, it was hard to tell what was true and what wasn't.

I guess because she didn't have any real friends, she often rambled on about herself and her "shitty childhood" out loud to herself, which, unfortunately, made me a captive audience. It was like she was the star of her own one-woman shit-show. I learned at an early age that no matter how you're raised, there are just some things you don't ever want to know about your own mom, but I think Omzi took joy in the fact that I didn't want to hear what she had to say.

Now by no means have I come close to ever getting the full story, but over the years I was able to discover tiny shards of information that I have glued together to create a mosaic version of myself, helping me piece together the parts I want to see and remember. I read in a book once that women are considered to be mosaics because we have a mixture of two very different types of cells in our bodies, and men only have one. It was a great comfort and relief to learn that all women are mosaics, and it wasn't just me.

There are still some memories I consider to be forbidden, because they're way too painful to bring to the forefront of my mind. I know they exist, are alive and in living color, but there are barriers that I have built around them for my protection. They are my brain's version of firewalls. Once in a while, when I try to get too close to them, it feels like I touched an electric fence, or a hot stove, and the jolt is enough to ward me off again.

When Ellie Horvath was a kid, she was what people back then referred to as a ragamuffin. I remember that word because it's supposed to be a negative description of a dirty, crappy-ass kid, but it includes the word muffin, which, for me, conjures pleasant images of cupcakes, muffins, and perhaps melted butter or sprinkles.

Omzi told me that she stayed on the streets more than she did at home because her parents didn't care where she was, and it was a good way to escape her shit-brown home life. She never had clothes that fit and was usually smelly and dirty. From what she told me, she tried to get kids in her neighborhood to let her eat dinner or sleep over at their houses. Most times the answer was no, because people saw her and her family as trouble and didn't want any part of it.

When her father, Bill, was at home, he was angry and violently abusive to her mother, Susan. It was an everyday occurrence for Omzi to witness Bill ruthlessly abusing his wife, both verbally and physically.

After a couple shots of Jack Daniels, Omzi would often recount 'Billy the Bruiser' stories. She often spoke of the way her father would beat her mother if she left the house without him, or if dinner wasn't ready when he got home—and how it didn't matter that he came home at all hours.

The story I heard most often happened one breezy but warm June evening. It was Bill and Susan's wedding anniversary, so my grandma brushed the dust off a pair of high heels, donned a crisp, navy blue and white, lowcut summer dress, and did her hair and makeup in hopes of pleasantly surprising her husband. She worked all afternoon on a feast fit for a king and made absolutely sure not to break a sweat or smear her lipstick while she did it.

According to Omzi, who never said a nice word about anything her mother did...everything was perfect. The rolls were browning in the oven when her father came home with eyes overcast with clouds of gin and a smile that made his teeth gleam like a lighthouse.

He walked in, took one look at Susan, and told her furiously that she looked like a slut. After pushing her out of the way, he strode into the kitchen and lifted the lid from the roasting pan. With dirty fingers, he ripped free a hunk of meat, like an eagle using its talons to tear into its prey. A sultry breeze from the open window slow-danced with the delicious aroma of the roast. Juice dribbled from both my grandfather's hand and his chin, but he viciously told my grandmother that the meat was dry and tasted like a number two pencil. He grabbed her by the back of the neck and shoved it in her face so she could see how "overdone" it was. He demanded she take *her* overdone ass in the bedroom and put on more respectable clothes.

Susan did as she was told, but when she returned to the kitchen, she was met with the smell of burning dinner rolls. Bill went into a rage over the stench of the crescent-shaped charcoal bricks and slammed her into the kitchen wall, causing her beloved cuckoo clock to fly off the wall and smash on the ground. He then took the hot rolls and threw them at her one at a time—each one carrying its own insult. And since you can't have bread without dipping it in a little gravy, he poured that all over the floor for good measure, then he told her to clean up the mess and stormed out of the house.

He was an extra mean drunk, but at least when he drank there was also great possibility of his passing out, which kept him out of Omzi's room at night. I guess my grandma was too afraid to stand up to him, and so she allowed my grandpa to sexually abuse Omzi on a regular basis, but I don't know that for sure. Omzi said it was because both her parents were pieces of shit, which is why she ran away from home when she was seventeen and ended up in Niagara Falls.

Omzi told me she had an obsession with Niagara Falls that started when she was a kid in third or fourth grade after learning it was on a list for being a Wonder of the World. Anything that was dubbed a Wonder of the World immediately had Omzi's attention, and her intrigue with it simply grew from there. She told me that she constantly thought about running away to Niagara Falls, and figured she could work on the Maid of the Mist, which is a boat that takes tourists in bright yellow rain gear for a ride around the Falls.

These stories often stunk of booze, cigarettes, and maybe a little improv, but she did end up there, and, at first, landed a job as a waitress at the Niagara Falls Convention and Civic Center. She said she made pretty decent money working the events at the Convention Center, (and she didn't spend a dime on anything that she didn't absolutely have to), but the money was only part of the reason she chose to work there.

Omzi liked to control things. She controlled how much food she allowed herself to eat, how much money she spent and saved, and every other aspect of her life that she could. She had my grandpa's anger, but it was more than that. She was what I have heard people describe as a psychopath. She had a sadistic side to her that couldn't be sated by simply controlling things like money, food, and her lovers. She craved something more, something or someone that would be hers and hers alone, that she could control and abuse in any manner of her choosing, and at all times.

When the adults around me tried to describe Omzi in a polite or professional way, they would say she was mentally ill, but in an evil way that even medicine couldn't fix. It has been explained to me several times, by a variety of sources, that she wanted to unleash a wrath of controlled abuse and terror on a person that she had full access to, and who she believed couldn't resist her maltreatment. All of the information that I pieced together about Omzi from counselors I have had to see over the years to help me cope and move forward, as well as the American Psychiatric Association's *Diagnostic and Statistical Manual of Mental Disorders*, was nothing compared to what Omzi told me herself, usually just before passing out on filthy bed sheets littered with clothes, magazines, and empty Jack Daniels bottles.

Using her place of employment as a hunting ground for potential sperm donors became a sport that brought her a great sense of joy and purpose in addition to a paycheck, until it also ended up being the cause of getting her fired. She unabashedly called the idea brilliant (since she saw nothing wrong with it) and fully admitted to securing the job for easy access to the hundreds of professional men (or candidates) in town for a conference or convention in their respective fields. Many of them were far away from home and, when they weren't attending boring meetings concerning the latest technical or scientific developments or current status in medicine, law, or academia, were ready to play.

Back then, Omzi blended into the environment by coloring her hair honey blonde and wearing heavy makeup to highlight her best features. She wore black stockings and high heels and poured coffee…just like all the other women who worked there. But Omzi wore her skirt a bit shorter and held men's gazes a lot longer than anyone else, which is why they often gave her their room key. She reveled in the fact that she could control notable men who were held in such high regard for their intellect and abilities. The sexual pleasure meant nothing to her in these scenarios and was no match, as her plan came to fruition, for the sheer ecstasy brought to her by manipulating the bigwigs like a puppeteer.

According to Omzi, it was like shooting fish in a barrel, which apparently is supposed to be a super easy task—certainly getting knocked up by a stranger was easy as pie for her as well. Once the seed was planted, she could grow her own Chia Pet or bonsai tree, of sorts. She told me that she had the right to clip and prune her creation whenever it grew or blossomed too much. She had complete power and control of the little seed's environment, growth, and vitality, which she said brought her the ultimate pleasure.

I remember sitting in the kitchen one night, trying to finish a worksheet my science teacher had assigned for homework. Our kitchen was a disgusting mess of piled-up food containers—both used and unused—and kind of looked like a church rummage sale on crack, but the light over the table worked, and I had a spot at the table with enough room to sit and work without having to move too many things around.

I could hear Omzi clumsily making her way down the cluttered steps from above, stomping and swearing loudly the whole way until she stopped in the doorway. I was hoping she wouldn't see me doing any schoolwork, because it usually just made her angry that I was wasting time with anything that wasn't something that she had instructed me to do.

Although my back was facing her, I knew she was leaning on one side of the doorway, because I could smell the alcohol that oozed from her pores, and the 'Chk! Chk! Chk!' of her lighter startled me, even though it was a sound I was all too familiar with.

"Jesus Christ, c'mon already!" she yelled at the lighter.

It wasn't just the Jack making her talk funny. I could picture the cigarette dangling in front of her chin yet held firmly in between her lips.

Once it was finally lit and she'd taken a long, raspy drag, she came up behind me to see what I was doing.

"Whatchya got there, Miss Nora Fancy Pants? Is that science or something? Why are you wasting your time on that when you still have chores to do tonight?"

At times like this, I knew it was best to let her do the talking. I didn't answer, quite aware that the questions were rhetorical.

Anyway, she didn't pause for me to answer, then went on to say, "Did I ever tell you that your dad was a doctor? He was a brain surgeon, but obviously no rocket scientist because he was dumb enough to fall for my shit!"

I had heard the story many times before but sat still and listened without interruption.

I was told that my dad was specifically hunted and chosen at a neuroscience conference. Omzi spotted him at the long table of doctors seated in the main conference room while she served baskets of bread and filled water glasses during a lunch presentation. He locked eyes with her and, although the gold band on his left hand might have frightened a lesser woman off, she said she knew from the glint she saw in his hazel eyes that she could have him.

A few flirty smiles in his direction, and an 'accidental' water spill in his lap not only got her message across, it got him to excuse himself from the table to attend to his pants.

"It was like shooting fish in a barrel, and here he was supposed to be so smart. I waited for him to come out of the men's room and told him how sorry I was. We flirted and I told him I would do anything to make it up to him."

I put my pencil down and looked up at her at this point. I knew the story well, and it only occasionally varied in small details here and there. Sometimes if I looked at her when she told it, she would realize she was talking to me and wrap it up quicker.

"Can you believe that's all it took for him to give me the key to his room? He thought he was the one in charge, but it was me! I had him by the balls and he didn't even know it. That night I went up to his room, and after a couple drinks and a little fun, I cuffed him to the bed and told him I wanted to do something he would never forget."

This is the part that I would love to forget, but can't, because Omzi loved to tell me this stupid story over and over again. She finished her cigarette, put it out in an old I Can't Believe It's Not Butter tub filled with sand that sat in the container graveyard that we called our kitchen counter, and continued, "I rode him like a horse and when he was finished, I got dressed, threw the key to the handcuffs onto his chest, and left the room without as much as a 'how do you do?'!"

She always laughed at this part and shook her head like she was in on a private, hilarious joke with *herself*—and both parties were enamored by her wit.

"I know that was the night I made you. Plus, you have his coloring, hair, nose, and freckles. The only shitty part about it was it was the first (and last) time I got caught messing around. There was a maid, a total bitch, name of Valerie, that saw me come out of his room. She always hated me and turned me in to my boss. But fuck it. I got what I wanted."

I don't know how much of the story is true, but what I do know is that I was born nine months after that particular medical conference (I looked it up online) on November 15, 1995, to a beast. I also know for sure that I was an innocent with no idea that I would be raised in an intentional living hell.

From what I have been told, I was just twelve months old when Omzi moved us back to the big yellow house she grew up in, so she could take care of my bedridden, dying, grandmother. Omzi's dad had already passed away and her mom wasn't far behind him. Moving in with my grandmother and taking care of her in a state of rapidly declining health wasn't something Omzi particularly cared that much about, but living in her house with all her stuff and any money that might be left over most definitely was.

After getting what she wanted from the sperm donor in his hotel room, she had already given birth to me, and she started to hang out with some people who taught her the business of selling drugs to the tourists and locals. She had money saved and was making more of it by ripping off as many tourists as she could, but her ultimate goal was to profit in some way from her own mother's demise. So, it was a no-brainer for her to leave Niagara Falls with me, go home, and wait for her mother to die. But, much to her chagrin, my grandmother's death took much longer than she thought it would. She lived with us in the house, and required our care, for another seven years. This made life hard for all three of us, because if Momzilla wasn't happy, nobody was.

I had never met my grandmother before she was sick but

wished that I had. Maybe it was because she was tired and weak, but she was nice to me. There being someone else in the house besides Omzi comforted me somehow. She had a fragility to her, which I took to be kindness, (whether that was really what it was or not), and it helped me feel better about the sinister creature who ruled the house, and the pressure I was under to keep up appearances in the outside world.

For the most part, I loved spending time with my grandma. When she was still able to get around, we spent a lot of time together sitting on her front porch in big white rocking chairs. During the summer months, we drank iced tea and she read to me from the thick, hardcover romance novels that she loved so much. I loved how my grandma actually listened to what I said, and seemed to care about what I was doing and the things I was interested in. She always told me things that made me beam with pride.

Things like, "Nora, you are such a precocious little girl." And, "I can't get over how incredibly smart you are. You are truly wise beyond your years."

When the leaves started to change colors and became the perfect accessories to the yellow house, my grandma would sit wrapped up in blankets, and we would listen to music or play cards. At night, before she went to sleep, I loved when my grandma let me undo the tightly wound bun she wore during the day, so I could brush her long, gray hair. She would sit on the edge of the bed in her long, cream nightgown with tiny blue flowers around the collar, while I kneeled behind her with a huge brush made of boar's hair. Her beautiful, thick hair flowed around her delicate shoulders with each long, careful stroke I made, and I often thought she looked like an angel or a ghost.

One of my favorite days with my grandma was when she was still healthy enough to leave the house. It was the last time she and I ever went someplace together.

She and I walked into the grocery store with a long, hand-written shopping list for the ingredients to bake a cake. I had never eaten a cake that wasn't bought from the store, and the only time that happened was at school when someone's mom brought one in for a kid's birthday. This bit of information seemed to really bother my grandma, so she said we were going to bake a cake together.

I will always remember how excited I was to make a cake for absolutely no reason with her from scratch, but the time together in the store finding the ingredients is what meant the most to me and will forever reside deep in my heart. I have such a vivid memory of her taking my hand in the parking lot. I looked down at her boney hand holding mine. For some reason, I loved the bluish-purple veins that bulged beneath her spotted brown skin like fat earthworms in the soil. I wanted to squish them with the index finger of my other hand, but, instead, I kept walking and tried to mirror my grandma's sense of purpose. It was like we were two spies on a secret mission to search for, locate, and retrieve the items on our list.

My grandma wanted white cake, and I wanted chocolate, so we compromised and got boxes of both kinds of cake mix, and chocolate buttercream frosting that came in a can with a red plastic lid on it. It was going to be a cake with layers. A layer cake is what my grandma called it. I had never had one before.

She said it was okay to cheat a little by getting the premade stuff, and that we could still say the cake was homemade because we were making it together at home.

I ran with excitement to the open area outside of the short grocery aisles to look for the eggs. My grandma slowly pushed the cart into one of the aisles in search of some kind of oil to go into the cake mix, while I located the eggs and eagerly pulled a carton out of the cooler.

I turned to run back to where she had gone to show her the ones I had chosen but tripped on my own untied shoelace. It felt like I was watching the carton fly out of my hands in slow motion as the eggs crashed like bright yellow grenades all over the floor, so shiny and bright. I could see the look of horror on my own face when my knees hit the ground.

I thought my grandma would be furious and that I was going to be punished and beaten by Omzi when she found out, but when she came out of the baking-needs aisle and saw me, her face got soft instead of hard. She told me it was okay and that someone would clean it up. I couldn't believe it, but she wasn't even mad at me. She said it happens sometimes, but that I needed to slow down and try to be more careful, especially if I was carrying eggs.

When we returned to the house to bake and frost the cake, I was so happy that Omzi wasn't home, but nervous about the fact that I didn't know where she was or when she would be back. The kitchen got really warm, and smelled so incredibly delicious, that it seemed like forever for the cakes to be cool enough to put the frosting on them. I didn't want to wait, but my grandma said we had to, or it wouldn't turn out right. So, we played Go Fish with a deck of cards that had a picture of Niagara Falls on them until it was time to frost the cake.

My grandma let me do it, and even though some spots were kind of bare while others had enough frosting for two cakes, it was the most beautiful cake I had ever seen. My grandma said she would pour us both some milk and get a knife to cut the cake while I got plates and napkins.

I was digging through a cupboard to find actual paper napkins, when I heard the back door open and then slam with a *whap*. Omzi came into the kitchen and, although my back was to her, I knew right away she was high on something. She often did crack and meth, and I didn't really know the difference, but I knew things were probably going to go really bad quickly.

"Well, look at this shit. Did you guys make a fucking cake? Is it my birthday and nobody told me?"

My grandma stepped in front of the counter where the cake sat innocently on a plate—she was like a rodeo clown trying to distract a bull after the cowboy has been bucked off of it. Her efforts to protect the cake, however, simply riled up the raging bull that was my mother.

"Why didn't you guys tell me it was my birthday? It's too late to try and surprise me, Ma. I already saw it," she said, her voice oozing sarcasm as she roughly bumped my grandma to the side with her hip. "Where did you get the shit to make this, or the money to buy the shit to make it?" She turned her attention on me, and growled, "Did I say you could bake a fucking cake?"

"No," I answered, but couldn't look at her or my grandma.

"No, I didn't."

My grandma tried to lighten the mood by saying, "We thought it would be fun to surprise you with it for no reason. Here, Ellie...sit down and Nora will get you a plate and a fork."

"Fuck that! And fuck your surprises! I didn't say you could do any of this. Nora, get over here."

It was only a few steps from where I was to where my mother stood huffing and puffing in front of the cake, but it felt like concrete was running through my veins and I could barely move.

"Jesus Christ, Nora! Sometime today. Get your ass over here *NOW*!" she screamed.

I found myself immediately in front of the cake, with Omzi's hand on the back of my neck. Without hesitation, she screamed, "Since you want it so bad, go ahead and have it!" and she forced my face into the middle of the cake. I felt tears mix with frosting and chunks of cake entering my mouth and nose as I coughed and screamed for her to stop.

"I don't want to spoil your fun, but okay, I'll stop."

She let go of my neck and waited for me to lift my face, which was now covered with smeared frosting, cake, and snot. She pointed her finger into my face, and I have never seen her laugh so hard in my life. It was a laugh fueled with anger and contempt.

She used her right index finger to scoop a tiny bit of frosting off my left eyebrow and gave it a little taste. "Not too bad, guys! This is like a real party now—you know why?"

No one answered her, but she told us anyway.

"Well, for one thing, Nora here looks like a fucking clown. And it sure as shit isn't a party until something gets broken!" As she made that final declaration, she picked up the plate covered in the ugly white and brown remains of the cake and hurled it against the wall, where it smashed, obediently illustrating her point.

Her chest was heaving, and her voice was rough from yelling and maybe smoking whatever she was on. She wiped her hands on her jeans and stomped out of the room as she said, "There; *now* it's a party."

As she left the room, she must have taken my memories of what happened next with her. Omzi's anger and her breath, made hot with bourbon and whatever else she had been taking, had changed the mood and the feelings in the kitchen from pleasantly warm to unbearably blazing. I can remember pulling my soaking wet body out of one of the nasty barrels of water in our basement, but I haven't ever been able to figure out exactly how I got there, or what happened in between the kitchen and the basement.

My grandma was so horribly sick after that day, and because she was too weak to talk, she wasn't able to fill in the blanks for me. I'm sure I was ordered to stop the waterworks and go down to the basement to wash the mess off my face and clothes. It's the only thing that makes sense of how I got down there so quickly, and why I was submerged in the water barrel. And truthfully, I don't mind not being able to remember the bad parts about that day, since my grandma died so soon after it happened, and I have held on to the bits of happiness and love that I felt before Omzi showed up and ruined it.

The night my grandma died will also forever remain embedded in my brain as one I will never fully forgive myself for nor forget. I started sleepwalking and having the most vivid nightmares around the time that my grandma passed away. I don't think I will ever know for sure what happened that night or how much of it was real, but I know my life changed forever when I lost my grandma.

I had an actual bedroom in the house, but I wasn't allowed to sleep in it. Omzi and I shared a bed in her room, and while we were asleep together, I heard sounds that reminded me of the time I found a litter of kittens under a neighbor's front porch. Their long, drawn-out squeals were unlike any grown-up cat meows I had ever heard before. They sounded so lost and lonely, and the squeaky 'mews' that seemed to be coming from my grandma's bedroom sounded just like those baby kitties.

I was scared at first, and thought I was hearing things, like I often did. I pressed my pillow around my ears and tried to figure out if I was having one of my crazy nightmares, or if I was fully awake, but either way, the noises didn't stop, so I got out of bed and quietly walked down the hall.

The door to my grandma's room was half open, and I could see the moonlight illuminate the foot of her bed. I pushed the door fully open slowly because I was scared of what I might find—it was often so difficult for me to tell the difference between what was real and what was a nightmare.

When I stepped into her room, the covers were pulled over her head and she looked like a mummy in a tomb under her blankets. I began to think that the noises I had heard were my grandma's last breaths, and I couldn't help but wonder if Omzi had killed her and then come back to bed afterwards.

I wanted to turn and run out of the room, but I had to see if my grandma was alive, and just making noises while she slept, so I slowly tip-toed to the side of her bed and pulled the covers away.

Her face was hauntingly gray in the moonlit room, and her mouth and eyes were both frozen and wide open.

Horrified, I tried to scream but no sound came out. Instead, I heard a thunderous roar escape from my grandmother's mouth, as a thick, black funnel of flies exploded from her cavernous mouth. The fear in my heart jump-started my feet and I started to bolt out of her room, but grandmother grabbed me by the elbow and said, "It's still too dark to see."

I jerked my arm loose and took off down the hall.

The next thing I remember is waking up to an empty bed. I made my way downstairs with hesitant steps, not really knowing what to expect. Omzi was leaning over the kitchen sink, smoking a cigarette. When she heard me come in, she took a drag, blew it out, and said, "Your grandma died last night."

Like a punch to the gut, I was overcome with the feeling deep in my core that I just lost the only friend I had in the whole Universe. I was petrified that the only buffer I had from the wrath of Momzilla no longer existed. I was also left with guilt about how she spent her final days on earth. Omzi had been horribly abusive to my grandma, and she would hurt me if I tried to intervene or help my grandma in any way unless she specifically told me to do something for her.

She usually let her sit in dirty diapers and suffer the agony of bed sores and diaper rash, but the day before she died, she must have been in a good mood, because she told me to change grandma's diaper.

I'm ashamed to even think about that particular time I changed it, because I was impatient and mean to her for the first and last time. I knew that Omzi was going to take a nap, and I wanted to sneak downstairs into what I called the toy room. This was the room where Omzi kept all the stuff I wasn't allowed to play with. Sometimes she would buy things at Goodwill—toys, stuffed animals, or old Halloween costumes—and say they were for me, but then to punish me, she wouldn't let me have them. She put these items in one of the forbidden rooms in the basement, where they would sit in the dank and dark, silently torturing and taunting me.

I didn't want to help my grandma on that particular day. I took out my frustration on her with impatience and a bad attitude, and I actually told her that she should just die already. The guilt hovered over my head like a perpetual black cloud, just biding its time to have its vengeance on me.

4

It's the ass crack of dawn and I'm waiting for my coffee maker to create the magic juice that turns me into a human being and keeps me from killing people throughout the day. I flip through my phone to update my running playlist with some hard-hitting Clutch tunes like 'Electric Worry' and 'The Regulator,' mixed in with some emotion-plucking Lumineers and a few folksy songs by The White Stripes and The Raconteurs. For good measure, and to maintain my eclectic spirit, I sprinkle in some Drake, Disturbed, Lizzo, P!nk, Madonna, A Perfect Circle, Rob Zombie, Beastie Boys, Blink-182, and Britney Spears. I like a kickass, eclectic variety to keep my mind busy while my legs turn over rhythmically through the miles.

Since Nathan is the lead vocals and guitarist for a pretty hardcore indie rock band called Undressed Enema, I do a quick search for their new release he told me about called 'Sink of Solitude.' If I can find it in the next minute, I'll add it as well. His band has a large, loyal local following, and for some reason, is also extremely well known in their genre in Japan. I enjoy his gigs when he plays around here, and I can always count on his shit to jack up the pace of any run.

It's still dark outside as I chug down a little coffee and pet Chaos before heading out. Chaos jumps off the kitchen counter and winds around my leg, purring louder than a bulldozer. For a split second, I consider skipping my run and crawling back in bed with her. She makes me feel momentarily weak, and, in a stupid way, resentment flashes behind my eyes, but disappears as quickly as it came. I pick Chaos up and hold her to my face to kiss her soft ears.

"Nice try, but you can't keep me from getting my miles in, you little butthead." I scratch her under the chin a bit, and stroke her silky black fur from the top of her head all the way down the length of her back and off the end of her tail, before shaking a little dry food in her bowl, and gently placing her on the floor.

She looks at me like I'm an asshole, and then turns to her food, taking out single morsels at a time and placing them on the floor. Loud, individual crunching sounds are my cue to pop my ear buds in, crank up the music, and head out. I can't stand to hear people eat. And yes, to me, Chaos counts as a person. She means more to me than most humans I interact with on a daily basis ever could. She has the kindest heart and when I look at her, I see an innocence and purity that can move me to tears. We can trust each other, and that's something that I can't say about anyone else in my life. In fact, that Nathan has a key to my apartment so he can help me take care of her when I'm at the firehouse on a twenty-four-hour shift makes me feel both at ease and anxious simultaneously.

When I was a kid, stuffed animals were my friends, and I considered them to be real. I talked to them, cared for them, and did all I could to protect them, because they made me feel some semblance of what I thought love might be. Today, having Chaos has become essential to my soul's survival in its own special way, because I tell myself that no matter how crazy I feel at times, if I am kind enough to care for her, I will never have to worry that the beast that lives within Omzi has been passed on to me.

When kids are little, they think a watermelon will grow inside them if they swallow the seeds—I secretly harbor the fear that a very dark seed has been planted in me by Omzi and, if left unpruned, it will grow out of control like an ugly, wicked weed.

It became her mission to have a seed planted inside of her for the purposes of evil, but I'm determined to keep my potentially malevolent soil unfertilized. I only occasionally consider how sad it is that this is a legitimate fear of mine. Don't make me say it out loud—we've all seen the movies. We know how monsters begin to hone their skills and satisfy their hunger for darkness, first with animals, before they graduate to inflicting unspeakable harm on something bigger.

I step out into the crisp morning air, and the smell of impending winter brings back memories of that night I took off running in the cold. Every time I start a run, especially when it's cold, the memory of that night whooshes across my heart like a ghost or a dark gray shadow. It's like the cold, dry air and the lingering memory are in competition with each other to see who can steal my breath first.

I begin to run, focusing my attention on matching the rhythm of the music to the meditative beat I create with each foot strike on the pavement. I know my run will grant me everything I need to feel renewed, and that afterwards my head and heart will be clear enough to face the day.

Truly, the only things that can quiet my mind and help me feel like a human are running, my cat, creating art, and a few other extracurricular adult activities that I have taken a particular proclivity to. Even after all these years, and with more psychotherapy than anyone could fathom, I still have a lion's share of trouble with nightmares, concentration, hypervigilance, and what I like to refer to as 'black holes.' My episodes with black holes and hallucinations aren't as bad as they used to be, but they still tend to rear their ugly heads in times of great stress, or if I'm triggered by something that brings me directly back to my childhood faster than a ride in one of Stewie Griffin's time machines.

When I run, I can usually let my mind wander. Even though I'm hypervigilant about my surroundings, when my breath is going hard and fast, my mind often slows down and ruminates over current puzzles or floats through memories. It has taken a lot of time, with many failed attempts, to discover just the right combination of antidepressants and anti-anxiety meds to help me learn how to ride the dragon, but without my own personal coping mechanisms added to the mix, I would be in a much worse and more fragile place, which is pretty hard to believe, but true.

This run I start puzzling over my black holes, and my mind drifts to when I lived in a Residential Treatment Center (RTC) for a short period as a teenager. There, I met a lot of kids who dealt with their trauma and abuse by using drugs of every kind. One of the girls on my wing used to talk all the time about how much she loved falling into a 'K hole.' I had no idea what a K hole was, which of course she couldn't believe, so she was more than willing to sing its praises by telling all about the euphoria, hallucinations, and floating sensations you feel if you take a high dose of 'Special K.' Apparently, she loved ketamine because it made her lose time and blocked out all the pain she was trying to get away from. It also fucked with her ability to control her body, and her interaction with the world around her, which is why she ended up in an RTC.

At that time, she and I were referred to by the other residents, and even staff, as the star sisters, because we looked exactly alike, and everyone said we shined too brightly to be in lockdown. Her name was Darcy and we formed a bond that, at the time, we both thought could never be broken. We truly began to feel like sisters. We did everything together, and we got each other. She fully understood my black holes; why I experienced them; why they were necessary. I understood her trauma, her addiction, and the internal conflict she battled daily.

I have never taken ketamine, and although they aren't drug induced, I think my black holes are similar to Darcy's description of a K hole. I've seen enough counselors and read enough books to know about coping mechanisms. The black holes aren't exactly complete blackouts, per se, but they are definitely my mind's way of dealing with the extreme pain and trauma I experienced as a kid.

Despite the crisp air, I've worked up a sweat and the endorphins are kicking in, so I give myself a mental "way to go" slap on the ass. I'm smart enough to know that I can't decide not to have issues or, for that matter, mental illness, but I *can* decide to be a good person, or at least the best person I can be, while dealing with the aftermath of being raised the way I was. I'm an extremely strong-willed and highly intelligent individual, and I made up my mind a very long time ago that neither my mother's monstrous treatment of me as a kid nor her DNA would make me any less of a person.

I like to think of myself as a blank slate, and the artist of the canvas that is my life. This is part of the reason I love art so much. Art doesn't have to be perfect in order for it to be beautiful. In fact, it's in the imperfections where true beauty, complexity, and uniqueness can be found. On the off chance that I think I feel bugs on my skin or hear voices in my head, I remind myself that I'm a work of art and they are simply sources of inspiration to create from rather than to destroy with.

My apartment is pretty bare, and the only décor on the walls are drawings and paintings that I have created—with the exception of one framed piece, which is a poem I discovered in the library while I was supposed to be studying for the written test to enter the firefighter training program. I was immediately sucked in by the theme of resilience, how a person can become courageous by embracing life and basically telling despair to go fuck itself. It spoke to me because it went beyond the poet's bravery during the time of the initial suffering and focused on using the limitless fortitude of the human spirit as a shield against future adversity.

The poem hangs in a rich wooden frame in my tiny living room above the beechwood easel I ordered from Italy after my first few paychecks at the fire department, so I can see and read it every day. It wasn't long before I'd memorized it. Many times, when I need to drown out voices in my head, or I need extra motivation on a run, I recite the poem to myself and it brings me great inner strength. The words are powerful, and sometimes I think that long dead Victorian poet wrote them specifically for me:

Invictus by William Ernest Henley

Out of the night that covers me,
*   Black as the pit from pole to pole,*
I thank whatever gods may be
*   For my unconquerable soul.*
In the fell clutch of circumstance

I have not winced nor cried aloud.
Under the bludgeonings of chance
My head is bloody, but unbowed.
Beyond this place of wrath and tears
Looms but the Horror of the shade,
And yet the menace of the years
Finds and shall find me unafraid.
It matters not how strait the gate,
How charged with punishments the scroll,
I am the master of my fate,
I am the captain of my soul.

I fend off and deal with my inner demons pretty successfully with a combination of these words, running, expressing myself creatively with art, and taking my bag of tricks out on the town every once in a while. With consistent use of those organic and holistic methods, in addition to twice-weekly therapy sessions with my psychiatrist, and prescriptions for your garden variety medications, I'm basically just like every other human roaming the planet. Well, that's quite a stretch, but I do my very best with what I've got. I'm determined to not allow my mother to win by having any control over, or influence on, the way I currently live my life. And as far as I'm concerned, considering what I've been through, that's pretty fucking triumphant.

I intentionally keep my social circles (if you can call them that) extremely small, since it's easier to contain my anxiety over relationships (and about appearing normal) to as few people as possible. I have Chaos, Nathan, and my best friend, Ronnie, who is like family to me, since she's part of my crew at the firehouse, and having the firehouse as the home I never had makes my life so much easier.

I get back from my six-mile run and feel a surge of peace and power wash over me, a runner's high, a Zen-like sensation mixed with a sense of strength and focus—both mentally and physically. Kind of like the aftershock of a good orgasm. I feel alive, free, in control, and strong: all the things that are absolutely essential to my well-being and mental health. And, believe me, it's not a coincidence that they are also essential to the well-being of anyone who has to have contact with me, because oftentimes, without my runs, I feel like I could crawl out of my skin, and while I'm at it, peel back the skin of any asshole that has the misfortune of pissing me off that day. Just ask any of the guys at the firehouse. The first thing they say to me in lieu of a proper greeting (like as "Hi" or "What's up?") is "Did ya get a run in today?" I actually find it funny and endearing to be known as the house runner.

Growing up, I had no idea that being intelligent, agile, strong, and athletic was something I could use for anything other than invoking the horrendous wrath of my mother. Running is a time when my thoughts and feelings become a stream of consciousness that I let flow wherever it wants. I let my inner dialogue continue without me as I listen to the music and channel any negative energy through my breath and the machine-like turnover of my legs.

I jog up to the duplex I share with my boy toy, buddy, or neighbor, Nathan. It's hard to explain the extra burst of energy that washes over me, but I feel his presence and energy inside the house, presumably asleep, while I briefly stand there sweating and breathing heavily. We have a connection that I can't deny, but labels are something I rebel against, especially when it comes to my own sexuality or the people I choose to fuck. Unless a famous producer is at my door with a contract for a record label (never mind the fact that I have zero musical talent), I would have to say labels suck donkey dick and have no place in my life.

Simply stated (as if anything relevant to my life could ever be simple), Nathan is a dude who lives below me. I rent the space above, and he has seen my space below, if you catch my drift, but now we are just good pals. Amigos. Shit, who do I think I'm kidding? Forget it...I'm just going to stop trying to explain what we are to each other, and simply quantify our relationship status with the tired old 'it's complicated' cliché.

I walk into the house and glide past his door (only half trying to listen for any movement behind it), then I hit the stairs up to my apartment two at a time. When I get to my door at the top of the wooden stairs and around the tiny, charming spindly banister, I can hear Chaos batting around the catnip pineapple I bought for her the other day. I don't like to get her toy mice because they freak me the fuck out, so I always opt for cartoonish looking things that don't have anything to do with your typical feline's innermost desires.

I stride in and laugh out loud as I catch her trotting by with the little green and yellow pineapple guy in her mouth. While I stand heel to toe and pry my running shoes off without untying them, she shows off a bit by throwing the little dude in the air with a muscular flick of her neck. She swiftly hooks it with her claw, like she's nabbing a bird in flight. Her grand finale includes a few more air hockey-like bats of the pineapple just before she stabs her front teeth into it and proudly prances out of the room. "Damn, Chaos, that must be some good shit in there, huh? You're a goofy monkey," I say to her backside. Suddenly I realize that I know exactly where the expression 'You think you're the cat's ass' comes from.

I open my fridge, which is eternally devoid of food, and grab the pitcher of water. Getting a glass out of the cupboard and making it 'dirty' isn't something I feel like dealing with, so I just chug the water—a little too eagerly—straight from the pitcher, causing the excess to run out of my mouth, down my neck, and into my already soaked sports bra. Great...like trying to get out of these things even when they aren't drenched isn't already like wrestling a boa constrictor.

I need to get into the shower and grab some food before my shift. I rip my cold, clammy clothes off and toss them in the laundry before I turn on some music and let the water run to warm up before I step into the spotlessly clean bathtub. The cleanliness of my apartment is in stark contrast to the hellhole I was raised in, and I celebrate the difference silently every day.

My post-run body is cooling off rapidly. I rush around the apartment getting ready for the day, and my naked skin responds to the air with goosebumps that make me shudder. I push the memories I associate with cold, naked goose-bumpy flesh, and grab my phone to text Nathan.

Hey

He responds,

Hey Kara Goucher

I can't help the stupid smile that creeps over my lips as I read the text and quickly send back:

Creeper! How did you know I was running?

I immediately follow with a second text that includes a middle finger emoji, as well as:

Dude, you can compare me to that long-distance running Olympic rockstar any day of the week.

He responds,

Maybe you could run as fast as her if you didn't have those heavy-ass Dumbo feet. I knew you got up to run when I heard you clomping around up there like a herd of elephants.

I think to myself how full of shit he is. I'm like a ghost up here. It's ingrained in me to be as undetectable as possible in the house. I know he keeps a close eye on me. It used to creep me out, but now if I'm in the right mood, and the right frame of mind, it can be somewhat comforting.

I send back,

Hilarious, asshole. Maybe you wouldn't hear me clompin' if you didn't have those Dumbo-sized ears. You still good to take care of Chaos while I'm working?

I get a thumbs-up emoji with an elephant. Then he says:

Do you really have to ask? I have never let you down before. Your little angel is all set.

I send the thank you hands emoji back, throw my phone on the bed, and step into the steamy shower. It never ceases to amaze me how the warmth of the water and the clean, soapy smell of my shampoo can still make me feel like I'm doing something bad or indulging in a forbidden pleasure. I remind myself that guilt isn't generally involved when normal people take a shower, and I make a mental note to bring this up again with my therapist.

As a way of defying my guilt, I stand under the water longer than I need to. I lower my head and look down at my body while the hot water relaxes my muscles and eases my mind. I watch the little rivers of water pool around my feet and I think back to the first time Nathan and I hooked up.

We ran into each other at the Juice Box, both a little drunk on tequila. I was with Ronnie, but she went home early and, as usual, I wanted to stay. I didn't want to face another fitful night of sleep. Anything was better than the possibility of night terrors, even if it meant going home with Nathan. Even before the shots of Patrón, I could already tell he liked me—maybe a little too much—which is always the kiss of death (strike one). He's also a sweet dude who is admittedly seeking a real relationship (strike two). And on top of it all (no pun intended), he's my downstairs neighbor (strike three). The poor dude has three major strikes against him, all of which should outweigh his amazing hair, super-hot body, and sexy, strategically placed tattoos.

That first night a year ago is a little foggy, but I remember stumbling into his living room and taking turns awkwardly removing articles of clothing while trying to make out. Normally I couldn't care less how a guy decorates, and it takes a lot to creep me out, but I was strangely uneasy in his apartment. The less I had on, the worse I felt because of all the eyes on me.

"Who the hell is your decorator, Norman Bates?"

He laughed...but I wasn't kidding. The stuffed heads and black eyeballs protruding from the walls started to sober me up and turn me off.

"My dad and I hunt together, and we believe that you shouldn't discard any part of the animal, out of respect for its soul."

"Well out of respect for *my* soul, and my G spot, I'm going to cover their faces,'cuz I can't stand them looking at me. I feel like they're accusing me of something."

"Yeah—they're accusing you of being too fucking hot. Now get over here and forget about them."

After he passed out, I wiggled my way out from under his arm (which felt not unlike a lead pipe on my chest) and made my way up the stairwell that connected our apartments, telling myself that if I did him again, it would have to be at my place. While simultaneously feeling sorry for them all, I wanted to punch all of those deer and fox heads in the face.

I got in bed and texted Ronnie.

Thanks a million for leaving me there tonight. I ended up fuck-

ing Nathan!

Not surprisingly, she was up, and sent a text back immediately:

Whatever, slut is what she sent, with an emoji of an eggplant. Then she sent a couple more with a bunch of LOLs after each one.

You knew that was brewing for a while

You gonna break his heart too?

As I read it, I could just picture the face she made while typing it. I'm sure she made her big doe eyes even bigger, and somehow rounder, while she jutted out her plump bottom lip in exaggerated false sympathy.

I shake my head at myself for even thinking about all this shit in the damn shower an entire year after that first time. Omzi would have told me to wash that man right out of my hair. I hate that I can remember that too. Sometimes, just sometimes, I wish I knew how to love humans.

Each time we fell into bed together I told myself it would be the last, but I was just lying to myself. The truth is, he's too sweet and cares about me too much. Those two facts alone are enough evidence to prove that there's something inherently wrong with the dude. I've never even shown him my bag of tricks. Well, that is to say that, although he has seen me going out wearing my little black backpack purse of power, I have never shown—nor used on him—the various contents of the black leather sack I causally throw over my shoulder before heading out on a hunt. Ronnie doesn't even know about my bag of tricks. The only person who knows about it, other than the people who end up on the receiving end of my bag of fun, is Doctor Sharee.

Ronnie and I are the only two female firefighters in our station, our county, and the two neighboring counties as well. We took our written and physical tests on the same day, went through training together, and almost immediately bonded like sisters. Ronnie is my best friend. She's also my only friend, since I keep to myself as much as I can, keep my social circle very small, and have been told that I'm beyond what people would refer to as a 'private person.' She's really cute and funny, but I would never ruin the sanctity of our friendship by trying to sleep with her, even though she's a lesbian and has teased me on a drunken night or two, calling me her straight-girl crush. We are family, and since I never really had one, at least not one that cared for me or had my back, I won't ever jeopardize that with sex that I can easily get from someone I'll never have to see again. (Unless he happens to live at the same address as me, of course.)

I can remember reading her last text message with a cocky grin on my face. Since her questions were rhetorical, I texted back:

whatever, bitch

and then put my phone on the nightstand and rolled over to try and sleep nightmare free.

As I step out of the shower and towel off, I think about how long ago that night seems, and how much has happened between Nathan and I since then. It feels like much longer than a year ago. The dynamics of our relationship, or lack thereof, have changed and evolved so much.

When our leases were up for renewal, I chastised myself for the flicker of happiness that involuntarily warmed my belly like hot soup when he told me he signed for another two years. I hoped my eyes didn't defy me by communicating anything more than I wanted them to as I told him I had done the same thing.

"Dude, I mean, I would have to be stupid to move," I said as breezily as a socially awkward person has the ability to do. "The house is only two blocks from the fire station, and we couldn't ask for better landlords."

All of that is the truth and then some. I think our landlords are absolutely the cutest little Greek couple, who not only allow me to have Chaos, but are also quick to attend to anything that goes wrong with the house or property, and the rent has only increased $100 per month since the first time I signed with them. I usually hate people who are nosey or prying, but they have an endearing way of asking me how I am. The sweetly innocent comments they make communicating their delusional hopes that one day Nathan and I will become a couple don't even rake my skin the way they would if anyone else on the planet made them.

"Two beautiful young people, both single. Ripe fruit right there for the picking. Such a waste," Mr. Stavropoulos will say, shaking his head incredulously, while Mrs. Stavropoulos smiles and playfully smacks his shoulder while exclaiming, "Mind your business!"

It would probably have broken their baklava-laden hearts to know that the very day they said those words to me for the umpteenth time, while I signed the dotted line to renew my lease, was also the day that I fucked Nathan for the truly 'last time.'

5

Learning to remain as inconspicuous as possible was made much easier due to the fact that I was being trained by the best. Omzi was a master of trickery and was simply a pro at looking like something she was not. Case in point, she masqueraded quite well as a human, only shedding her outer skin when she was at home. She was also incredibly adept at winning over anyone she considered to be in charge or who had any type of authority. Doing meth and crack made her inner skin even uglier than it was before she got into using drugs, and I would say she was a wolf in sheep's clothing, but that would be an insult to wolves.

On several different occasions, teachers called Omzi into school to talk about various concerns they had about me. Sometimes it was my lack of participation, or that I was too quiet and reserved that concerned them. Other times, it was my exhausted or disheveled appearance, or that I didn't complete or hand in my assignments that prompted a call home.

Regardless of the reason, every single time she went into my school, Omzi would squeeze into the shiniest and most mesmerizing snakeskin she could find and charm the pants off the ones who were supposed to be doing the snake charming. She was quite adept at making the school staff think that I had trouble sleeping, or that my bad behavior was due to the loss of my grandmother, and other sleight-of-hand type of excuses. So much so, that by the time she walked out of the building, the teachers were apologizing for bringing her in and holding the door open for her on her way out.

The next day at school, the same teacher who might have been the slightest bit worried about me, was instead telling me to "mind my mother" or "try to behave at home, Nora." You had to hand it to her...she was really good at being bad. One teacher even sent flowers to our house with a note that said she hoped that Omzi had a good day! I almost shit my-self.

She hadn't had to work for a year now, because she had collected a large inheritance when my grandma died, and she'd also started to make money (or at least save it) by pimp-ing me out to her boyfriend and his friends in exchange for drugs when she felt the need.

From an outsider's perspective, it probably looked like I had a really great life, and that I was, in actuality, another un-fortunate and heavy cross for my poor mother to bear, after having to care for her ailing mother for so many years. She did an excellent job making it look like her controlling and abusive behavior was actually the doting of a concerned, over-worked, and underappreciated single mother.

On a daily basis, Omzi would tell me to "mind my Ps and Qs." I never quite understood what that meant, and pictured little green peas swirling in a big bowl of alphabet soup with some orange carrots and a bunch of Q-shaped pasta noodles. Was I supposed to keep an eye on them, so they didn't drown? Didn't they have an adult figure in their lives who could mind them? Why did everything in my life have to be so damn con-fusing?

I can remember the low, clenched-teeth way she would say things that could stop me in my tracks much faster than yelling at me ever could. Her gritty voice reverberated in my ears as she wrenched my elbow and pulled me up so that her lips skimmed the hairs that stood up on the back of my neck. "Power comes from not being seen," she hissed so coldly, it made the blood in my veins freeze. "You will be well served to remember that, Nora Elaine Horvath."

As far back as my mind will allow me to reach, I can't recall a time in my life when I wasn't being abused by the thing that was supposed to be my loving mother. She started to sexually abuse me when I was just six years old. It was when I reached nine years old that I could feel her frustration and anger compound, and although the sexual abuse lessened a little, the physical abuse became much more ruthless and violent. The kind of relationship I had with her, and the way she abused me was all I knew, so I had no idea that everyone else in the world didn't live the same way that I did.

In the beginning, the physical abuse was a slap or a pinch, but it quickly escalated to the most inhumane things she could come up with. She was always fuming and irate with me for the slightest of things. If I couldn't find my coat, or anything that I needed for school in the hellhole that we lived in, or if I didn't clean well enough for her liking, I was subjected to any number of painful punishments. When I couldn't locate my shoes, for example, she would make little cuts on the bottoms of my feet with scissors or broken glass.

Another form of punishment was making me eat rotten food. Our refrigerator was a frightening, overstuffed garbage can of black mold and brown, soupy streams of goo that used to be something edible, but had become a revolting muck, unfit for even an animal's consumption. I wasn't allowed to throw anything away from our refrigerator, and if I was caught trying to get rid of something particularly smelly, that thing would be my next meal. Don't even ask me what happened when I puked it up.

Cleaning the house was a joke, and in attempting it, I was simply being set up for failure. After my grandmother passed away, the entire house had become a hoarder's paradise and was littered with garbage, nonsensical clutter, and rotting food, which rendered it impossible for me to attain the goal of getting it clean. This is precisely why it served as one of Omzi's favorite methods of punishing me.

There were paths carved out through each of the rooms like an indoor haystack maze at a fall fair. When I was in the house, I wasn't allowed to wear clothing, no matter how cold it was, and no matter where and what she was making me clean. Part of my cleaning duties included doing our laundry by hand in the basement. Even during the time when our washer and dryer actually worked, I had to wash the clothes in buckets and metal tubs that sometimes had dead mice floating in them. If I didn't get the laundry done properly (which was impossible), I was punished in a variety of creative ways. Sometimes she would make me eat liquid soap from a big metal spoon. I didn't mind choking down the nasty-ass soap as much as the alternative, which was being locked inside, and forced to sleep in, one of the horrible basement rooms that weren't off limits. There was a tiny room just off to the right of the laundry room with a cold and dirty concrete floor that I was forced to sleep in while the centipedes and mice terrorized me. It was right next to the room I referred to as the toy room, and as I lay on the floor, I could picture all the unused toys in the adjacent room, like some kind of warped, polar opposite depiction of childhood.

Omzi called the room she put me in the playroom because "if you want to play you have to pay," and if you were put in that room, you paid dearly. Although the names toy room and playroom sound fairly similar in nature, *believe* me when I tell you, there's no way in hell anyone could confuse the two. Out of all the punishments and abuse I endured, being locked in the playroom was by far the worst and scariest. I hated hearing the screeching of the mice and having to smell my own shit and piss in the bucket she so kindly put in the corner for me to use as a toilet. The most excruciating and horrific part about it was when I tried to sleep. The mice, and even sometimes squirrels, would make their way into the room in droves, presumably to get warm, and claw their way up onto my naked body. They would sit on me and scratch at my chest, stomach, arms, and legs. Centipedes wriggled out of the damp, dark corners and crawled all over my skin and in my hair. Their quickly moving legs made me feel insane with an itch that couldn't be scratched hard enough. I would scream and cry in the most animalistic ways until my throat was raw. I was so petrified of the playroom; I didn't even want to think about the horrors or forms of torture lurking behind the doors of all the other rooms I *wasn't* allowed in. They were locked, but the fear of what I would find, and of the punishment that would follow if I were caught, was enough to keep me from even trying to get into them.

I was a kid, so of course I was curious about anything that was considered off limits. I had read in a book once about opium dens in the olden times in China. They fascinated me for some reason, and I wondered if Omzi had an opium den in one of the forbidden rooms. I imagined that one day she would force me to have sex with her in that particular mysterious room while rotund men and women watched, lounging on big, colorful, opulent cushions and smoking opium dealt to them by the lizard-like monster.

When I wasn't creating ridiculous phantasy scenarios, I wondered if there were dead bodies in those rooms. It wouldn't have surprised me to find out that my mother was a serial killer like the ones in the movies I watched with her all the time, and that there were bodies, or at least parts of them, buried in the forbidden rooms of our basement. Maybe there were metal surgical tables, drains dug into the floors, and huge shelves with canning jars full of fingers and eyeballs that lined the walls. Flashes of Leatherface from the *Texas Chainsaw Massacre* would often come to mind. There were millions of nightmarish scenarios that I could come up with for why Omzi had rooms she kept only for herself, and none of them would have come as a shock to me if I had discovered any of them to be true.

As a child, there has never been a time in my life that I didn't feel fear, or when I felt truly safe or loved. I have many memories of abuse that stand out in my mind, but what seems to take front and center among it all, and will probably always haunt me, is the hopelessness that hung over me, and followed me like the eyes of a phantasmagorical portrait throughout my double life.

Omzi had an arsenal of old-fashioned ways to phrase things, loving to use a good old adage in place of a more up-to-date vernacular every chance she got. Her father, Bill, was a wellspring of these crazy expressions, and Omzi had no choice but to learn them verbatim from him. One of her favorite idioms was, "Nora, you're cutting off your nose to spite your face!" She told me that this meant I was deliberately trying to anger her by doing things I knew damn well were wrong and would result in horrible punishment. She said I must like getting punished, since I was willing to do such stupid and spiteful things for no good reason. I learned this expression pretty early in life, and that self-destruction was apparently in my wheelhouse, when all along I just thought I was trying to be happy. It became blindingly clear that anything that might bring me happiness or positive attention had to be put a stop to or ruined by Omzi, and that it would also result in one of her many grandiose punishments.

For instance, she knew how much my drawings and paintings meant to me, which is exactly why they were used against me. My art and my stuffed animals were my everything. I needed them like I needed air. They were a sanctuary I used to escape and heal, which is exactly why it wasn't unusual for me to be force fed paper as a meal. If Omzi found me drawing when she didn't say I could, she would rip the page up and make me eat it. Sometimes she would torture me beyond anything I thought I could survive by taking my stuffed animals away and hanging them from the banister in our front hallway. She knew I thought they were real, so by killing them, she was able to threaten me and rip my heart out simultaneously. She would point out to me that if she could kill them, it wasn't far-fetched to think that I could be next. My knees would buckle, and I would be wracked with grief as I stood below my little friends while they swung from delicately crafted nooses, handmade especially for them. I would have rather been forced to eat an entire set of encyclopedias than to have seen my animals left hanging for days, their tiny voices screaming in my head the entire time.

I was about nine years old when the announcement sounded over the loudspeaker at Ben Franklin Elementary School on another cold and dreary winter day. "Attention, Students," I imagined Miss Crainbridge gushing into the silver microphone that perched on the gigantic wooden desk in her office. She was such a petite woman, and I often wondered if she knew how ridiculous she looked behind that heavy oak monstrosity. "Ben Franklin Elementary has had the distinct honor of being chosen to participate in a national art forum and contest presented by the Presidential Scholastic Art Association! The winner of this prestigious contest will receive a trip to our nation's capital, Washington D.C., where their art will be displayed in a special section of the Smithsonian for an evening, in addition to a $5,000 grant that can be used for art lessons or put away for high school or college tuition."

My usual slumped-over, half-asleep stance changed in a split second, like a hot fire poker had been placed behind my back. I could feel my heart race, and my brain already began creating a masterpiece behind my sky-blue eyes. Is this what happiness feels like? Maybe even love? I don't know, but my hand shot up the moment we could express interest in participating in the art contest.

Omzi's number one rule was not to be seen, yet, ironically, she gave birth to a kid who was constantly referred to as scholastically gifted, artistically talented, as well as beautiful. I was careful not to point out that if she wanted me to be a little dumber and less attractive, maybe she should have gotten knocked up by the carny who operated the tilt-a-whirl at our town's Fourth of July festival instead of a neurosurgeon. But, hey, what do I know about such things?

The compliments and accolades I received made her even more determined to make me suffer, as if this wasn't already her life's mission. She did what she could to keep me ugly, but even lack of hygiene and crappy clothes couldn't disguise my natural, baby-blonde hair, big blue eyes, and the light dusting of freckles over the bridge of my pale nose and cheekbones that I always hated, but that other people seemed to find adorable. She was constantly angry that I wasn't blending into the background well enough for her liking, and it certainly didn't help matters that I was already two grade levels ahead of my class in every subject.

On the day that the contest was announced, I went home right after school and immediately finished my chores and homework. Omzi was busy watching TV while she laid in our bed and ate pistachios, making even more of a mess with their shells. She probably thought I would take much longer to finish the list of chores she told me to do, which gave me time to sneak away to my room and start my art project—I had moved enough of the garbage that surrounded my unused bed to create a space where I could draw and create. I stole crayons, colored pencils, oil pastels, and paper from school in small increments so that no one would notice and stashed them under my mattress for special occasions such as this.

I knew damn well that Omzi wouldn't allow me to enter the contest, and that trying to 'peacock' for some stupid prize would get me into the kind of trouble no one in their right mind would even believe. My entire existence was one that no one would believe, but none of that mattered to me at the time, because creating art overtook any fear of repercussion from Momzilla.

I worked day and night on a drawing of Niagara Falls when I could get away with it, but in my feverish perfectionism, with one day left before we had to hand in our submissions, I messed up a bit of gray and white shading on my drawing and let out an instinctive (and very loud), "God *damn* it!"

That did it. Omzi reacted like a bunch of dogs guarding their house when they detect the mailman approaching the door. She came barreling into my room, barking the whole way down the long hallway. I heard her coming, but she was unusually fast when fueled by rage.

She caught me with the unapproved paper and art supplies in hand. Since abuse wasn't something I knew as a term or by definition, but instead, as a way of life, I knew what was coming. At first, she stood over me, breathing her hot breath on the back of my neck, as her brain mulled over the multitude of ways she could inflict pain on me.

Knowing how cheap Omzi had always been, and how much she loved money, I feebly explained that there was a contest with prize money and a trip if I won. That was a mistake. Winning meant standing out. The first thing she said was, "You just have to cut your nose to spite your face, don't you?" She went into her room and found the Swiss Army knife she used to slice the apples she ate in bed. The blade was already out and looked shiny and sticky as she handed it to me by its red handle.

She said, "Go ahead and cut your nose."

I just looked at the knife and then slowly reached out and

took it from her.

"Do it!" she screamed. "You're only hurting yourself more by wanting to stand out—but if you insist on cutting your nose to spite your face, then do it, God damn it. If you don't, I'll take the corkscrew out of that thing and shove it up your ass." I knew this was not an idle threat. She had put things inside of me as punishment before.

Slowly and painfully, I dragged the knife through the middle of the constellation of freckles that resided just above the tip of my nose, but apparently didn't cut hard or deep enough to please her. Omzi violently snatched the knife away from me with one hand, and pulled my head back using a fist full of my hair in order to complete the job to her satisfaction. She carved a short, albeit deep cut over the surface scratch I had previously made, and I watched as blood poured out of my face onto my drawing, adding too much red that wasn't at all part of my original design.

Omzi turned to leave, but not before she alerted me to the fact that my dinner would be my blood-soaked drawing, which meant I wouldn't have anything to enter into the art contest. This hurt more than having to eat my own work, and Omzi knew it. She told me (if anyone asked about my nose) to say I had been coaxing a big can of baked beans from a high shelf in the pantry with my fingertips; that it got away from me, tumbled down, and landed on my nose with the edge of the rim. As she walked out of the room, I could hear her snarling, "Gluttony kills more than the sword, Miss Nora!"

If I even had a 'normal'...this was it. I never knew any different except for when I got glimpses into the lives of the kids at school, or in my dance or art classes—Momzilla had to keep up appearances by keeping me just active enough in the same things that good moms kept their kids busy with. A bad mom would never take the time to bring her child to dance lessons and special art classes, right? Wrong. My mother would sit and watch me closely at all of my extracurricular activities, which made her appear to be the doting and caring mom. Later she would make me pay dearly for every misstep or misspoken word that occurred while I tried my best to be both present and unseen. She was always careful to leave marks in places that couldn't be seen or, at least, explained away. No one ever guessed she was a drug, alcohol, and child abuser.

When you have been brought into the world for the sole purpose of being abused and tormented, you have to learn how to fit in and blend with the outside world, while constantly working to keep the insanity inside of you bottled up with a snugly fitting cork: a virtually impossible task for any human, chameleon, or monster. Sometimes I wasn't sure which one I was.

I fell in love with art as a way to channel my emotions without having to voice them out loud. When I stood in front of the short, plastic finger-painting easels for the very first time as a kindergartener, it was a feeling like no other. I can remember it like it was yesterday. They were lined up in three perfect rows, each with a large, brownish-white rectangle of paper neatly fastened from the top with a shiny, fat metal clip. I stood before the expanse of blank paper as my mouth fell open in awe of the sheer, yet thrilling, possibility of it all. The other kids around me dug right in, and unabashedly jammed their little fingers into the tiny, fat pots of paint that smelled like melted crayons mixed with the inside of a church. Their messy fishing expeditions resulted in pure glee as they pulled out huge globs of paint that they held in the air and studied for a brief moment, like a freshly harvested booger from their nose, just before they smeared it in circles on the paper. With no apparent rhyme or reason, they continued this process until they created a big brown circle of sludge that dripped heavily down the weakened paper, causing it to warp and buckle under the heavy layers of paint.

I couldn't fathom how they were able to decide which colors to use, and where to put them, or that it didn't bother them that their paintings looked like a bunch of smeared baby poop from a dirty diaper. I wanted to use all of the colors, and also none of them, for fear that what I pictured in my mind would somehow be completely ruined on its journey from my brain to my fingers and, ultimately, on to the paper. It didn't take long for that fear to subside, however, once I was urged to begin my project by the teacher and told, "You can't do it wrong." I had never heard those words before. I couldn't do it wrong. The freedom of it all was almost too much to handle, and yet it was the start of my absolute love of art and everything about it.

As I got a little older, I was introduced to what felt, to me, like a secret world of art that I had never known. Over the years, art class introduced me to oil pastels, watercolor paints, clay, mixed media, and so much more that I felt like my senses were working overtime as I walked out of each class. None of the other subjects in school made me feel this way, except maybe gym, and the fact that I was told I had a talent for art was truly just an added bonus.

Every new school year, I made sure to endear myself to the art teacher, like it was my job. I was always the first to volunteer to pass out paper or other supplies in the beginning of class, and I stayed after school to help wash paintbrushes or take care of anything else that needed to be picked up or cleaned. The art teacher was always appreciative, and the more time spent in the art room meant I was spending less time at home: whether I was with Omzi or in foster care—I simply felt more at home in the art room.

When I was in eighth grade, my favorite art teacher of all time, Miss Vega, and I were in her classroom after school on an unseasonably warm November day. The windows were open to let in some much-needed air. The loud clicking of the radiator competed noisily with the shouts and laughter of the kids outside as they ran to catch their rides home. A warm breeze ricocheted off the orange and brown leaves of the trees, sending them on their final, slow float to earth, then wafted into the room, which reeked of an odd combination of glue, old paint, that stuff the janitor sprinkled everywhere after someone barfed, and adolescence, a smell I found simultaneously gross and comforting.

That afternoon, I was cleaning up scraps of clay left on the desks and workstations by the kids who had just created pinch pots before dismissal. I took my time picking up the small pieces until I could form a little ball of clay. It was kind of fun and peaceful to create a continuously bigger hunk of clay by pressing into the ball all the bits and pieces that were scattered about. Watching the hunk of clay in my hand grow into something that was considered useful and desirable again by squishing it together with the pieces that may have been deemed worthless, and discarded otherwise, was extremely satisfying.

As I continued this process with each different color of clay, I found myself wishing I could bottle the way I felt in the art room, so I could drink it down whenever I needed to feel peaceful or happy. It was just then that Miss Vega interrupted my thoughts and asked me if I wanted to do an extra credit project. "Umm, do bears poop in the woods?" I said awkwardly.

She said, "I'm pretty sure they do, but I've never actually seen it happen."

We both got a chuckle out of that, and she continued, "Anyway, I know you don't need the credit for a better grade, since you already have all As in this class, but you seem like you're really passionate about art."

"I really am. It's what makes me feel normal," I responded. "Plus, I don't think extra credit can ever hurt, even if my grades are already good. Thanks for offering it to me!"

"It's no problem, Nora. You remind me a lot of myself at your age. I didn't have a lot of friends, and kind of felt like an outsider at times, since my parents didn't speak English."

I was shocked to hear her say this but listened intently and let her continue.

"The other kids never saw me as one of them, and my parents made things worse for me by adhering strictly to their Mexican culture and traditions, with no attempt to incorporate some of the American ways, even after living here for many years. We only spoke Spanish at home, and I was expected to help my mother with the garden in the summer, the cooking and housework, as well as taking care of my grandpa, who lived with us. Like I said, I didn't have a lot of friends, but I had art and books, and that made me feel like I could be part of different worlds, and have a more colorful life, without having to leave our house."

I pushed tightly fitted blue lids on three little plastic tubs of clay, to keep them separated by color, and from drying out, and said, "Wow, you and I really have a lot in common. I helped Omzi, I mean, my mom, take care of my grandma too. She lived with us until she died."

One at a time, I placed the tubs of clay on the classroom shelf next to a single remaining package of sculpting clay that hadn't been opened yet, and continued, "I think I understand what you mean about how art transports you without having to go anywhere. I actually think art is better than being popular and having lots of friends, because it's whatever I want it to be and helps me express how I see myself in the world without having to be seen by anyone in real life. It's like a superpower or something."

Miss Vega reached into her canvas tote bag and pulled out a large book that had a striking woman with beautiful flowers in her hair on the cover, and said, "Well, that's kind of what I had in mind for this particular project. I was thinking you could take the next couple of weeks to read about an artist I would love to introduce you to. Her name is Frida Kahlo. Once you have read about her, the assignment would be to write a couple paragraphs describing what you learned, or how you felt about her, and then to paint a self-portrait. I would grant you fifty extra credit points for doing so, which would bring you up to an A+ in this class."

As she handed me the heavy, glossy book, I could tell before I even had it in both hands that I was going to love Frida Kahlo. The painting of her on the thick cover was so beautiful that just looking at it made me feel like I was being sucked into my Mother Ship by artistic alien beings from another Universe. Vibrant shades of red, yellow, blue, and forest green comprised and surrounded the unique and mystifying woman who stared up at me with eyes that conveyed both pain and strength. Her intense look of survival and pride, although fire hot, sent an icy chill up my spin. Above those eyes were dark caterpillar eyebrows that looked like they were drawn in with a Sharpie marker all the way across her forehead.

As I processed Miss Vega's amazing offer silently to myself, my typical internal conflict and chaos jump-started like a Harley Davidson. How the hell was I going to carry this expensive book around without bringing unwanted attention to myself, let alone be able to afford a canvas, brushes, or paint for the project?

It was as if Miss Vega read my mind, because her next outpouring of words echoed around my ears while my still-sticky, clay-covered hands grasped the book so tightly that my knuckles turned a yellowy shade of white.

"I would be happy to let you do the work after school, if you like. You can leave the book here and read it at whatever pace you decide is enough to complete your essay. When you are ready to create your self-portrait, simply let me know if you will be using oils or watercolors, and I will be happy to supply you with the canvas, brushes, and paint supplies."

I was still looking down at the book, petrified to look up at Miss Vega, for fear that she would see the gigantic dopey tear drops that began to sting the corners of my eyes. I tried to hold them back, but one of them betrayed me as it got so big and heavy that it seemed to take a whole year to fall with one, loud splat on the hard cover of the book. Without looking up, or trying to wipe the tear away, I told her I would love to take on the project and I thanked her.

So as not to make direct eye contact, I shifted my glance over to the small pinch pots that the students had left in messy rows, waiting to be glazed. Miss Vega was kind enough to pretend not to notice the tear when she took the book back from me, and she said, "Great! You can find the book right here on the bottom shelf next to my desk. Just don't write in it and be sure to put it away when you are done with it each time. Oh, and by the way, did you call your mom Ommy or Omzi, or something earlier? That's so interesting! Is it another language, like German, maybe?"

I looked down and decided to pretend to tie my already laced-up sneaker. Quickly I sputtered, "Okay, thanks so much! I have to get going, but no, it's not German, I think I was just so excited that we had so much in common, I misspoke. Thanks again, Miss Vega. You have no idea how much this project means to me."

With that, I gave her a quick, sheepish glance as I grabbed my backpack and practically ran out the door.

* * *

I had no idea, at the time, just how life-changing that moment was for me, how much Frida Kahlo would influence my life, and that because of her (and Miss Vega), art would be added to my kickass 'self-medication arsenal' as an adult.

I dove headfirst into the extra credit project, and what I learned about Frida Kahlo in that book simply reinforced and solidified all the reasons I experienced love at first sight when I saw her. We were kindred spirits.

On the last day of school before Thanksgiving break, I sat in my last period class watching the clock on the wall slowly tick off the seconds before the bell. I suppose the other kids in class were looking forward to break for reasons that I simply couldn't relate to, like cozy family Thanksgiving dinners and going out with friends for late nights filled with fun and laughter.

I couldn't wait for the damn bell to ring so I could haul ass to Miss Vega's classroom and give her my essay. We didn't have a computer or a printer at my foster family's house, so I took great care to form big, loopy, hand-written words with my favorite blue pen on some college-lined loose-leaf paper my foster mom had bought for me at the beginning of the school year. I'm left-handed, so as much as it killed me that the pages didn't look perfect due to indigo smears and heavy ink blobs where I stopped to rest my fatigued hand, I couldn't help pulling the slightly bent and crumpled paper from my folder for the umpteenth time to read what I had written. I figured it would help the last few minutes of class pass a little quicker to read it again, and although I knew it by heart, I enjoyed pretending to read it through Miss Vega's eyes, and reacting to my insight and eloquence as I imagined Miss Vega would.

The only downside to handing it in today was that I wouldn't be able to start my self-portrait until we came back to school after break, but at least I could use that time to plan my painting. I was halfway through my essay when the final bell shrilled loudly. The other kids jumped up from their desks and bolted out the classroom door, with me right on their heels for once. I didn't stop at my locker or to chat in the halls like they did, partly due to the fact that I didn't have friends to chat with, but mostly because I couldn't wait a minute longer to place my essay in Miss Vega's small hands. It is a rare occasion that I am proud of myself for any reason, so this day meant everything to me, and I was beaming brighter than the sun. It felt like I was floating on a cloud all the way to the art room.

The door was shut, but not locked, so I pushed it open with a huge smile on my face and darting eyes as I looked for Miss Vega, but she wasn't there. I didn't have art that day, so it wasn't unusual that I hadn't seen her during the school day, but I fully expected her to be there the second I walked in the art room, with my essay beginning to wilt in my now-clammy hands. I thought she would be back any minute and was probably in the bathroom or the teacher's lounge getting a cup of tea or something, but after I had waited for half an hour, she still wasn't there.

I looked around the room one last time and made sure no one was there to see me approach her desk. I argued with myself about leaving the essay on her desk, but decided it was the right thing to do in case she came in during the break to do some work. I used a giant, black stapler as a paperweight, and left the essay in the right-hand corner of her desk, in front of a small papier-mâché globe and some yellow and red flowers made of pipe cleaners and tissue paper. It was the perfect place, since it would stand out to her, but not to anyone else.

My essay went like this:

Frida Kahlo was a Mexican artist that became well-known for her self-portraits. She was born on July 6, 1907 in her family's home in a small town outside Mexico City. She died on July 13, 1954. When she was six years old, she got a disease called polio. Because of the terrible illness, her right leg ended up being much thinner than her left leg, which she hid from everyone by wearing long skirts. When she was 18 years old, she was horribly injured and almost killed in a bus accident. Her spine was crushed and disfigured, and she endured a lot of pain and loneliness, so she began to paint in the hospital to occupy her time. She used her terrible pain and suffering as a theme for many of her paintings and showed that you can transform pain into something good. In The Broken Column she painted her spine as a column that was completely shattered. She had nails hammered into her body and her face. In her rebellion and defiance, which I loved so much, she refused to just sit and suffer. Instead of being a victim, she created beautiful paintings of herself on canvas. There is so much hope and energy in her art that it seems to come to life through each stroke of her brush. Her paintings conveyed things that were way beyond words about bodies, death, and pain and forced me to reflect on womanhood, shame, desire, and self-hate. Reading about her life and seeing her paintings was like looking at a reflection of the parts of me that feel alone, invisible, and like a freak. Her paintings illustrated the fact that there is great risk in visibility, but because she painted herself, she had the power to decide how she wanted to be seen. Her art screams out, 'I am here even though I am not seen,' but also says that even when we decide to make ourselves visible, we aren't truly seen.

Oftentimes, we don't want anyone to recognize us for who we really are and what our lives might be like. Most people my age try to blend in, while others, like me, don't even want to be seen. As a female, a teen, and someone who feels like a chameleon among colorful crowds of people, I look around and think about how I can see everyone so clearly, but they don't see me at all. We all share space together, yet they see through me like tracing paper. I often ponder which of the following is the worst: to be an unseen hidden secret, or to try to remain unseen in plain sight… or both? Frida Kahlo made me realize that I can learn to recognize the beauty and the good inside of myself no matter what obstacles I face. I can choose to blaze my own trail, to write my own story, and to recognize my strengths above my flaws. I want to leave evidence of my existence on this planet with my art like she did. Maybe, like Frida, I can find strength to move forward by becoming my own muse. If I can do this, it will be easier to accept the ugly parts of me (inside and out) that I don't want anyone to ever know or see.

I love (and can relate to) her quote that goes: "I used to think I was the strangest person in the world but then I thought there are so many people in the world, there must be someone just like *me who feels bizarre and flawed in the same ways I do. I would imagine her and imagine that she must be out there thinking of me too."*

I am so grateful to Frida as an artist, woman, and a human being. Her paintings made me walk down a street called Recognition. She helped me to recognize and accept hidden pieces of myself, and for that I will always be grateful. Maybe I can hone my fiery interior and use it to light up the world around me—like she did—instead of trying to burn everything down.

Miss Vega, thank you for introducing me to someone so bold, defiant, and strong. I will forever be grateful to you as well.

The first day back after Thanksgiving break was snowy and cold, but I barely noticed the somber grey sky and icy crunch under my feet as I climbed the concrete stairs and flung open the double doors of my school. Instead of heading to my homeroom, I went straight to the art room to see what Miss Vega thought of my essay and let her know about my carefully thought-out self-portrait I planned to do in oil, starting that day after school. But when I reached the art room, I didn't even need to step inside to know that something was different. The lights weren't all turned on, like they usually were, and there was a perfumed smell that I didn't recognize.

When I walked in, I was greeted by our principal, Mr. Woodland. He must have seen my face fall with disappointment but kindly asked how my break was anyway. I could feel a little lump building in my throat but managed to croak out, "Where's Miss Vega?"

"She had a death in her family and needed to take a leave of absence."

Almost too desperately, I responded, "Well, when is she coming back?"

"I honestly don't know, Nora, but we are working on getting a sub for the rest of the school year. I'm hoping she will be back next year."

My heart was pulverized like Frida's spine on hearing this news, and to make matters worse, I felt a good amount of shame for being so selfish. I didn't want to cry in front of Mr. Woodland, nor did I want him to know about the extra credit project or why any of it mattered so much to me.

"Oh. Okay. I'm sorry about all of that. I just came to grab this essay."

I searched his face for recognition of what I was referring to and thanked my lucky stars that none registered. I snatched the essay, which was in the exact place I had left it and bolted out of the art room.

I felt betrayed by Miss Vega, even though deep down inside, I knew she had done absolutely nothing wrong. Although I lost a lot of love for school and art class that day, I promised myself I would remain grateful to her, and to Frida. I told myself that one day I would paint that damn self-portrait, and that it would be savage and phenomenal—just like Frida herself.

6

My nose still sports the little scar in a thickly healed line of skin resembling a crescent moon laying on its back. I still tell people it was a can of baked beans that cut my nose. I'm too tired to make up anything else, and I can't even giggle anymore when a lover tells me it's cute, or that it looks like a moon surrounded by my freckly stars. I don't let anyone kiss it, even if they ask me very nicely. It's amazing to me how many people will break up with you—or never want to see you again—because you tell them to fuck off for wanting to kiss the tip of your nose.

Boop!

Nope—next!

This probably sounds insane to all the normal people of the world. Is there such a thing...or is normal simply a subtext for 'you just don't know the real me'?

As a kid, I wasn't at all sure what normal was, or if I even wanted it, now or ever. If it did exist, that is. Maybe with a family and boring shit to worry about like taxes and good school districts, you don't have time to think about the past or remember the pain. Sometimes that sounds amazingly serene and, well, comfortable...and then there is that other side of me that snaps me back to reality. It only takes a second for me to remember that I'm perpetually anxious and restless, with a quiet darkness that some would consider scary and perhaps even a bit insane. Serene just may not suit me. This side of me wants to beat the shit out of myself for even considering a normal lifestyle, but I take comfort in knowing that I can live my life my way and still be a person that both myself and society would consider to be good. I think the rebellious part of my psychological makeup enjoys fitting in with the normal people wherever I go, but it also knows deep down that I'm far from normal in any way. I'm chock full of wanderlust, as well as good old-fashioned, unadulterated lust. However, with my escape through running and gym workouts at the firehouse, along with my extracurricular nighttime workouts, I tell myself I can keep those urges from blowing my cover and consider them to be my own personal forms of medicine. Hell, I can chit chat with a soccer mom at Whole Foods as we bag avocados and commiserate over the extremely short window of time between their unripe, hard-as-rock status, to disgusting, brown mush. Maybe on that very night I'll be drinking whiskey at a sex club while the same soccer mom's husband finger bangs me on an avocado-colored sofa. Who knows?

I am a powder keg of both darkness and light ready to blow at any time. I'm a passionate, anxiety-ridden, provocative, detached, social, reclusive, sometimes ugly person wrapped in an attractive outer casing. Being what people deem as beautiful can often allow you to get away with a lot but pretending to be all things can turn you into a complicated and quite conflicted individual.

I love everyone and hate the world (and everyone in it) all at once. It's not easy to be a living, breathing paradox while unequivocally fending off unwanted attention by only allowing people to see me in the manner of my own choosing. I suppose, ultimately, this is what all people do, right? All humans present a persona to the world that reflects how they want to be perceived. They certainly don't share their darkest thoughts and impulses and behaviors with the world...but they still have them. So, really, I'm just a *bit* more extreme than most people, but otherwise essentially not all that different in this regard. Or so I tell myself.

I often feel a sort of envy for snakes, because they can shed their own skin and slither away from the last version of themselves and start again. My 'medicine' helps me achieve what snakes can, but without having to actually peel away my skin and leave it in a disgusting, dried-up heap for some poor schlep to happen upon.

When the urge gets too great, and the ache washes over me, I know I need to attend to it. I need my medicine. If I don't feed the desire, I run the risk of being devoured by a painful darkness from the inside out as it feasts voraciously on my inner resolve and any shred of normalcy or virtue, the only sliver that I might think I possess. The more it eats away, the emptier I feel, making it virtually impossible to ignore the need to fill the hollowness inside.

I don't waste time feeling any sort of guilt over these episodes, since I'm not really hurting anyone—unless they want me to. There's no sense in wasting time with guilt when I have already spent much too much time doing just that over the years before I stumbled upon this therapeutic way of satisfying the hunger inside of me for skin, pain, pleasure, and control. I mean, there are worse things I could be doing, and hell knows I've already had most of those things done to me.

To actually be myself, and not feel bad about who that person is, has become the magical remedy to what has for so many years felt like a deep sickness within me. By employing absolute control over another human being once in a while, I can maintain a steady sense of mental wellness and clarity. Like a drug addict who needs a hit to get straight, my personal antidote for these empty, aching episodes does the trick, at least temporarily, and I return to an even keel. Finding people is the easy part of the hunt—having patience and not devouring the prey is the hard part. I need to take a lesson from Chaos and play with my food a little before tearing into it, morsel by tasty morsel, but patience isn't one of my virtues.

In preparation for a night on the prowl, I like to take a long bath. I light candles and throw a silky scarf over the lamp next to the couch in my living room. The scarf has little white sugar skulls on it and projects the perfect amount of moody glow around my otherwise plain apartment. Decorating has never been something I have understood, which isn't surprising, considering the hoarder's hell I was raised in, but I love my own drawings, and of course my warrior's poem. Every time

I throw the scarf over the lamp, I think about what a horrible firefighter and hypocrite I am. I notice Chaos eyeing me from her favorite spot on the back of the couch cushions with what I interpret to be an intense look of haughty derision on her little face. I remind myself that she's not really judging me, and begin undressing in the living room, then the kitchen (stopping to pour some wine) so that by the time I reach the bathroom I'm fully naked.

I like to study my own body in the mirror. I try to look at the entire thing objectively, as if I could step back, away from myself, and take in every inch as a stranger would. How would I seem through their eyes? This is something I have always wished I could do. Forget super strength or X-ray vision; seeing yourself from someone else's honest and clear point of view would be my superpower of choice.

I pull my trusty bag of tricks out of the bottom dresser drawer and dump its contents onto my bed. My comforter sinks in a little from the weight of the cuffs, gum, condoms, belt, strap-on, dildo, lube, cock ring, and collapsible spreader bar—you never know what you might need. Sometimes a night on the prowl requires everything in the bag, while other nights nothing is used at all, but I believe in being prepared at all times.

I pick up my phone and notice a text from Nathan, which makes me wonder if that man has a sixth sense or a spy cam in my apartment. It's like he knows I'm feeling freaky. It says:

getting pizza and gonna watch horror flick if you wanna join

I text back,

can't – going out with Ronnie, but thanks

He answers with,

cool

and I leave it at that.

I place my phone and the Ball Mason jar that I drink my red wine out of on the edge of the tub and sink down into the hot, sudsy water. There is no way in hell anyone could ever put me or my personality or behavior into any one category or type, but I think my choice in bath oils is slightly on the stereotypically feminine side, and I love it. Recently I splurged on some super expensive shit I found on the Internet, and I have to say it has been worth every penny. The abuse I endured as a kid has left me with many issues, as well as phobias and hatred and disgust for certain smells, textures, and tactile sensations. I praise sweet baby cheeses that sumptuous bath oil and smooth, slippery skin are not among them. There are times I get into the bath, inhale the sexy fragrance, watch some porn on my phone, and I don't even make it out for the night.

I begin to feel mesmerized by the voluptuous feel and smell of sweet almond oil, jojoba seed, and avocado oils layered with luxurious and exquisite aromas of roses, crushed violet leaves, and hints of fresh lemon.

I shake the excess water and oil droplets off my fingertips and bring up a little porn. Tonight, I choose something lesbian, as it lends itself so perfectly to the warm, wet, slippery softness of the bath. I play a game with myself to see how long I can stand watching and listening without reaching down between my legs to manipulate my engorged clit.

I sip my wine and turn over onto my stomach, holding the phone just above water level. I like having the waterline cover my mouth and nose while I simultaneously fight the urge to both cum and breathe. I notice I begin to involuntarily buck ever so slightly against the bottom of the tub and tell myself it's okay as long as I don't use my hands and I don't climax.

For a brief moment I consider texting Nathan to come upstairs so I can blow his fucking mind, but I know that's just my hormones going into overdrive. I want to cheat and touch myself, if only just to let out one incredibly explosive underwater moan: a deep guttural release of sound that could only come from an animal. Instead, I abruptly stand up and towel off.

While I get dressed, I drink down the last few sips of smoky, yet jammy-tasting Cabernet Sauvignon (my second major splurge for a good night on the prowl). I already know where I will go, and I begin to pack my bag of tricks.

Sometimes I hit a bar or two before I hop on the bus that takes me to the seediest part of the city, a playground of cheating spouses, drugs, darkly lit bars, and poor life decisions. It's located far enough away from my everyday life that I have no real concern of seeing people I know.

There are a couple sex clubs to choose from two blocks down from the bus stop, and I feel like I'm almost running to get there. I'm walking so quickly that I'm afraid the friction in my tight jeans will get me off before I arrive at Alley Cats, my club of choice for this evening's prowl. I like the place because you don't have to have a membership, and no one cares if you participate or just watch. Anything goes, and I can quickly and easily find a man, a woman—or both—to dominate without explanation of any kind, or directions having to be doled out. Tonight, I'm too impatient for any of that nonsense. I want to fuck—I want to devour someone hungrily and swiftly.

I walk past the bar and only half consider ordering a drink. I have a bottle of water in my bag of tricks if I need to rehydrate, but don't want to waste time chatting up a bartender.

My favorite room is the furthest one in the back. As I make my way through the club, it's darker than a moonless night, and the vibration from the music takes hold of my head. The throbbing between my silky, freshly oiled thighs keeps time with the thundering backbeat of the music. My eyes adjust to the dark, and I begin to see shadows moving, and outlines of bodies on various types of furniture, in an array of sexy, silhouetted positions. I strain to hear the pleasure sounds of the people I'm watching, but sadly the moans are drowned out.

When I reach the back room, I survey the talent. There are four men and three women on a tall, oversized bed engaged in a heated orgy. My eyes are glued on them as they writhe as one. Heads are thrown back, and necks are being held tightly and choked in delirious pleasure.

I take a little winding metal staircase slowly up to the platform that overlooks the bed. It's extremely dark up there, but I can see people sitting on velvet chairs or propping themselves like birds on the edge of the platform to watch. I peer over the edge, and for a split second, the people below look like a vat of maggots. I close my eyes and shake my head as I step away from the balcony's edge.

I turn around quickly and open my eyes, and that's when I spot the outline of an intriguing and most definitely well-built guy standing against the wall behind me. I take his hand and push a chair up to the balcony's railing. Without words, I direct him gently to sit, and he obliges. I take off my shoes and open my bag of tricks.

I'm quite good at seeing in the dark with my hands. I stand before him and place my hands on his inner thighs. He answers me by relaxing his legs and letting them fall open. My fingertips very lightly trace the outline of what could be misconstrued in the darkness as a baby's arm, leaving me to smile to myself as if I just won some sort of nonexistent lottery for dick size.

I leave one hand on the throbbing between his legs as a move behind him. I lean into him and kiss his neck, while both my hands explore their way up from his groin and sweep across his muscular abs and chest. When they reach his smooth, delicious throat, I pull back a bit and massage his traps. He seems to be both melting and hard, all at once.

Still without words, I communicate my desire for his arms to come back to meet me, giving them a light double tap on his elbow. He raises his arms and locks his fingers behind his head like he's going to do a few sets of sit-ups. I hold his hands together right where they are and pull his head backwards so I can kiss his mouth. There is a passion in our kiss that ignites a fire within me that can only be put out in one way. The cuffs come out and I work quickly to get them secured to his wrists while our tongues teasingly keep tempo with the music.

After cuffing his hands behind his head, I straddle his lap, and remain standing while facing him head on, and can't help but think that he looks a bit like a winged gargoyle on one of the old, ornate buildings downtown.

I think gargoyles are sexy, so I undo the button and zipper on his pants and pull them down to his ankles. He has no underwear on, and I'm thoroughly pleased by the way his member springs out at me and stands at attention like the old pop-up books I loved so much as a child. I knew that when I opened them the contents would jump out at me, but it still provided an immense thrill.

I pour a little lube in my hands, rub them together to warm it up, and then kiss him while stroking him with a warm, gooey hand. I yank my pants down with my other hand and deftly maneuver myself out of them while he pulses beneath my strong, smooth grip.

I can feel his need and his ache, and, just for a couple seconds, I step back a little so we can look at each other, before I lean into him to feel his body and his skin on mine. I press myself into him and absorb the shock it sends through my clit.

While I put the condom on him, I very gently lick his nipples. Once it's on, I push away from him and turn around to face the balcony and the amazing pile of bodies below. I lean back and tap his cock a few times so he can feel my wetness and warmth. I don't leave him out in the cold very long. I grab hold of the balcony with both hands and position myself so that I can watch the show as I plunge down hard and ride him in a reverse cowgirl position. It feels both animalistic and beautiful. He can't touch me, and I can barely stand the absolute control I have over him for the short time it takes both of us to explode. I open my mouth to let out a scream that no one can hear, and it feels like the most incredible release anyone could ever experience. A full-body shudder moves through me and I can feel him trying to catch his breath. He's dying to grab me, and I know he wants to slam his tongue into my mouth while he explores every inch of my body, but I haven't uncuffed him.

In a minute I have my clothes back on, and my bag packed up like a doctor who just finished a house call. I take a second to drink some water and pop a piece of gum in my mouth. I stand behind him and pull his head back by his hair. I kiss him with closed, sex-plumped lips as I undo the cuffs. The second they're off, so am I, and he's left sitting in the chair with his pants around his ankles, cum spilling out over his inner thigh, not knowing quite what hit him.

7

It's not as if the thought of running away had never entered my mind before. When I was really little, I never even considered it, but over the years, and especially when I reached double digits, the thought began to pop into my mind more than ever before. I thought about the kids I went to school with, and the ones in my dance class or swim lessons. In very brief moments of self-pity, I considered the lives of those kids with wistful envy. They probably thought they had big problems: like having to set the table for a family dinner, doing their homework, or having their phone taken away as a punishment. As I poured myself some punch at my own personal pity party, I couldn't help but wonder if their only sources of pain or fear would include picking out the wrong shoes to go with an outfit, embarrassing themselves somehow in the lunchroom at school, or not being liked back by their big-time crush. Of course, there was no way of knowing for sure. Maybe they had actual problems, but I could never think of any that came close to the war that, on a daily basis, waged in my brain and ravaged my heart.

It might seem like a no-brainer to just run away. Most people would probably wonder why I hadn't done it years ago, and would consider it insane for me to feel an ounce of trepidation while even considering it. Yet it's not that cut and dry. She's a monster, but she's still my mother, and there's a messed-up sense of loyalty that goes along with that fact. I can't explain it, but something made me feel guilty and shameful when I thought about leaving. The most substantial emotion that kept me tethered, however, was fear. It's beyond amazing to me just how powerful fear and terror can be, and how much she must have used them to control me—I mean, the way I was living stretched way beyond the borders of Stockholm Syndrome. In essence, I was quite effectively held in a cult with only one member.

My list of fears was longer than Santa's Naughty List and included lots of words that began with the letter R, such as: revenge, retaliation, and repercussions. These are words that no kid should even know, let alone physically experience.

There was a myriad of other reasons I had stayed and endured for so long, but when I tried to understand them, they became soft, blurry voices in my head, and made me question myself for wanting to leave. One of these voices would tell me that I was completely mistaken and there was nothing at all wrong with what I was experiencing. It made me consider the possibility that every kid in the Universe was brought up exactly like this, and I would be a complete fool—and in very big trouble—for running away to complain about it. Imagine how embarrassed Omzi and I would both be when the powers that be proved to me that the world is like this for everyone and I was just being an ass. This idea seemed exceedingly plausible, particularly when I was at my most tired and confused state, and as a result, I remained anchored to the yellow house and all that came with it.

Another muffled voice I often heard was actually the hardest to decipher, because it sounded as if I were underwater whenever it reverberated in my head. While submerged, I had no trouble holding my breath, and if I kept my eyes open, I could watch the never-ending waves caused by sumo wrestlers doing cannonballs off the tongues of giants as they lapped at the shoreline of my brain. But because my ears overflowed with the sounds of high-pitched, faraway echoes, I needed to strain in order to decipher everything that was being said. The message I received became less about actual words, and more about a feeling, like that of a strong, magnetic pull. This particular voice made me fear the outside world, and so stopped me from wanting to leave. I became petrified that if I consciously tried to break the gravitational pull that caused the waves in the first place, I would no longer be able to survive underwater, and I would drown in my own sweat and tears.

The loudest and clearest message I have ever received, however, was on a chilly morning as I walked to school and the Universe itself spoke to me. I had my ratty old ski hat pulled down over my ears, but I could still hear the message as clear as a bell. Omzi had found my puffy, army-green parka at Goodwill, which, by even the most basic outerwear standards, was basically useless. It had a stupid broken zipper that always got stuck halfway up, leaving a big gaping mouth that made me feel like my own jacket was laughing at me.

My gloveless hands were jammed as deeply into my pockets as they would go, and I was taking my time getting to school, counting the cracks in the sidewalk as I walked. The sky was a crisp, nautical blue that could almost make you forget where you were if you looked up long enough. Bitter gusts of wind quickly reminded you, however, in case you did forget, as they blew clouds as big as elephants in a blustery game of hide and go seek with the sun.

Every once in a while, I would look up and squint at the figure of a woman pushing a stroller up ahead of me. For some reason, she caught my interest, and I decided to walk a little faster to catch up to her. Why the hell I had any interest in her was beyond me, but I was compelled to see what she was doing on my route to school that day when I had never seen her before.

When I was almost directly behind her, I could see that she had a tall, confident posture, and the way she walked looked happy. That in itself was odd to me, but so was her stroller. It was smaller than a regular one, and I could see that it was sort of square-shaped and enclosed with a zipper that went around the top of the black lid. I thought for a minute that it might be one of those dog or cat strollers that I have seen on TV shows, but no one in our town had ever had one that I knew of.

My legs had a mind of their own by this point, as they worked like firing cylinders to pass the woman so I could see what the hell was in that stroller. We were now side by side, and she turned to look at me with the brightest smile and warmest eyes I have ever seen. Both of her gloved hands were gripping the bar on the stroller, and her arms were completely stretched out in front of her as she proudly pushed what I now saw was a creature of some sort, but not a dog or cat.

I could see there were clear plastic windows on the sides of the enclosed compartment, and a netting that served as air vents as well. I felt like I couldn't help myself, and with my curiosity on high alert, I stepped in front of her so that she would have to stop and talk to me. It was so unlike me, but there wasn't anything normal about the entire situation as it was to begin with.

Her smile remained on her face as she kindly greeted me with, "Hello!"

"Hi," I said, not looking at her for very long, because I couldn't take my eyes off the creature in the stroller. I couldn't believe what I was seeing, and as I stared at it, this crazy sense of happiness and freedom bubbled up within me like hot cheese on a pizza.

There was no point in trying to be polite, or make small talk first, so I just blurted out in astonishment, "Is that a rooster in your stroller?!" (I mean, c'mon! A freakin' rooster! In a stroller!)

"She's a hen, actually. But yeah. Her name is Nora."

My mouth dropped open like I was a Venus flytrap ready to catch a snack. No way in hell there is a hen getting pushed in a stroller in front of me on the way to school, and she has the same name as me. I had to be sure I wasn't dreaming, so I pinched the palm of my right hand as I asked if I could pet her.

As the woman unzipped the lid for me, she said, "Nora means light and honor. I named her that because she's like a star, and she has come to be a light in so many people's lives."

She pulled the top back and held it as an invitation to pet the bird. I put my hand in and stroked her feathers. She sat calmly in a little bit of hay that was scattered on the bottom of the encasement and peered up at me with a confidence I didn't realize was possible. I thought about all the people I tried to insult over the years by calling them a chicken, and realized I needed to improve my trash talk game.

"My name is Nora too," I told the woman, and I suppose the hen as well.

"Oh my gosh! I can't believe it! It must be meant to be. What are the odds?"

"She's very soft," I said.

"Yes, and she's molting. She's still getting her winter feathers in."

"Does she like being in the stroller?" I asked, even though it was fairly evident that she loved it.

"Oh yes! Nora loves her stroller, and she knows when she goes in it, she will be visiting people and making them happy. I take her to schools and the children read to her. It's something I developed to show how animals of any kind can bring a sense of calm and joy to people, and it encourages the kids to read. I also have a bunny, a snake, a dog, and a squirrel that I bring...but never all at once," she laughed.

"A squirrel? Is it friendly?" I said incredulously.

"Oh, yes! His name is Carl and he's actually the most requested animal I have. Well, we'd better get going. Nora has work to do. It was very nice talking with you," she said, while zipping the lid and providing a slight amount of pressure on the handlebar, which was my cue to step out of the way.

"Yeah, thanks for letting me pet her," I said as I stepped out of their way and let them by. Even though I was giddy with what felt like I just downed a handful of Omzi's happy pills, I stood there, slightly frozen by the whole encounter, and watched them until they were too small to see anymore. Was this some kind of crazy sign from the Universe to consider running away? To become free as a bird, even if that bird can't fly? I felt like it was too weird not to mean something significant.

Later that same extremely windy and cold Tuesday night, Momzilla had me doing the mountain of dishes that piled up in our kitchen sink from the meals she allowed herself, but not me, to eat. Our house (I could never call it a home) was a crazy and disgusting mess of old mail, boxes, plastic containers of God knows what—dirty dishes, plastic bags full of filthy clothing, piles of newspapers, magazines, stacks of vinyl records, rotting food, old furniture, and old Styrofoam coolers that I was afraid to look in because I feared they might contain human organs or body parts. And that was the tip of the iceberg.

These were the things you could see on the surface at first glance, but there was so much more that was buried underneath the mountains of filth and painful memories that will surely one day overflow from every window of the big yellow house. Our shower broke, and instead of fixing it, Omzi used the tub as another catch-all for more junk. The toilets, dishwasher, and kitchen sink were all messed up, clogged, or unusable, so I was forced to figure out how to get the toilet to flush by using a convoluted system of tubing and buckets that I dug out of a pile of junk in my room. Sometimes it worked, and sometimes it didn't.

I couldn't get the kitchen sink to work, because, although I was considered a gifted student, I was by no means a skilled plumber. I wished I didn't have to live in a house that had buckets of dirty water stinking up the basement, even if that was the least of my problems.

Because of our crappy conditions, I became kind of afraid of water. The water in our basement always stood ready and waiting for me—in buckets, barrels, and, sometimes, puddles—to either clean something with or to swallow my face when it was held under the surface until I felt like passing out. I have heard that some people find the sound of water comforting and relaxing. For me, it stirs up thoughts of drowning or being engulfed in dizzying waves, unable to determine which way is up. Dreams of overflowing toilets, capsizing ships, or being trapped in the rat-infested sewer systems of New York City often take hold of me while I fist fight the Sandman.

The last time I had a dream of this sort, it was even *more* messed up than usual. When I woke from it, I not only believed it had actually happened, but I was completely freaked out because I wasn't *at all* where I expected myself to be. The dream started in a small boat that I was rowing through the hallways of my school, that somehow opened up into a giant swimming pool that was infested with sharks. Everything around me was dark, but the water glowed a deep shade of red, as if it were lit by underwater light bulbs in the shady part of Paris.

The sharks began to slam into the boat, which created huge waves which crashed over my head, sending blood-like water to slowly pool in my lungs and around my ankles. I couldn't bail the water out fast enough, and the boat began to sink in slow motion.

Just before I was torn to bits by the sharks, I found myself standing on a starting block in a bathing suit at a swim meet. I hadn't trained, and my suit was too small. Old wooden bleachers were full of screaming spectators, and I saw that I was waiting for someone to complete their leg of a four-person relay. All six lanes had one person in them, freestyling furiously with someone poised and ready to dive in as the anchor of the relay, while the rest of the swimmers cheered their team on from the slimy, wet deck behind the blocks.

A sudden and very odd hush came over the entire pool area, and everyone started pointing at me. I began to feel like I was drowning in ugly jeers, taunts, and laughter. I looked down and noticed that I had the most unruly and incredibly embarrassing amounts of thick dark hair sprouting from my bathing suit, that made the front look like I was harboring a wig from someone's Halloween costume in my crotch. The hair completely covered the insides of my thighs, and the longer I stood there, the faster it grew down my legs and onto my feet. I had no other choice but to jump off the starting block and try to hide the hideousness under water.

The water was freezing cold and took my breath away. My heart raced and chlorine burned my eyes, which were screwed shut, until I heard a whirring sound followed by a loud thump and click. I pushed off the bottom of the pool with both feet, only to hit a clear, plexiglass cover that trapped me underwater. I was now the only person in the pool, but I could see everyone from the deck and bleachers standing over me with dishes, forks, knives, cups, and dead rats, which they began to throw at me. Everything flew from their hands in slow motion, and I watched in horror as the items made impact—one at a time—with the clear ceiling of my underwater prison. Each

wet, greasy-looking rat bounced and slammed into one another in ugly and twisted ways. Instead of letting me out so I
could breathe, everyone just stood there, and I could see their
happy and maniacal faces while thunderous sounds of laughter echoed underwater as I began to drown.

Just then I found myself fully awake. I bolted straight up
and sucked in huge amounts of air as I frantically grasped at
everything and nothing around me. The school nurse immediately ran over and tried to calm me down. I tried my best to act
like I was okay, but I had absolutely no idea how I had ended
up in the nurse's office. I still kind of expected to be dripping
wet with highly chlorinated water, or to see her holding a cup
or a fork in her hand, but everything was business as usual in
the small, sterile room.

I certainly couldn't ask her how I got there, and why I
wasn't drenched...so I took a quick sip from the glass of water
she got for me and went back to class.

That horrid dream came to my mind again as I was doing
my usual house cleaning, in the nude, like always. I had to carry the dishes down to the basement to do them in the laundry
buckets, since our kitchen sink was useless. I fantasized that
one day I would overcome my fear of water, and that I would
have a clean tub, toilet, and sink in my house.

I purposely made lots of trips, carefully balancing the dishes as I navigated the steep, wooden stairs. Part of the reason
I took such great time and care with this chore was obviously to avoid the horrible punishment if I so much as chipped
a cup. But the biggest reason was to bide time to formulate
an escape plan in my mind. Having my "ducks in a row," as
Momzilla would say, seemed like the best course of action if
I wanted to get away both successfully and unscathed.

The water in the buckets was frigid and made it difficult
to get the dishes fully clean. I only had my raw, red hands
and fingers to chip away at the crusty food left on my grandmother's old white and yellow daisy plates.

When I finished the last spoon, I sat back on my heels for a
minute to admire my work. I had done a pretty amazing job,
I must say, considering the conditions. But the time for small
victories was over, so I began the process of bringing the piles

of plates, cups, forks, knives, and spoons back upstairs to the kitchen.

My mother was laying in our bed, eating an apple with her favorite paring knife and watching *Law and Order,* when the deafening crash shook our entire house. It was my very last trip (literally) up the steps, and although I was being ultra-careful not to go too fast, I was hugging a stack of seven plates (along with a couple spoons and forks) close to my body, just below my chest, and somehow miscalculated the distance between the last two stairs.

The top of my left foot caught and sent me flying forward in what I can only imagine might have looked like Superman. My arms were stretched straight out in front of me, and my legs kicked back behind me as I was catapulted through the doorway of our basement. It felt like I was frozen in midair, and I had plenty of time to watch as the dishes and cutlery traveled in slow motion from my hands, through the air, and against the wall, where everything shattered into a million pieces, including the last little shards of my life—that never fit together in the first place.

8

When the sun actually shines during the winter in Upstate New York, I swear it feels absolutely magical. Chaos is stretched out like a long, furry tube in the heat of the sunbeams that spread across my bedroom floor. The bright, warm sunlight (combined with the amazing run I just had, and the fantastic fucking the previous night) makes me feel almost superhuman. A positive surge of energy washes over my body that feels amazing, but also makes me very nervous. I do love to feel this good, but when I do, a little voice inside tells me that I don't deserve it, and that for every good feeling I have, something equally as shitty will come my way. And *this* is exactly why I see Dr. Sharee twice a week.

I need to get my ass moving and out the door, especially if I want to stop by Tarts & Vicars for a latte with an extra shot, and some innocent barista flirtation before my therapy session and twenty-four-hour shift. I gather my shit together in a hurry, but I take the time to pet Chaos and plant a quick kiss on her hot, Dorito-shaped ear before I run out the door. Her short black hair feels hotter than an oven beneath my touch.

"You're gonna bake yourself to death in this sun, ya little fart face."

She answers me with a bit of a mew and rolls over.

"If you say so, Biscuit Butt," serves as my retort. "I'll be back really soon, I promise! Just gotta get my work done and then I'll be back."

It's not always easy for me to work the hours that I do, especially when I put in OT. I remind myself again that it's a good thing I have Nathan to check in on Chaos, to be sure she has her food, water, and proper amounts of snuggle time, basically whenever I need him. I repeat this fact to myself every time I want to kill the dude for being overbearing, intrusive, or just plain irritating. The popularity of his band (both here and in Japan, for some fucked-up reason) has really been picking up. Undressed Enema has been headlining a lot of decent-sized shows, and their gigs in bars and clubs have picked up a ton as well. The last time Nathan stopped by to see if I wanted to hang out, he said that they might even book a short Japanese tour next summer. But no matter how nuts his practice and playing schedules get, he always makes time to help me out when I'm at work. Anxious thoughts about what I will do with Chaos if and when Nathan goes to Japan try to creep into my cranium, but I chase them away with a saying that involves crossing a bridge at the appropriate time. Instinctively, I cringe upon the realization that just such a saying would make Omzi proud.

I often wonder just how much snooping Nathan does when he's alone in my apartment. Thankfully, there isn't much to see, and although it wouldn't be the worst thing in the world if he saw my bag of tricks, I wouldn't consider it to be ideal either. If the dude has big enough balls to rifle through my shit when I'm not home, it would serve him right to be horribly embarrassed by anything he found. I just hope he isn't in here sniffing my dirty workout clothes or anything like that. Even I have standards. And if I'm being honest with myself, he's the first person I thought of when I couldn't find my favorite silk scarf the other night. I always keep it in the same place. When I realized it was nowhere to be found, and that I would have to go without the moody little skulls and sultry, slippery feel of it, a flash of anger went through me that I immediately associated with Nathan.

I know he doesn't mind helping me with the cat (mostly because he loves my *other* kitty), but he has often said to me how much he thinks it would suck to work for twenty-four hours straight. I can understand why he would say that, and if

I had any other job in the world, I would probably feel exactly the same way. But honestly, as corny as it may sound, what I do isn't just a job; it's actually a huge part of who I am.

I love my Engine 7 B-shift crew family. Of course, there are a couple guys who can be real dicks, but you're going to have that with any job. The entire fire department is the supportive family that I never had until I became a firefighter. And like all good families (unlike my biological one), even though everyone doesn't always get along, when it comes down to it, everyone always rallies for one another no matter what. I would go so far as to say that the department is an extension of ourselves. We hold each other to high ethical standards and have our own code of conduct for one another, which brings me an enormous sense of comfort and pride. And God knows, I've never been invited to, or attended, so many weddings, birthdays, graduations, or holiday parties in my entire life.

I feel extremely fortunate to have passed my paramedic exam so easily and nailed the written and physical tests to get into training and hired at such a young age. The fact that I'm a woman never dawned on me as a deterrent to go after this male-dominated profession, although Nathan has voiced his opinion about this aspect of my job. In fact, I didn't really think about it until I actually started working in the firehouse.

Clearly, Ronnie and I have separate sleeping quarters and we change in a different locker room than the guys. Aside from that, however, we do everything else that they do, including working out together in the house, cooking and eating together, maintaining the rigs, cleaning the house, and even tending to the landscaping. I'm certainly no stranger to cleaning bathrooms and doing difficult chores, so all of it seems like a vacation compared to what I was used to.

A couple of the guys in our crew have taken both Ronnie and I under their wing: making sure no one fucks with us and doing all they can to ensure that we're treated as equals. My buddy Mike is one of these guys. He's been on the job for a lot longer than I have and is about ten years older than me. We have a mutual, albeit funny respect for one another. We both have a dry, sarcastic sense of humor, and he loves to pretend to hate me. When I walk into a room, he makes a face like someone farted, and says, "Oh shit, there she is." Or, "Here comes trouble." But after a tough call, or at the end of a killer training class, he's always the first one to come over and fist bump me without a word.

My absolute favorite duty I have been given is one that doesn't even qualify as a job in my book. It's an absolute joy and pleasure, in all actuality, to have been assigned the responsibility and care of our house dog, Roger, whenever I'm working. I actually hope for and love overtime because of *him*, rather than for the extra money I can earn. He was named after the last original fireman in our department, Captain Roger Dodkins, who retired a few years back. A man extremely well-respected for his bravery and integrity, Captain Dodkins was truly the last of his kind, and my Roger Dodger is absolutely the *first* of his kind, at least at our firehouse.

He's a big, handsome blue-nosed American Pit Bull Terrier who was rescued from a vacant warehouse building two weeks before I joined the department. He has his own page in our firefighter's fundraising calendar (Mister October, thank you very much) and rides the rig proudly in every parade. Hell, the big, goofy meatball has more Instagram followers than everyone in the whole department put together.

Roger and I were both newcomers to the house at the same time, and it was love at first sight for me and for the giant alligator head of a dog as well. The guys were all too thrilled to hand over his care, especially his dootie duties, and I was more than happy to take them. That being said, Roger helps every firefighter in the crew. When we get back from tough calls, he is always there to comfort us. Roger knows to get out of the way each and every time the alarm goes off, but no matter what, the big hunk of love is waiting by the door for us when we return. Once in a while, I even sneak him into my room at night to snuggle me and help me sleep. Other than Chaos, he's the most precious living being in my life.

* * *

When I step into Tarts & Vicars, I'm greeted by the pleasant smells of ground espresso, fresh croissants, and a touch of cinnamon wafting through the air. The buzz of the busy café rivals the caffeine buzzes of the many quasi-hipster patrons who dot the establishment, diligently glued to their phones and tablets. The place is alive with loud music, the whistling of the espresso machine, and a unique brand of coffee-induced energy. Tarts & Vicars is always packed, night and day, because it has a liquor license and serves wine and booze in addition to coffees, gourmet pastries, and chocolates—and also because it's cool as fuck. Aside from being a PMS paradise (due to the killer chocolate selection), the musical playlists are also eclectic and amazing, and they have truly mastered a European vibe that so many other places try to achieve but fail at miserably.

I stop in on a regular basis after a run or before work or therapy for the awesome and unique variety of lattes. I'm not ashamed to admit that I have a major caffeine addiction. I absolutely love a good coconut milk triple shot latte after a long run—but let's be real here, shall we? The biggest motivating factor for me to go out of my way just to grab a coffee, in addition to caffeine, is that I'm currently hooked on the stimulating flirtations poured out by a gorgeous Barista named Maya. Getting my coffee here is, in essence, like doing a daytime hunt, one which takes much more time and patience than my adventures in the dark. Just because I don't have my bag of tricks with me doesn't mean I can't go for a prowl every now and then without it. We have flirted shamelessly during some of my past visits, and I feel that perhaps today I'll get a muffin as well as coffee.

The shop is bustling, so the line to place my order is pretty long, which I mistakenly surmise as the perfect opportunity to study Maya undetected. The hiss of the espresso machine sounds like shrieking voices in my head, but I shake them loose with a quick nod that I cleverly disguise as an adjustment to the hood of my jacket.

She looks over at me and catches me staring. I don't flinch, although I want to because, truth be told, I feel like my bones have vaporized, and the area between my legs has swelled like a bee sting. She's one of those girls who is so pretty it actually hurts to look at her. Maya is kind of a girl next door, Lululemon type with a slick, high ponytail, athletic build (with perfect posture), and an ass that could make a stone angel weep. It seems to me that underneath the squeaky-clean surface is the perfect amount of bad girl trying to get out, as evidenced by the singular black and gray tattoo of a wolf and gypsy sitting under a full moon on her forearm, and the adorable little hoop ring in her right nostril.

I hold her gaze while she flashes me a smile as hot and powerful as the sun itself. I picture myself pressing her up against a wall from behind and feeling her heart pound against my chest. I lean in to kiss her neck and the delicate area behind her ear. The sounds she makes send me into an erotic orbit. My fingertips sweep the sides of her breasts and her ribcage ever so slightly as she arches her back and slowly peels off her yoga pants. I'm in a fog of my own sexual desire when the dude behind me gives me a slight tap on the shoulder and tells me to move up. It's my turn to order and I'm standing there like a jackass holding up the line.

I laugh and jog up to the register, where the cashier is waiting to hear what I want. I feel like the whole damn place must know what I really want, and that they can all see and smell the pheromones oozing from my pores. Somewhat awkwardly, I place my order, give the guy my name, pay, and then gladly step down to wait for my drink, which gives Maya and I an opportunity to chat.

"Since you're such a devout latte girl, have you ever tried our turmeric latte?"

I look at her like she just grew an extra head. "I have no idea what that is."

She squints her eyes a bit and nods her head toward the specials listed neatly in blocky, handwritten letters on a large chalkboard. "I don't think they describe it on the menu properly. It's actually an exotic and delicious elixir that creates a sense of comfort and wellbeing."

"Well, shit. I still have no idea what it is, but you sold me. I'll get one next time for sure."

"It's a gorgeous day today, huh?" she half yells over the noise of the machine.

"Yeah, they don't come often enough around here," I respond, maybe a little too quietly.

She smiles and says, "So true. But hey, this is Utica, baby. What do you want?"

Beneath her work apron, she's wearing a body-hugging tank top, and I thoroughly enjoy watching her arms and shoulders flex and catch the light as she manipulates the frothier. I crack a huge smile and tell her, "There *is* something that I want."

She tilts her head to the side, squints her eyes at me again, and cocks a single eyebrow as she deftly dumps all three espresso shots into my cup at once and says, "Oh yeah?"

I know she thinks she has me, but I say, "Yeah. I've always *wanted* to know why they call this place Tarts & Vicars, but I've never asked."

She throws her head back and laughs, confirming that I didn't even come close to saying what she had expected me to say. She takes her time while she carefully places the lid on my drink and writes my name on it.

As she hands me the cup, she extends her index finger and purposely drags it across my own while it changes hands. I feel an electric shock roll through my entire body like an ocean wave. An eternity passes, and I half forget what I'm even doing here. She explains that the owners are from England, and that Tarts & Vicars is a type of costume party where the people either dress as a tart in revealing or sexy clothing, or they dress as a vicar, priest or member of the clergy.

"I guess it's kind of like a good versus evil thing, like a shot of espresso versus a shot of whiskey. Sometimes you need one, the other...or both! They also really liked the idea of naming their American shop something they would never call it in England."

"Ah, that would explain the Union Jack hanging behind the bar, and the cool, European feel to this place," I answer.

"Exactly! Have you been to England?" she asks super enthusiastically.

"Nope, but I've read about it, and I've seen *Bridget Jones Diary*," I say lamely, but she laughs politely anyway. "So, they wouldn't call their coffee shop Tarts & Vicars in England, because everyone there would know the real meaning?"

She giggles and says, "Probably not, but we're known for

our *heavenly* raspberry *tarts*, so the name could still fit anyway."

"I love it!" I say, as I start to back away, because I know she's busy.

Just as I'm starting to leave, the dude at the counter yells out, "Hey Maya...we're getting a little backed up here."

She smiles and says, "Duty calls—and I hope you will too."

I just say, "Okay, see ya," and walk out of the shop. The cold air and blinding sun make my eyes water, but not enough to keep me from seeing Maya's number written underneath my name on the cup. She has also scribbled 'call or text' and drawn a little smiley face with its tongue hanging out, causing me to practically float to my doctor appointment. I realize, quite gleefully, that I'm the hunter who just became the prey.

* * *

Dr. Sharee's office is located on a little tree-lined street next to an urban park with a playground, about a mile away from the firehouse. The location is perfect for her, truly suiting her personality.

I walk past the empty park and try to keep my thoughts positive by picturing Maya's smile. (And, for the love of God, that ass.) If I look at the swings, teetertotters, and slides, even the brightest sunny day can't keep me from feeling a tinge of darkness—playgrounds in the winter depress me and bring back crappy memories.

Both my hands are wrapped around the coffee cup to keep them warm, so I direct my attention to the smiley face and tongue drawn in black marker, which has now slightly smeared under my grip. The face is pulled out long and exaggerated, making it appear to be moving. It reminds me of one of those animated flip books.

I'm staring at the tongue, with fiery thoughts of Maya's warm tongue intertwining with my own, when it suddenly turns from black to red. The happy face is suddenly demonic, with a forked tongue that's wildly flicking up at me from the cup. The strangest shriek escapes me, and I involuntarily hurl the cup from my hands. If I hadn't felt the high-pitched squeal reverberate in my own throat, I would have thought someone else had expelled the horrific sound.

I'm only a couple yards away from the door to Dr. Sharee's office, but I stand frozen in my tracks with eyes as big and round as above-ground swimming pools and frantically look around to see if anyone has heard or seen what just happened. At first, I think I want someone there to bear witness, to say they saw it too, but when I see that I am alone, I'm relieved that the incident will remain my secret, like it never happened at all.

The whole street is empty except for a single, brown, bushy-tailed tree squirrel. He scurries over, props himself up on his hind legs, and unleashes a barrage of obnoxious chirpy grunts to scold me for the mess I've created on his icy sidewalk.

I look him in his beady little rodent eyes and say, "Save it, punk."

He cocks his head to the side in a manner I thought was reserved for birds, and flicks his tail, which I interpret as his way of telling me to fuck off.

If it hasn't already been determined that I'm officially bat shit crazy (and believe me, it has), I'm pretty sure the smack-down that I'm currently engaged in with this squirrel would sufficiently dispel any shade of doubt in that regard. So, thoroughly convinced that no one is around to hear it, I say, "Aren't you supposed to be hibernating or something? Crawl back into your hole, dickhead."

He comes down from his hind legs, chitter chatters at me one last time, then picks up my cup with his teeth and takes off.

I stand still for a minute and sweep my eyes back and forth to be absolutely sure no one has seen this incredibly insane episode. Once I'm positive that I'm alone—and that Skippy is back up in his nest somewhere—I silently confirm with myself that I will make no mention of this whatsoever in my session.

As soon as I step into Dr. Sharee's warm, inviting office, I instantly feel much better. It's been a long, crazy morning, and it's only 8:30 a.m. Even after all of that, I'm still a little early for my appointment, so I try to shake away the residual stress of my hallucination as I sink down into a cozy, overstuffed chair in the waiting room. Dr. Sharee doesn't have a receptionist (which I love) and there is a separate door for patients to exit after their session in order to ensure privacy. When her door is shut, it means she's with someone.

I can kind of hear muffled voices behind the door, but I don't strain to listen. I'm still jacked up, and I make a conscious effort to settle down so that I'll be fully recovered by the time the door opens.

It's at times like this that I realize how happy I am to have such an incredible psychiatrist whom I truly like and feel comfortable with. She's not just a great doctor, she's an amazing person, and in a way, she is everything that I'm not but would love to be.

Dr. Sharee exudes a positive energy and kindness that is palpable. She has a bright and shiny personality, but not in an annoying cheerleader on amphetamines sort of way. I like the way she listens with care and then dishes out some no-nonsense, constructive suggestions to help change my behavior or mindset in a way that makes me think it was all my idea in the first place.

I have issues with boundaries (duh) and although I have never told her, I have often wished that she was my mom. If I let her know about these stupid, childish feelings, I'm sure she would say it's some form of transference, not uncommon for people like me with mommy issues. She would probably do so in much nicer, more flowery terminology, but that would be the gist of it.

The door to her office clicks open and she stands in the middle of the doorway with her usual warm smile that makes me think of cookies out of the oven or my cat curled up in my lap. She's always barefoot, no matter what time of the year it may be, or how cold it is outside.

Her inner office space is like a sanctuary that has expertly married a bohemian decorative mix of looks from Anthropologie, a Peace Corps hut, and a Day of the Dead celebration with a touch of Venice Beach Surf Shop. When I step into her office, it feels like I have boarded my mothership. Pillows with Indian prints, Turkish throw rugs, plants with giant green leaves, and African masks coexist beautifully with skulls, dream catchers, salt lamps, and a bold Mexican-inspired color scheme.

Dr. Sharee is wearing a boho chic outfit of flowing, chalky-white cotton pants and an oatmeal-colored tank top, that combined with her short, platinum-blonde hair and the sun filtering behind her, gives her an almost angelic appearance. If I told her that, she would find it hysterical, so I keep my observation to myself.

Every time I see her, I can't help but think that she looks like Jessica Lange and P!nk had a love child—if that were actually possible—and she's a grounded, calming, beautiful, badass combination of them both. She's also the type of woman who has no problem telling you her age. Sometimes she puts me in my place when I question whether or not she can relate to how I feel, or to some of my sexual exploits, by saying, "I'm fifty-one, but I wasn't always this age, and I'm not dead yet."

Much like the doctor herself, the office décor is worldly, unique, bold, artistic, colorful, calming, vibrant, and so much more. The first time I stepped into her office, I felt transported to another part of the world, and even with everything there was to absorb and to look at, my eye was immediately drawn to a small, ornate frame on her bookshelf that contained a copy of 'my' *Invictus* poem. That was when I knew this chick was my spirit animal, even if she occasionally pissed me off, or made me dig into places in my mind that I didn't want to revisit.

I have been assigned by Dr. Sharee to keep a gratitude journal, where I write lists of the things that I'm happy about or grateful for. At first, I thought it would be a little too cheesy and not at all effective, but I have come to realize that it's one of the best therapeutic tools I have ever been given. My gratitude journal is a potent supplement to my other forms of medicine, and it helps me manage my stress, boosts my self-esteem, and keeps me from ruminating on negative thought patterns. Of course, Chaos and Roger Dodger are always on my lists, but one of the things I am most grateful for was being referred to Dr. Sharee by my Chief in the first place.

There is still a huge stigma attached to mental health issues in the first responder services, but due to the number of suicides that have occurred in our department alone over the past few years, our standard roundtable talks after a call are now slightly more focused on how we feel. If anyone needs additional support, resources are offered. Still, a lot of the guys think it's shameful to receive help from a shrink, and that only someone with a screw loose would need it. Even so, thankfully, seeking support has become much more accepted in our firehouse.

I know I need it more than most, for obvious reasons, but I hope that sooner rather than later having mental health problems will be completely stigma-free, and that all first responders will get the support they need to offset the difficult jobs we love to do. So many firefighters are racked with guilt, playing the calls that ended tragically over and over in their heads. As if our equipment isn't heavy enough, most of us walk around every day with the extra burden of wondering what we could have done differently to change the outcome of some of the grisly calls that haunt us like ghosts. And then there are the times when not knowing if you saved someone is even harder than knowing you didn't. A lot of the time, we respond to an accident with the squad, and help care for people before they're transported to the hospital. They're alive when they leave us, but not knowing what happens after that can feel like torture.

We tend to be the ones who show up on everybody's absolute worst day, and it's virtually impossible not to absorb the grief of the people we help. In a strange way, I'm almost grateful for all the shit I've been through, because it has made me the tough, resilient freak of nature that I am, and seeing shrinks and getting help for my issues is my wheelhouse. I have basically been raised by mental and behavioral health professionals, so seeing a doctor to talk about my dreams or interpret a Rorschach inkblot test is no big deal to me. Hell, every time I start with a new therapist, I consider how many poor, innocent trees have sacrificed their lives for the gigantic stacks of case files and court documents my time in the social care system as a child has resulted in.

The office door clicks as it opens, and I stand up so quickly I feel a little lightheaded. I pretend not to feel the headrush and hope that the big, toothy smile I give her makes me look more stable than I feel.

Graciously, Dr. Sharee steps back, allowing me to walk through the door. She greets me with, "It's good to see you, Nora."

This particular greeting is both purposefully and intentionally given to me, and every time she says it, I visibly cringe.

She extends a hand, offering me to sit, while she gets comfortable in her velvety, dark purple chair, sitting with her legs crossed underneath her.

She's a strong, fit woman, but with a petite stature that makes her appear younger than she is. I know she's a pretty amazing athlete, and she played women's lacrosse at University of Michigan, but I wonder what kind of workouts she does currently. One of these days, I might actually ask her, but I haven't decided if it's inappropriate to do so.

She sits perched like a little cross-legged bird, expertly balancing her notepad on one knee, and asks me how I am.

I tell her I'm doing okay, and she answers me with a smile. I know this is my cue to elaborate, so I add, "I'm still having that crazy dream with the toilets and the centipedes. I hate when I can't sleep. It makes me feel crazier than I already am."

"You're not crazy, Nora. You have experienced significantly more trauma in your short twenty-four years on this planet than most people do their entire lives. I would say you're handling everything in the most extraordinary way that you can. I think a lot of your anxiety still stems from the unrealistic standard you have set for yourself at work, while at the same time trying to fly beneath the radar, as well as from your desire for control in your life."

"I'm not fucking Nathan anymore," I say abruptly.

She laughs and says, "Oh! Okay, we're switching gears, I guess."

"I get so confused with my feelings for him at times, but I can't admit that to him."

"Why can't you admit it to him?"

"Because he's too sweet and sensitive, which I like sometimes, but mostly it makes me want to punch him in the head. If I tell him that I get confused about my feelings, he'll latch on, and I can't handle that. Keeping him at arm's length, and as a friend, is the best way for me to manage my relationship with him, I think."

"You might be right about that."

"Can I ask you something?"

"It's your dime, sister...and um, isn't that why you're here?" she says with a smile.

"It's gonna sound New-Agey and weird."

In a compassionate and sincere voice, she says, "Well, this sounds interesting. Let it rip!"

I take a minute to gather my thoughts in an attempt to express them as accurately as possible. "Okay, have you ever felt like you were wrestling with the duality of self? Like you're entrenched in a battle for this single-beam, center-stage spotlight of consciousness? Oh my God, forget it! Spewing this happy horseshit just makes me want to puke. *I'm* not even buying into what I just said, so how can I expect *you* to buy it, let alone help me figure it out?"

She gives me the head tilt that tells me she's considering everything I said and responds, "I don't think it's horseshit at all. The duality of self is complicated and extremely unsettling, but it's not a crock. Keep going with this train of thought, Nora."

I take a long breath in and try to sort out what I want to say. "I guess I feel like I'm battling a constant fluctuation in my emotions: like the furthest extremes of both good and bad moods are constantly duking it out within me."

"So, what I'm hearing you say is that you often feel like two very separate people inside one individual. Is that right?"

"Yes, and if I'm being honest, which I know is the whole point of my being here, it scares me."

She furrows her brow and asks, "How so?"

"So many reasons. Mostly because I worry if I can truly trust myself—when I see, hear, or even feel certain things, I don't know if it's real or not."

"That could stem from the fact that you were punished so severely for the things you saw and heard as a child, or even for letting *yourself be seen* in terms of your talents or ambitions. To make matters worse, your mom often said you made up or lied about the things you heard and saw."

I pause and absorb her words like a sponge. "I guess that

makes sense for why I don't trust my own perceptions at times. We have discussed it many times that I don't fit the bipolar diagnosis, but when I get like that, it makes me think of my friend, Darcy."

"Your best friend and doppelgänger from when you were in Residential Treatment?"

"Yes."

"Why does it make you think of her?"

"Well, it's a long story, obviously, but from what I know, she came from a good home, but got caught up in the drug scene and skipping school, and all that. She was partying one night with a group of friends and was sexually assaulted by one of the guys while she was passed out. She said the more her parents tried to help her, the more she pushed them away, acted out, and did drugs. She stopped going to school altogether when one of her counselors told her, mistakenly, that she was bipolar. The misdiagnosis made her behavior even worse, and after being caught with drugs multiple times, a judge sent her to residential treatment to complete a program that included both counseling and rehab."

"And how do you think that relates to you?"

"Well, I know how shitty it is to feel like you aren't being seen for who you truly are. Sometimes people judge you and the things you do without knowing what you have been through. Like, 'there's a reason underneath it all for the shit I'm doing, asshole.' But then, you can't win, because when people do find out that something bad happened to you, and they see your shitty behavior, they judge you for *that* too. They stamp a bipolar diagnosis, or whatever new and hip explanation they can come up with at that time, on your ass, so they can tell you who and what you are. They want to cross shit off a little list and put you in a specific box without really understanding what's going on with you as an individual, and it pisses me off. Wait, does that make sense?"

"Yes. It makes perfect sense. But do you think you might be the one who is stamping the diagnosis on yourself?"

"Kind of, yeah. I spend so much time trying to hide my feelings and my past, that when it manifests in aggressive ways, I worry that maybe I have something I'm not addressing. I do worry that I might be bipolar or something."

"You aren't bipolar. If you were, it would be okay, and we would address it, but in my expert opinion, you aren't."

"That's pretty much what the therapist at RTC told my friend, and I think she was right. I hope you're right about me too. Well, either way, I often think of her manic episodes when I feel certain ways."

"What ways are you referring to?"

"Like what I said earlier, that one day I'm full of joy and the next day I'm consumed with dread. I feel like a prisoner in my own body. It's a horrible feeling, like I'm stuck on an amusement park ride that never ends, and all I want to do is get off and get away from everything. Then I get super frustrated because it's impossible to get away from yourself. Sometimes I feel very strong, usually when I'm at work or working out, but other times, I can't tell if my body even belongs to me. It's like I leave it sometimes."

"That's why I don't think 'duality of self' is bullshit, as many might say it is. I think we all have two sides, and you rely on both of yours to cope with the trauma you experienced as a child."

She sits up a little straighter and says, "You can feel in doubt of everything in your life one minute and the next, believe in absolutely everything. That doesn't mean you are bipolar. You are allowed, and, in fact, *need*, to feel, Nora. You are allowed to *see yourself* for who you are and accept both your light and dark sides. In fact, being able to recognize and address all of this is true progress, in my opinion." She stops because I burst out laughing.

"What's so funny?"

"I just can't believe you said my 'light and dark sides'."

"Why? Too *Star Wars*?"

"That's funny, but no. I told you how Darcy and I were called the star sisters, but I never told you about the self-esteem-building exercise we did once in group therapy, where we looked up the origin of our names and then created posters with drawings based on what our names meant.

I discovered my name was of English, Greek, and Latin origin and it means 'light; woman of honor.' When Darcy looked up her name, she found that it was of Irish and Gaelic origin, and that it meant 'dark.' She really took it to heart, like we were two halves of the same person, but I was the good half, and she was the bad one. She was pretty depressed about it for a while after that, and then she ended up going AWOL. I always wondered if it was my fault somehow that she ran."

"I'm very sorry to hear that, Nora. I know that when you live in residential treatment, there is often difficulty maintaining boundaries and individuality. It may not have felt like it at the time, and although you became very close and bonded over shared feelings and emotions, you and Darcy were two very different people, and it certainly wasn't your fault she ran. It's a shame that whoever conducted that exercise didn't look up the meanings of everyone's names beforehand. Just saying."

I nod my head in agreement.

"I actually felt so bad about it, I asked the staff if I could paint a mural on the wall of the entrance to the girls' wing, because I thought it would help cheer her up. I put together a proposal and did a mockup drawing, and the big bosses loved it and granted me permission. They said it was good for my therapy, but I knew that it would also make the facility appear more progressive in its treatment, and a bunch of shit like that. So, they bought the paint and brushes, and I did a really cool black background that looked like a dark, inky sky with ruby red planets scattered around it. In the middle, I painted star constellations and stardust in the shape of two girls who were holding hands and dancing on the Milky Way. Then I added the Martin Luther King, Jr. quote: 'Only in the darkness can you see the stars.' It turned out so beautifully, that a guy from the newspaper came and took a picture of it and did a pretty cool story about it too. I was just happy that Darcy saw it before she ran, and that it made her happy again."

"That's amazing. You're such a good friend, and a talented and creative artist too. Going back to your feelings associated with duality of self; I know that the emotional unrest can be extremely overwhelming, but the good news is, it doesn't have to be a life sentence. It might be hard to believe at times, but you aren't a prisoner of your mind, your fears, or even your past. You *can* take control of the fluctuations and regulate your mind. And *you,* my dear, are stronger and smarter than anyone I know, which is why overcoming this particular type of mental state is completely and positively achievable."

"And my meds can't hurt either, right?"

"Yes, your medication is only going to help as well."

"Wow, thank you. I actually feel so much better."

"Well, *you're* doing all the work. So, from what you said earlier, it sounds like you're still running and getting to the gym on a regular basis, and it's helping quite a bit?"

I tell her that I am, and that I'm almost religious about it. "Fitness really keeps me centered and focused."

"Good! I'm happy you're keeping up with that mental house cleaning so your moods and emotions can remain as uncluttered as possible. Now, how is your gratitude journal coming along; did you bring it?"

Sheepishly, I say, "No. I was in such a rush to get out the door." *I'm grateful for you,* I think to myself.

"That's okay...next time. We've covered a lot of ground during this session regarding your mood fluctuations, nightmares, how you view yourself in the world, and how others view you as well. We're just about out of time for now, anyway, but be sure to list at least ten things per day that you are grateful for so you can keep your head and your heart in a positive place. You can rewire negative thinking by focusing on all the incredible people, animals, experiences, and things that you already have in your life."

When I leave her office, this morning's hallucination, as well as the calamity with Skippy the squirrel, are ancient history. I feel recharged and ready, with my head in the right place, to start my shift at the firehouse.

9

Free crack being handed out on the street couldn't even tear Omzi away from an episode of *Law and Order*, but the sound of breaking dishes sure as shit could do the trick. The last few chips of porcelain were still making their way to our filthy hallway floor when I heard her yell angrily, "Nora! What in *the* hell is going on?!"

At that moment, as she came barreling down the steps from the bedroom we shared, with the Swiss Army knife and a chunk of apple still in her hands, I knew that the cuts on both my knees from landing in the rubble on the hallway floor were the least of my worries. From the look of horror on her face, one would think she actually had feelings, and that the mess before her was a basket of dead kittens instead of a few broken plates.

"This is the straw that broke the camel's back, Nora Elaine Horvath! You know what? A long time ago, some dumb ass said, 'Don't throw the baby out with the bath water,' but that's exactly what I should have done with you."

My knees were burning from the fresh cuts. I knew damn well that anything I did at that point would only antagonize her and exacerbate things further, so I just remained still.

"Get up!" she screamed furiously. Christ Almighty, girl, is it possible for you to do anything right? How hard is it to wash a few dishes and put them away properly? Huh?! That's *it*! I'm throwing you out with the bath water."

She grabbed me by the hair and dragged me sideways

through the kitchen to the back door. I very rarely protested any of her punishments because that only brought me more pain and trouble, but I was naked and bleeding, and it was cold and dark outside, and worst of all, I knew how Omzi's mind worked.

"I'm so sorry I broke the dishes. Please just let me go clean it up!" I pleaded.

With a tightly wound fist, she held my hair in a long, painful ponytail as she used her other hand to forcefully jerk open the scratched-up door and throw me out, onto the back porch. By now her face was lobster red, and I realized she was going to make me stay out there to die.

She told me to sit on the porch until she came back but didn't give me any indication of when that might be. The back door slammed shut so forcefully that the window in it shattered, causing glass to rain down on my head and naked body. Tiny shards decorated my hair like an evil tiara, while jagged chunks threatened to slice me up with every move I made.

I'd almost jumped out of my gooseflesh skin at the sound of the crashing window, and I figured the whole neighborhood would soon come running to see what happened. No one came. I was already shivering like I had fallen through a hole in the ice of a frozen lake when I heard the heavy clunk of the lock and saw the light go out in the kitchen. I was quite literally afraid for my life and tried my best to concentrate on what to do next, but every coherent thought in my head was shaken loose by the incessant chattering of my teeth.

The back porch was covered with a slanting roof, but it wasn't screened in, and the railings and back steps had been broken for years. Bits of paint were barely hanging onto the splintery old boards by the skin of their teeth, and I felt the loose flakes mixed in with broken glass beneath my fingers in the dark.

In an effort to stand up, I got on my knees, but immediately fell back on my heels as the pain ripped through my entire body, causing me to cry out into the night like an injured wolf.

There was no way around it, as I couldn't rely on my shaking legs alone to get me up. I was going to have to use my hands to prop myself up before my legs could be invited to the party.

Trying to put as little weight as I possibly could on my fingertips and feet, I slowly made my way to a standing position. I couldn't see it in the blackness that surrounded me, but I knew blood was now coming from my hands and feet too, and not just from my knees.

I wasn't sure how far the glass had scattered, but I was pretty sure I was standing in the midst of it. So, with a deep breath, I used every bit of strength I had to leap out of the sea of broken glass, hoping to fly over the sharks and piranhas and land further along the porch without being bitten. I managed to clear most of it, but I felt a nibble or two upon landing.

The night was strangely quiet, and if it weren't for the unbelievable horror I was currently experiencing, it may have been described as serene. It was then that it dawned on me; if I stayed out here, and didn't die of hypothermia first, the flakes of paint—and maybe even the glass—would most definitely be my next meal.

I bit my lower lip as I turned and looked out into what I knew was our backyard, but I couldn't see a thing through the black blanket of sky that was draped over it. I didn't have my getaway plan quite ready yet, and I really wanted to be better prepared, but it was clear that the exact day and time for me to run had just been chosen for me, and before I could talk myself out it, I leaped off the porch and took off into the darkness.

The cold night air and my pumping adrenaline made me feel both manic and superhuman. My bare feet crunched through the frost as I ran, but it was nothing compared to the pain of the cuts and bruises I was accustomed to on the soles of my feet.

The nearest police station was located across the street, diagonally, from my school, which was a little more than two miles away from the yellow house. I knew exactly how to get there, even in the dark, so I wasn't worried about finding my way. It was the fear of what would happen if the monster caught me before I reached my destination that threatened to paralyze me.

My nose and eyes were running like a faucet and I kept wiping at them angrily with the backs of my hands. I couldn't stop myself from craning my head over my shoulder as I hauled my body forward, fully expecting to see Omzi's headlights at any moment.

Running forward and looking back may not have been the smartest thing to do, especially in my unstable condition, but I wanted so badly to remain unseen. What if one of Omzi's friends saw me and called her? If she drove up and yanked me into her car, she'd probably drive me straight to Niagara Falls and throw me into the dark, crashing water, never to be seen again. She'd probably tell everyone I ran away or that I was staying with some relative or other because of my horrible behavior, and of course, everyone would believe her.

Once I was about a mile away from the house, it became impossible to remain completely covered in darkness because of the warm glow cast by the streetlights and local stores, though they were now closed for business. In the hope that no one would see me, I tried to steady my breathing and my legs as I willed myself to be as small and invisible as possible. My best efforts, however, weren't enough to conceal the ugliness of a ten-year-old child running naked in the street at night.

Although I had almost reached my school, and the lit-up POLICE sign was in sight, I continued to dart my watering eyes from side to side in constant surveillance, and that was when I tripped off a curb I didn't see. Then, when the headlights coming toward me began to slow down, the fear of God (or Godzilla) struck me like lightning.

I couldn't see what kind of car it was, but out of the corner of my eye, I saw it pass me in what seemed like ultra-slow motion. I swear, Omzi could have watched three episodes of *Law and Order* in the time it took for that damn car to drive by. Then it turned on a dime and came back around.

Despite the freezing-cold night air, panic washed over my entire body in hot, prickly waves, and my ears hummed so loudly I couldn't hear myself think. I saw the empty playground at my school and darted to the left, hoping the person in the car would lose sight of me, or think I was a deer, or maybe a drunk.

One of the slides had a plastic tube around it that we all loved to hide in and climb on at recess. I thought back to the times that Omzi would pick me up late in the afternoon after my dance class, and I would see groups of older kids hanging around it to make out and smoke.

When I dove inside the chute, I felt my bloody knees catch and pull on the cold, dry plastic. I climbed up to the enclosed, covered landing at the top, where I tried my best to silence the huffing and puffing that could have easily blown down all three of the Little Pigs' houses—even the brick one. (That punk-ass wolf had nothing on me.)

Gravel crunched like granola as the car came to a rolling stop in the parking lot attached to the playground. In my mind, I pictured it parked between the fading map of the United States and the two hopscotch courts that were painted on the cracked asphalt.

When the door of the car opened, it felt as if the world stopped turning, and time froze like the snot that ran from my nose was beginning to do. I buried my face into my knees, mixing hot tears and fresh blood with cold, semi-frozen boogers.

My senses were in overdrive, and I could clearly hear the driver get out of the car in a heated rush. The thundering sound of footsteps made their way directly to the slide, and I knew that if whoever was out there didn't kill me, having my heart explode inside my chest would certainly do the job.

I didn't recognize the woman's voice that echoed inside the slide with a loud, and seemingly concerned-sounding "Hello?"

I stayed motionless and didn't respond.

The woman stuck her whole head, and part of her body, into the slide. She yelled, "Are you okay?"

I hoped she got stuck in there like Pooh Bear, so I could go down the ladder on the other side and take off, but I remained frozen and silent.

"Hello?! Are you okay?! What happened?!"

I willed her away with my mind.

"Hon, I saw you running over there, and I just want to help you. I have a sweatshirt and a blanket in the car. Let me at least get you wrapped up and warm."

I pressed my lips together and squeezed my eyes shut, confident that if she was answered with crickets she would give up and go away. To my horror, a couple hiccup-like sobs managed to escape from deep within me and bounced around loudly inside the walls of the slide.

"Sweetie, I know you're up there and I can see some blood. I just want to help you before you freeze to death. It's dangerous to be out here like this at night. If you don't want to come down, I can call the police to come and help."

I have no idea if I was being defiant or docile when I answered, "Go ahead—that's where I was trying to go anyway."

"Oh my God, what happened? Let me help you. My name is Margaret. Who are you?"

"Nora," I managed to snivel.

"Nora, how old are you?"

"Ten."

"My Lord. What am I going to do? I can't just leave you here."

"Sure, you can. Just get in your car and pretend you never saw me. It's always better not to be seen."

"I don't know what all that is about, but I already know you're up there and you need help. I was on my way to the store for some cigarettes when I saw you streak by."

"You shouldn't smoke. It's bad for your health," I said.

When I said that, she responded with a deep laugh that sounded so warm and kind, the invisible barricade I constructed around my heart melted into a puddle—just like Frosty the Snowman did when he was locked in the greenhouse by the bad guy at the end of the story.

"Nora, what if I grab that sweatshirt and blanket out of my car and toss them up to you? You can put them on, slide down, and then we can go to the police station together."

"I'll take the clothes and stuff, but you don't need to go to the police with me."

"I'm sorry, hon, but I absolutely couldn't live with myself if

I drove away before you got the help you need, and I knew that you were safe and sound. I wouldn't be able to sleep at night for the rest of my life."

"Shit, I know what that feels like," I said earnestly.

She let out a funny, dry cackle of sorts, and said, "I'll be right back."

When she returned, she was breathing kind of hard, and I could hear her sniffling from the cold. She poked her head into the slide again and yelled up at me, "Okay, here they come!"

The sweatshirt came first. It was a really huge Buffalo Bills hoodie, which was good, because it fit me like a long dress. When she tried to throw the blanket, it must have been too heavy, and got stuck about halfway up. The smell of mothballs was introduced into the air of my ill-chosen hideout, and I imagined that Margaret was probably kind of old. I figured she couldn't be worse than Omzi by any stretch of the imagination, and that if I came down, and she was really bad, I could most certainly outrun her.

"Oh crap, hon. The blanket didn't make it. I can try to get in there, yank it down, and throw it again for you."

I told her that I was still trying to get the sweatshirt on, and that I would grab the blanket on my way down in a minute. I was hoping the little lie would buy me some time to weigh my limited options. I was positive I could sneak down the ladder on the back side of the slide to make a break for it undetected, particularly since she had jammed herself pretty well into the small, circular opening. But I was frozen all the way to the bone, and my feet and hands had joined my knees in a painful and stinging bleeding frenzy. I couldn't bear the thought of having to continue running and hiding throughout the rest of the night, and I most certainly couldn't go home and face the torture that would be waiting for me there—especially if Omzi knew I stepped one foot off the porch. But because I'd told this lady my name, and that I was going to the cops, I was terrified of that option as well, for fear of being dragged back to hell.

Ironically, one of Omzi's favorite sayings popped into my head—I realized that I was indeed up shit creek without a paddle. Once I decided what I was going to do, I pushed off the sides of the slide and shot down so quickly that I ran into Margaret with both feet at the bottom.

She stumbled back a little and put one hand to her chest like she was startled. Unless you were a complete psycho and couldn't feel emotion, I think the sight of me (even in the inky black darkness) would have scared the crap out of anyone. I was malnourished and pretty tiny for my age, and my cheeks, eyes, and forehead were completely smeared with blood.

She slowly exhaled the deep breath she was holding, and with it came what sounded like the words "Holy shit." I could tell she was trying to hold herself together for my sake, and I appreciated it so much. I had never had an adult try to help me before then, especially not at the expense of their own comfort level.

As if I were a butterfly, whose wings she was afraid to damage, she delicately took the blanket from my hands and placed it around my shoulders. With one hand hovering in the air near the small of my back, and without saying a word, she gently guided me to her idling car, and I was actually happy to feel the sting of the heat against my frozen skin as I got in and sat down.

Margaret pulled out of the playground parking lot and we made our way across the street to the police station in complete silence. During the short journey, pain, stiffness, and exhaustion began to overtake me, and I suddenly believed I understood how it might feel to run one of those marathon races I had read about at the library. After parking the car in yet another lot, she got out and ran around the front of the car and helped me climb out of the passenger seat. She tried to remain calm, but I could tell she was frantically looking for a patrol car—or someone outside to help us—but the lot was empty.

I leaned on her as she maneuvered my limp body into the brightly lit precinct house. The lobby was smaller than I imagined it would be, and aside from a few chairs, it was empty. There was an older-looking cop behind the huge plexiglass window, doing whatever he was supposed to be doing before being forced to deal with me. I'd watched a million cop shows and movies with Omzi and could tell right away that he was one of those dudes on the verge of retirement and didn't want to catch any additional paperwork.

I prayed to God and the Universe that Omzi wasn't already in there with them, somewhere in the station convincing everyone that I was a miserable wretch who'd run away and needed to be institutionalized.

As he looked up and saw us, I tried to determine from the look on his face if Omzi had beaten me to the punch, but he was obviously an incredible poker player, and he gave nothing away.

10

As I make my way into the station, I'm still on a high from my encounter with Maya at Tarts & Vicars and have all but forgotten about the craziness that took place before my therapy session. And just when I think the day can't get any brighter, out of the twenty-three or so firefighters and officers on duty when I report to work, the very first to greet me this morning is my favorite one of all: Roger. The minute he sees me walking in, he comes trotting over with his patented bowlegged Pittie wobble, and I can barely contain my joy.

"Roger Dodger!" I call out. "Get over here, ya big handsome devil!"

I crouch down and grab him on both sides of his blocky cranium and flop his ears the way he likes. He responds with a grunt followed by a very athletic downward stretch.

"Nice yoga move, Roger. Are you ready to quit yawning and start pulling your weight around here? Let's get that giant noggin' of yours inside and get to work."

He looks up at me with his goofy smile and we head into the main part of the house. I'm just about settled in when the first call of my day arrives, from someone who has smelt gas near the intersection of Devereux Street and Genesee Street. With multiple buildings around that location (including the Utica State Office Building), and without more information or a more specific location, we respond prepared for 'anything as a worst-case scenario.' But when we arrive at the scene and investigate, it turns out to be a false alarm. It's not unusual for our unit to be dispatched for one thing but come to find something completely different—or nothing at all.

A couple hours later, the next call that comes in turns out to be a false alarm as well. We have top-notch dispatchers who gather as much information as possible, but a lot of times people call in from their cars to report a fire when they see smoke, but they don't really know where it's coming from. Omzi always said, "Where there's smoke, there's fire," which might hold true for rumors and shit, but it doesn't always hold up when it comes to actual fires. Sometimes when there's smoke, it's actually a controlled burn of leaves, or someone is just grilling dinner in their backyard.

The second false alarm takes us about forty minutes to complete. When we get back to the station, my buddy Mike writes up the report and Ronnie and I help to ready the truck for the next call.

Before dinner, we all hit the gym for a scheduled workout. Everyone on duty usually works out at the same time, but we often pair up with a partner for all of our sets and intervals. Ronnie and I almost always partner with each other, because we lift the same amount of weight, and it gives us a chance to chat a little and catch up.

She's loading plates onto the bar for the bench press as she says, "I'm thinking about getting a second job to make extra money on my days off. Maybe I'll bartend at the Juice Box or something."

"Really? Sounds like a good idea. I should probably think about making a little extra as well."

"I bet you could sell your artwork."

"My art? No way! I highly doubt anyone would spend money on it."

"Hell yeah, they would. You're super talented, my friend. Give yourself more credit."

We're both quiet for a minute, saving our breath for each time we press the weights. Ronnie finishes her set and takes a long drink from her water bottle. I pull the front of my shirt up to wipe at the sweat on my face and say, "I need to ask you something."

"Oh boy, this sounds serious. What's up?"

I pause, maybe a little too dramatically, and begin to say, "Do you ever feel—"

"—not so fresh down there?" Ronnie interrupts, and laughs so hard she says she's going to pee herself. The reference to the outdated douche commercial with the mother and daughter having a heart-to-heart chat *is* pretty fucking funny; I'll give her that, so I join her in her fit of laughter.

She's still bent over and cracking herself up when I pull myself together and say, "No! I'm being serious."

"Okay, I can do serious. What's up, for real?"

"Do you ever feel like the job is too much?"

"I guess; sometimes, yeah. I mean, it's stressful, but I can't picture myself doing anything else. What about you?"

The million-dollar question.

"It gets to me sometimes, I guess. What if the time comes when I can't keep up or keep it together?"

"You mean, like, physically or mentally?"

"Maybe both."

I often wonder what it might be like for me to move away and start over someplace else, to be someone else and leave my horror-ridden hometown behind. But I can't do it. I have agonized over the reasons why I can't move away from this city and try to rationalize it with the fact that I don't have a lot of money, or I can't leave my crew, but it goes much deeper than that. The truth is that whenever I think about leaving, an unexplainable and debilitating fear washes over me until I can't breathe. I'd like to think of myself as strong and tough enough to fight it off, but it paralyzes me, and I stay.

I asked Dr. Sharee about it and she said it's a coping mechanism of sorts: an act of establishing dominance, because I don't want my mom to have control over me, even from prison or the grave. If I do move away, it has to be on my own terms. There's a difference between moving on and running away.

Ronnie interrupts my inner dialogue with, "Are you thinking about retirement already? We're way too young for that, don't ya think?"

"God, no! Girl, I still eat off paper towels just so I don't have to wash a dirty dish. Retire? That's a lifetime away. I can't think that far into the future. I get by in my little world on a day to day basis. Hell, I thought about maybe moving to another state once, and it stressed me out so much I had to run for an hour just to shake off the anxiety."

Ronnie says, "You've been inspiring me lately to run more."

I lay flat on the bench, do my final set, and say, "For real? I know it's not your favorite thing to do."

"It's not. I mean, I do it to stay in shape, but you know I'd rather lift. I just think you look lean and strong, and that's great, but it seems like it goes beyond that, which I think is so cool. I could use some of that in my life. Will you run with me sometime?"

"Hell yeah! Anytime, dude! And, yeah, running is an amazing attitude adjuster. I feel like a completely different person at the end of a run."

We switch spots, and while she positions herself on the bench beneath the bar, she says, "But it doesn't exactly suck that it makes you look good, though, right? You should show those legs off more often, girl! When was the last time you wore a dress?"

"Dude, shut up and finish your set," I say while laughing.

Everyone rotates the exercise they're on, so we move over to the squat rack and I set it up. Ronnie is getting a big kick out of teasing me and continues, "Seriously, do you have any clothes that don't look like you're on the way to the gym, or that you found while shopping in the boy's department at Target?"

We both laugh so hard a couple of the guys look over and give us the stink eye. When I catch my breath I say, "I'll have you know, Veronika Williams, that I do just fine with my look, and that it's known in high-fashion circles as athletic street-wear. It's a style, and it's straight off all the runways."

She shakes her head and says, "Did you say *run*way or *one* way? Cuz you're only dressing one way—and it's bad!"

"Whatever, dude. Maybe if I watched a few YouTube tutorials on fashion, eyeliner application, and makeup contouring, it would make me a better person?"

"No—you know what I meant...I'm just messing with you."

"Yeah, I know, I guess it's just a shitty reminder that everyone judges people on appearances. We base everything on how people look, but no matter what you do, you can't win. If you stand out too much it's bad, and if you blend in too much, that's bad too. Which way is better?"

"I didn't mean to upset you, Nora. Honestly, the best way is whatever is right for you. Oh, and that reminds me. You know that chick, Ashley, I was seeing?"

"Yeah," I say, "the one who would only fuck you if you showered first?"

"That's the one. We're done for good."

"Why, what happened?"

"You can tell me if I'm being too sensitive, but it goes along with what we were just saying about appearances and not being able to win with the way we look sometimes."

I take a sip from my water bottle and wait for her to continue as I hit the chin-up bar.

"We were messing around last week and she actually told me I need to lose a little weight!"

"I know you're not serious with that shit right now, dude," I respond.

"Unfortunately, I am, and it gets worse. She said that I'm too muscular and that when we're together sometimes it feels like she's fucking a man."

"Ronnie! Get the fuck out of here. Okay, now I'm pissed off for real! You are the most beautiful woman I've ever seen. I hope you told her she needs to stop starving herself because every time you're together it feels like you're fucking a bag of antlers!"

She laughs so hard she has to drop from the chin-up bar and bend over to catch her breath.

"I love you, girl."

"I love you too! I have your back no matter what."

"Me too," she says.

Everyone is finishing up their workout, and I lay down to do sit-ups. It's Ronnie's turn in the rotation to prep dinner with a few other guys, so she gets up to leave. Just before she walks out, she calls over her shoulder, "Want to hit the Juice Box next week when we're off?"

I don't skip a beat and answer, "Hell yeah! I'll wear my best hoodie!"

* * *

The smell of garlic and warm bread fills the air and makes my mouth water. Dinnertime chatter and the clanking of silverware and plates feels both comforting and homey. I get my coat and hat on, because I want to be sure Roger is taken out and fed before I sit down to eat my own meal.

On my way out the door, I can hear Mike giving Ronnie shit about making spaghetti with red sauce again. "You need to beef up your repertoire," he jokes.

"I know you're not telling me I need more beef in my life, Mikey!" she retorts.

Cromwell, our station's resident hard-ass, pipes up and interjects with, "Okay, you two, knock it off! Eat your food and keep that talk out of here. I'm going to pretend you were both talking about adding meat to the spaghetti sauce."

"We were!" Mike and Ronnie say in unison, and with matching grins.

Roger is a good boy and does his business pretty quickly when it's chilly outside—especially when he knows he's about to be fed. Back inside he gulps his dinner down like a champ, and I make my way over to the table to join the others. Before I can dish out a helping of noodles, however, our call alert system is activated, and everyone jumps up in immediate response.

The 911 call is from a witness to a high-speed two car collision where Burrstone Road and French Road intersect. We arrive at the scene to find an overturned, severely mangled Toyota. The Ford Explorer that struck it after running a red light has been totaled and will have to be towed, but the young man driving it was able to exit the vehicle on his own. He is badly shaken up and in tears when he admits to the police officers on the scene that he was texting and didn't see the light change.

The poor kid is a new driver and had begged his older brother to borrow his Explorer so he could pick his girlfriend up to go to the movies. He paces back and forth as he pulls at his medium-length, curly brown locks in shock and disbelief. But when he overhears one of the guys yell that the two passengers in the other car are a young woman and her infant child, and that they are still trapped, fear freezes him statue still.

The police take a report from him and try to talk him into going to the hospital to be checked out for possible internal injuries or a concussion, but he refuses to go. On the verge of hysteria, he frantically makes calls on his cell. What was supposed to be a night at the movies has changed into his own private horror show. He watches us in anxious anticipation as we work as skillfully and efficiently as humanly possible to extricate the young woman from her crushed car. When she is out, the paramedics put her on a stretcher and try to attend to the wounds she has sustained on her forehead, hands, and legs, but she keeps trying to push their hands away while screaming, "Get my baby, get my baby!" over and over again.

Mike and Cromwell go into overdrive as they expertly loosen the door enough to see the baby in her car seat, but not enough to reach the seatbelt. The baby's mother screams in fits of terror as Ronnie tries to reassure her, calmly, that the baby doesn't appear to be injured and that it's all going to be fine.

Ronnie takes her hand and asks her what her name is, and for the baby's name. In between stricken gulps of cold air, the woman replies, "I'm Kate and my baby girl is Lilith."

A split second of peace seems to wash over her as she says her child's name, but it leaves just as quickly, and she continues to let out the most excruciatingly painful cries of a mother torn from her child. Lilith was trapped in her car seat, and no matter what we tried, we couldn't get the seatbelt undone.

Cromwell and Mike are on their way to the rig to get the Jaws of Life when the car catches fire and the smell of gasoline permeates the air. The heat from the flames grips our faces like Satan's fingertips. We all work feverishly as a team to extinguish the flames and free Lilith while heavy, dark smoke fills the air. It's not as common as most people think for burning cars to explode (like they do in the movies) but it *is* possible, especially when the driver of the vehicle lets you know that she was on her way to a cookout at her parent's house, and had just picked up a newly filled propane tank for the grill.

There is absolutely zero time to lose. The guys try unsuccessfully to reach the seatbelt through a medium-sized hole they created between the smashed window and the crushed body of the car. They are simply too large to get as far inside as they need to be. Because the car is overturned, and the baby and car seat are inverted, it is impossible for *them* to reach the seatbelt, but I trust that my small stature will be the one thing that can make it possible.

The opening is beyond what anyone would consider to be a tight squeeze, but I push through it headfirst with everything I have, sending a jolt of dizzying pain into my body that momentarily steals my breath.

My efforts to move forward are impeded by jagged metal edges and broken glass that rips and claws at my face, helmet, and suit, but the smell of gas and the sound of Lilith's shrill cries from inside the car tear through my heart with a much sharper pain that makes me push even harder. If I wasn't sure before, I'm now quite convinced that something has punched a hole in the fuel tank, causing the leak and allowing flames to shoot inside the vehicle.

Regardless of my petite size, I'm very strong and athletic, and am able to reach the seatbelt. However, as I gently remove Lilith from her car seat, the fear that I might not be able to get us both back out again shoots through my mind like a bolt of lightning. The scorching flames in the car are a quick reminder that I have no time for doubt. I do my best to remove the bits of glass and debris from my jacket before covering her little face and head loosely with my sleeve and forcing myself backwards with every bit of muscle in my body and will in my heart.

The space is tighter than the inside of a barrel, and it presses my awkwardly bent arms to my sides and my shoulders to my ears. I can hardly keep a firm, yet gentle, grip on the crying baby. When I emerge from the wreckage, the paramedics take Lilith from me so they can reunite her with Kate and load them both into the ambulance.

Just as the doors to the ambulance slam shut, the Toyota becomes completely engulfed in flames, giving us barely enough time to clear everyone out of the way before it explodes. It isn't the kind of explosion that can be seen from space, shooting the hood of the car 100 feet into the air, but it is enough to rock the world of anyone within twenty-five yards of it.

We are able to extinguish the flames before the Explorer can catch fire, and by some freaky act of God or the Universe, there are no additional injuries. The police put up road flares and barricades to close the road, while we tackle the strenuous job of cleaning up the debris.

There is still a ton of adrenaline pumping through my system, and I feel an inner chaos that I try to contain and subdue, while keeping a brave face. I can't help but feel like this time *I* was the house made of sticks, and this whole experience was the big bad wolf blowing *me* down.

Because of the explosion, more people than usual have swarmed to the site of the accident, and of course WKTV NewsChannel 2 reporter, Amy Butler, has arrived with her camera guy to stick her microphone in anyone's face she can. She is proudly broadcasting live from the scene of what most people would consider a horrific car accident, basically sealing the deal that the story has potential to go national.

I see that she is interviewing Mike next to the rig, so I put my head down and try to duck behind him so I can start putting away some of the equipment. I think I am at a safe enough distance, but feel a firm grasp on my arm that pulls me back around to where he is standing, and I hear him say, "Oh, hey...*this* is who you should be talking to!"

He positions me in front of him and places his hand on my shoulder as he continues, "That car was a ticking time bomb, and this woman right here climbed in and saved that baby's life in the nick of time. She's a true hero."

Amy Butler practically squeals with delight upon learning this new angle to the story, and there is simply no escape for me at this point. She zooms in on me and puts me through a barrage of questions that make my head spin.

For the most part, I have no idea what I even say to her, because all I can think about is exactly how I am going to torture and kill Mike for doing this to me. I know he meant it earnestly, but he knows I hate being the center of attention, and this is the epitome of being in the spotlight.

I think I finally mumble something about how we all worked together to save the baby, and that it was truly a team effort (which is all true) just before turning and walking away from the giddy reporter. She has the camera guy pan in on me as I walk away so that she can do one of those schmaltzy voiceovers about real-life, unsung superheroes that can make a Hells Angel weep like a baby.

11

It felt like an eternity passed as Margaret propelled me toward the stern-looking dude behind the desk. Fluorescent lights hurt my eyes and overwhelmed me with fear, as well as a strange sense of guilt—it was obvious that his eyes had locked on me first, and then on Margaret. Out of the millions of things I wished for at that very moment, one was that I could read minds.

The blood on my hands and feet made a mess on the floor, making it difficult for him to maintain his poker face. I could see a flicker of acknowledgement behind his eyes that this was a serious situation and that nothing seemed to fit—including the sweatshirt 'dress' I was wearing. We hadn't quite made it to the desk, when Margaret half-shouted, "We need help!"

He introduced himself to her as desk sergeant Henderson and asked her, "How can I help you, madam?"

Margaret couldn't contain her false bravado for me any longer and started to break down in sobs as she began to explain to desk sergeant Henderson that she was driving to the store for some cigarettes when she noticed me running down the street naked. I actually started to feel really bad for her, because she could barely talk and had been doing so well holding it all together up until this point.

All of those *Law and Order* episodes I stared at as I laid next to Omzi, too afraid to change the channel when she passed out, seemed to have prepared me for this exact scene, because it all felt so strangely familiar. I remembered all the plots, and most of the dialogue, from every show even better than I could remember all the state capitals. I could swear I had been here before. This was the part when the twenty-year veteran city desk officer, who was about to retire to a little house in Florida, decided to call for backup because he didn't want to deal with this shit.

Sergeant Henderson put his hands up in an effort to slow Margaret down and interjected exactly what I already knew was coming: "Ma'am, this is clearly a very serious matter. You may have noticed the parking lot was devoid of police cruisers. I'm going to call for additional officers to respond to the station, and they will be able to help you. Please, just hold on and they will be here momentarily."

Margaret took my hand and, although I let her hold it, I didn't squeeze back. We just kind of stood there for a couple minutes, dumbfounded, before stepping off to the side where she had me sit in a chair next to the window to wait.

I don't know how long it took for Officers Webb and Serdynski to get there, but Margaret wasn't crying anymore when they arrived. Sergeant Henderson came out to the lobby accompanied by the two young cops and told me I could stay seated where I was. He said the nice policemen were going to chat with me while he and Margaret went over to the other side of the room to talk.

I looked at Margaret with eyes wider than the Grand Canyon, but with a tight-lipped smile and a gentle nod of her head, she communicated that it would be okay to do what we were told. Not quite convinced that I was in the clear, I watched her and the desk sergeant closely from the opposite side of the lobby. It was hard to tell what they were saying, but no one looked unusually upset, considering the circumstances. I saw Margaret dig in her pocket for a wallet, from which she pulled out her license. Because of the grand gestures she made with her hands and the intermittent glances she sent in my direction, I figured she was recounting the events of the evening.

My view became blocked by a uniformed set of legs. I

looked up into the eyes of a very kind-looking man who told me his name was Officer Serdynski and he introduced his partner as Officer Pete Webb. Officer Serdynski had light brown hair, dark eyes, and looked like a giant standing before me. Although his demeanor was gentle and kind, his broad shoulders and stance were somewhat intimidating at first. He could tell right away that he was overwhelming me a bit, so he crouched down while Webb grabbed a couple of chairs for them to sit on so we could chat.

Officer Webb placed the chairs at a safe distance in front of me, so I didn't feel trapped, and he made every effort to make me feel at ease. Webb was considerably shorter than his partner and, although he too looked strong and athletic, he had a much slighter build. The smaller stature and red hair and freckles made me think of a leprechaun, rendering it virtually impossible for me to be afraid of him.

Officer Serdynski asked me if I could tell him my name. His radio crackled a little bit, so he reached for it to turn the volume all the way down. He was giving me his full, undivided attention and I could tell he really wanted to help me. I knew I would never forget either one of these men for the rest of my life—their names and faces burned into my brain like a cow being branded. The looks of genuine concern on their faces were something I had only seen on TV or in movies—ironically, given by actors to other actors. No one had ever looked at me like that before. I wasn't used to it. I didn't want to trust them, but their warmth and kindness ate away at the already weakened walls that I had built over the years. Walls that once felt like stone and brick suddenly felt like a gingerbread house.

I looked from one of them to the other in silence as I made up my mind that Omzi was in fact not here. I had made it safely, thanks to Margaret, but I was still fearful for what would happen next. My guess was that I'd be put in foster care or be sent back to Omzi. Both of these options sent another round of anguish and dread coursing furiously through my veins. I pulled my legs up to my chest one at a time and yanked the sweatshirt over my knees before I tucked it under my feet, so that I was enveloped in a heavy, fleece cocoon.

Both officers waited patiently for me to speak and neither seemed angry with me when I refused to do so. I could see them taking note of the fresh blood on my hands and face, as well as the fact that I wasn't wearing shoes.

Webb leaned forward and rested both his forearms lightly on his knees as he explained to me that they both wanted to do everything they could to help me, but they needed a little information in order to make that happen. He was so authentic and trustworthy, and I was so tired. I was just so utterly bone tired.

"Sweetie, can you tell us your name or how old you are?" he asked.

I responded quietly, "I'm ten and my name is Nora."

"Okay, Nora. It's nice to meet you. Can you tell me where you live?"

After a much shorter period of hesitation, and with a very shaky voice, I answered, "621 Maple Street."

Serdynski kindly responded, "Oh, okay... not too far from here. Do you go to school across the street at Ben Franklin Elementary?"

I nod my head to say yes and he continued, "Nora, who else lives with you on Maple Street?"

I tell them I live with Omzi.

"Who is Omzi?" Webb asks.

"She's my mom."

"Okay. Anyone else?"

"Nope. Just me and Omzi."

With a cautious and gentle manner, Serdynski asked if I could tell them what had happened tonight, and that's all it took for the dam to break and the flood waters to come pouring out.

I described what happened in great detail and let them know that I had been severely abused by my mother (who I explained I called Omzi, short for Momzilla) for many years. Once in a while I would show them a scar to prove I wasn't lying, but I could tell by the looks on their faces that I didn't have to convince them.

While I was telling them the many things that I had endured at the hand of Omzi, Webb stepped away to make a call on his cell. There was a heightened sense of urgency I could feel that built up and began to fill the room as Webb ended the hushed cell phone conversation and immediately called for a squad.

I finished talking after what seemed like a long, long time and looked over to see if Margaret was still there. She was sitting in a chair, staring down at her hands. She lifted her head and saw me looking for her. She gave me a reassuring little wave, that I took to mean 'I'm allowed to leave but I have chosen to stay for you if you need me.'

Even with the hundreds of hours of TV crime shows I have watched, I somehow blanked out on what exactly a 'squad' was. The question was answered for me by the sudden arrival of three men wearing navy blue shirts with patches that read Utica FD 21. They showed up and gently loaded me onto a stretcher. I realized that a squad is what they call the firefighters who help in emergencies, and as they attempted to escort me out of the station house and put me into the ambulance in the parking lot, I revolted by screaming and kicking my legs as hard as I could. Margaret told me it was all going to be alright and that it was normal police procedure in this situation to have me taken to the hospital. She said it several times, and with vigor, which led me to believe she needed to be talked into believing it just as much as I did, if not more. The idea of the ambulance was overwhelming, and I didn't want to leave my new friends.

I looked at Officer Webb and cried, "I don't want to go in that thing! It was a big enough deal for me to come here with Margaret! I can't go to the hospital in an ambulance! Omzi will kill me!"

Webb tried to convince me that I would be safe, and that Omzi wouldn't kill me, but I wasn't buying it. I was having a complete meltdown on the gurney, because in my mind they had no idea how bad this situation was becoming for me. Sweat began to soak my hair and tears burned salty, wet treks through the blood on my face. I started to think that I had made a grave error in trusting any of these people, when Firefighter Brad Graham managed to calm me down and changed everything around for the better again.

He stepped back enough to give me breathing room but stayed close enough to show me he was there to help me and that he truly cared about my feelings. I could see it on his face, and from the look in his eyes, that he wasn't full of shit, so I gave him a chance to help me catch my breath.

He said, "Nora, I told you my name a few minutes ago, but there's so much going on, let me introduce myself again. My name is Brad and I'm a firefighter with the Utica Fire Department. Can we take a few deep breaths together to help us both feel better?"

I settled down enough to say, "Why, what's wrong with you?"

He laughed in what I felt in my gut to be the warmest and most compassionate way, and responded, "Well, for one thing, I don't like to see you so upset. It hurts me to see you like that."

I was sniveling at that point, but was no longer full-blown ugly crying when I said, "Why do you care? You don't even know me."

He said, "That's true, I don't know you, but it's my job to help you and I care about the people I am called to help. So, I care about you and want you to feel as safe and comfortable as possible. Also, I have a little girl who is a bit younger than you—she's six—and it would kill me to see her hurting and scared like this. I know I would want the person who was called to come and help her to do a really good job making her feel better in her time of need."

"That makes sense," I answered, through my post-sobbing tears and sniveling hiccups.

"I like kids, and animals, too. What's your daughter's name?"

"Her name is Sophie. Do you want to see a picture of her?"

"Yes. Do you have one?"

"Of course I have one!"

He pulled a navy blue and red Velcro wallet from his back pocket that he said he only used for work so he could carry his family with him at all times. The picture was kind of worn on the edges, probably from being shown to lots of other kids who were freaking out.

"Oh, she's really cute. I like her ponytails and her stuffed frog."

He laughed as he put the photo back in his wallet and tucked the whole thing in his pocket, and he told me that her grandmother came to the hospital on the day she was born with that stuffed frog, and it has been her favorite ever since.

I said, "They want me to go to the hospital, but I'm really scared."

Firefighter Brad patted my forearm like a dad, and said, "I know you are, Nora, and that's understandable. But I will ride with you, along with the two officers, and I will come see you while you are there to be sure you're okay. Do you think we can lift you into the squad now?"

"I guess so, but I want to ask Officer Webb something first."

"Go for it, sweetie," Webb said.

"Are you guys coming with me for the ride, and what's going to happen to me when I get there?"

"Wow, Nora, those are some pretty awesome questions!" Officer Webb replied. "We're going to talk to you a little bit more while we take you to the hospital to be checked out. You have some fresh injuries that really need to be looked at and taken care of. Okay, Nora?"

At first, I couldn't decide if it was comforting or annoying that he kept calling me by name, but I decided on comforting.

I told him and Officer Serdynski, "I'm still scared, but I'll go."

I looked back at Brad and said, "Thank you for helping me feel better. I don't usually freak out like that, or I'll get into big trouble."

He told me it was no problem at all, and that was what he was here for.

Before the police officers joined me in the vehicle and the doors slammed shut, Brad added, "It's my job," and it was at that exact moment I made the conscious decision to survive the whole ordeal and become a firefighter.

I didn't want to cry in front of them anymore, especially

in that cramped, well-lit space. I closed my eyes tightly to keep the tears from falling out and so I didn't have to look at them while they asked me more questions about Omzi and our house. They asked me if I knew where my father lived, and if I had brothers and sisters, but I kept my eyes shut and pretended that if I couldn't see them, they couldn't see me either. I told them that I never knew my father, and I had no siblings.

As an afterthought, I added that I had a grandma once, but she died.

We arrived at the hospital, where I was wheeled inside two huge whooshing doors, and down long hallways as people shouted things around me and the scenery passed by like I was riding in a car on the highway.

I arrived in a sterile and scary room, where my new friends Officers Webb and Serdynski assured me I would be in good hands and that I was safe.

Brad told me that he had to go for a couple minutes, but that he absolutely pinky swore to come back to check on me. The officers then tried to introduce a new guy into the picture, who I didn't want to meet, a man named Detective Joe DiMarco. Apparently, he was there in response to some kind of call that had been made about me. He reminded me of a teddy bear because he was big and burly (but in a huggable sort of way) and had round, dark eyes. He looked like he just rolled out of bed, with messy hair and a long, wrinkled raincoat.

Detective DiMarco approached me and said he wanted to help me. He said that he'd been doing his job for a long time, and had solved lots of cases, which I supposed was really good. I asked him where Margaret was, but he looked to the officers for the answer.

Serdynski stepped in and said, "Margaret has been cleared—which means she did everything she was supposed to do and is basically a hero—but we asked her to go home so that we could continue to help you at the absolute best of our abilities. If too many people are gathered around it makes it harder for us to do our jobs properly."

I told him I understood, but, truthfully, I kind of didn't. I silently wished that Margaret was still with me in this ice-cold room with all these adults. She would've warmed it up a bit with her presence, and I'd have welcomed her rusty laugh and the mixed-up scents of perfume, cigarette smoke, and mothballs that transported me back to our time inside the slide, which now felt like a lifetime ago. Instead of Margaret, however, a nurse came in and explained that the officers and detective were about to leave, but they would be back again later. She went on to say that she was going to do a rape kit, and she described what that meant, along with every step of the process in great detail. It sounded horrible, but I understood why she had to do it. I was again transported in my mind to one of Omzi's beloved *Law and Order* episodes. It was a little easier for me to handle everything that was happening, as well as the noises, words, and conversations that swirled around me, when I thought of it all as a script that was being performed by actors on the show. I laid back and tried to hear what the guys were saying in the hallway, but could only make out a single word here and there in between garbled sounds that remind me of Charlie Brown's teacher in the old *Peanuts* cartoons that Omzi made me watch during the holidays. Right before I heard all of their heels clicking on the linoleum floor as they marched together down the hallway, I caught a few words from Detective DiMarco—warrantless; entry; naked; fresh blood; search; perimeter.

The only way I could keep from focusing on the horrible things the nurse was doing to me was to go to a different place in my mind so I could escape the discomfort. I was a pro at this by now. I had done it so many times before, I was truly an expert at making it feel like I'd actually left my body. Most of the time when Omzi sexually abused me, and when she made me sleep in the basement, I would pretend I was a different person in a completely different place, and it was as if it was actually happening.

I decided to imagine that I was Officer Webb and I had been given the go ahead by my supervisor to visit Omzi without a warrant based upon the information I'd received from the little girl with her fresh cuts who'd been running down the street naked in the night. In this other world that I created in my mind, my partner Serdynski and I roll up to the big yellow house and he says, "Jesus. Look at this fucking shithole."

I say, "No shit. If I had to live here, I'd want to get the fuck out too."

Serdynski tells me to wait out front as he exits the vehicle and does a perimeter check. I sit and watch the house for movement, while he walks around to the back. Only a few moments after he disappears behind the building, I'm startled by my own radio as it goes off in my hand, and Serdynski's voice bellows into the police cruiser that Nora has been telling us the truth.

Broken glass smeared with fresh blood litters the entire back porch. He says there's absolutely no doubt that something went down here and that we needed to go in. I make the call requesting additional officers on the scene.

Detective DiMarco hears the call on his radio and shows up immediately, along with officers Edward Varvaro and Tony Garza.

With the arrival of the two additional officers on scene, we're able to set up a perimeter and then I, along with officer Serdynski and Detective DiMarco, cautiously approach the residence.

The steps creak and moan under the weight of our feet and we can't get over the shitty condition they're in. Serdynski says, "Jesus Christ, I'm gonna be pissed off if I fall through these fucking stairs."

I tell him if he laid off the donuts, he might not have to worry about it, but follow that up with, "For fuck's sake, the damn stairs are nothing compared to this shit. Take a peek in this window…it's fucking disgusting in there"

I step back so DiMarco and Serdynski can see what I'm talking about. I keep my flashlight trained on the inside of the window, as they hold their faces up to the dirty glass and gasp at what they see.

"Would you look at this shitshow. What the fuck happened here?" says DiMarco.

"For the love of God, I've never seen anything like it. Who the fuck lives like this?" Serdynski says as he tries to shake off his disgust.

Then DiMarco says, "Webb, you knock on the door cuz you

have a face like Howdy Doody."

"Howdy *Who*-dy?!" I retort.

In a frustrated voice, DiMarco says, "You know, you look like Richie Cunningham."

I say, "Who the hell is he?"

"Never mind," he answers. "It just means you look sweet and innocent. So, because you'll be the least threatening of the three of us, I want you to do the talking at first." As I knock on the door, I hear him muttering something about young people under his breath.

Omzi comes to the door and eyeballs the three of us but doesn't say a word.

I say, "Good evening, ma'am, I'm Patrolman Webb with the Utica Police, and this is Patrolman Serdynski and Detective DiMarco. We have reason to believe that something happened here tonight regarding your daughter, Nora. Do you mind if we come in?"

In an attempt to show her innocence, and because she thinks she's smarter than everyone else, she steps out of the way as she says, "Not at all officers. Please, come in."

From the entryway of the house, we all begin to take in everything we can, and it's obvious to all of us that something occurred here that wasn't right. The interior of the house is evidence of the most disgusting and extreme case of hoarding that any of us have ever seen. It's the stuff of nightmares and horror movies. Serdynski and I are still pretty new on the job, but to see a twenty-year veteran like DiMarco visibly shaken by his surroundings is beyond alarming and clearly one for the record books.

The smell in the house is overpowering and combines a unique mix of dust, urine, and greasy food, unlike any of us have ever experienced before. From where we stand, we can see that there is just barely enough space between mounds of junk, random items, and knickknacks to walk around. Milk crates, newspapers, furniture, clothes, record albums, old food, cans, and boxes full of who knows what, along with plastic containers, musical instruments, and even a plastic swimming pool are all piled in unnervingly tall stacks in the rooms we can see from the front entryway.

I clear my throat and say, "Ma'am, do you know where your daughter, Nora, is now?"

She says, "Well, yes. She's upstairs."

I respond, "Can we confirm that?"

She hesitates for a split second, and then says, "No."

"Okay, I say, then can you confirm that for us?"

She says she can confirm it and will be right back with Nora. She walks slowly up the long, horribly dirty and cluttered staircase, but returns again without her daughter. "I'm terribly sorry, gentleman, but Nora hasn't been feeling well, and she's in her room sleeping at the moment."

"She's in her room right now? And she's sleeping?" asks DiMarco.

"Yes. Like I said, she's been sick, and I told her to get to bed early and get some rest."

I say, "Ma'am, we have a young girl in the hospital right now who we believe to be Nora. Will you come with us to confirm that it is, or is not, in fact your daughter?"

She pauses again for a long time before she says, "Yes, no problem. I'd be happy to clear this all up so we can all get on with the rest of the evening."

The woman goes willingly with us to the hospital, and I can't help but think how strange it would be for a mother to leave her sick ten-year-old at home alone at night. As I walk toward the examination room with the woman behind me, I hear a doctor saying the girl's name repeatedly. That's when I'm pulled back into reality and realize there really *was* a doctor (and a nurse) standing next to the bed trying to get me to respond.

"Nora, can you hear me?" the doctor asked.

"Your examination is complete, and I need to let you know what we are going to tell the detective regarding your condition."

I told them that I was ready to hear what he had to say. Just then, everyone froze simultaneously, almost instinctively. We all looked over at the door as it opened and Omzi walked in with Webb, Serdynski, and DiMarco in tow.

Due to some warped sense of instinct, combined with nervousness, embarrassment, and sheer terror, I pointed at her and exclaimed, "Hey! That's my mom!"

Webb said, "Ma'am, you told me that Nora was in her room."

I was super freaked out for a minute, in part because Omzi was standing in front of me with the cops, but mostly because my black hole escape hatch fantasy must have been pretty fucking accurate!

Omzi went ape shit and began shouting about how I'm a psychotic kid whom she had to lie about in order to protect me from being institutionalized. You could see on her face that she suddenly realized she needed to reel it all back in a bit, because she had made the mistake of going off in public... in a hospital...in front of doctors and cops.

That's when Detective DiMarco, the most senior law officer present, said, "Ma'am, because you told us that Nora was in the house, and she's clearly here, you are under arrest for obstruction."

Before she got there, I thought the room was cold enough to store meat in, but her presence made it feel like the inside of an igloo. It was suddenly so quiet, the only thing I could hear for a few seconds were the beeping and buzzing tones that resounded through the hallway and created a symphony of typical hospital sounds.

Omzi tried to get me to look at her. I could feel her eyes burning into the side of my head, but I stared straight down at the white hospital blankets that covered my legs.

She tried one more time, saying, "You're truly making a mistake. You've got no idea what she's like to live with."

No one responded to her at first. I still refused to look in her direction, but I heard Webb Mirandize her as she was led from my room and taken into custody pending bond. During times like these, I wished I wasn't so damn precocious. I imagined how nice it would be to not know or understand what the fuck was going on.

12

The rain taps out a rhythm against my window that keeps time with the drumming in Chaos' chest. She takes full advantage of the fact that I'm standing still by plopping her body onto my foot and batting playfully at my shins and ankles with a curved paw.

I stand in front of the window near my easel and stare outside at nothing in particular. Three tiny silver rivers gather in my line of vision like neat rows of cocaine. I watch the droplets compete in a contest of strength and speed and become a fan of the team furthest to the right because it is the only one not cheating—when the other two teams started to fall behind, they would merge with drops of water from the sidelines, which resulted in more weight, faster speed, and ultimately, a first place across the finish line. The rainwater races hold my attention for longer than they should, especially since my team loses every time.

I take a step back from the window and gently pull my foot out from under the fuzzy blanket that Chaos has become. My hands are wrapped around my favorite earthenware mug, one that I bought at a farmers' market with Nathan, and I'm careful not to spill any of the molten hot, iron-black liquid on her little noggin'. My eyes are drawn to the steam that slowly winds around like a stripper on a pole as it rises from the cup, teasing me before I can take a sip. I decide to add hot coffee to my gratitude journal today.

While I hold my face over the white steam, my mind goes to long, early-morning runs in the summer when the sun rises and envelopes the earth in a warm hug. Before my eyes, the dew turns to mist and rises straight up from the earth like it's coming from Mother Nature's first cup of morning coffee.

I walk over to my small, rustic-looking coffee table and set the mug down. The clouds outside my window have become even darker and seem to hang low and heavy from the sky like over-ripened fruit. The coffee table, and the steaming hot cup of coffee, suddenly transform into a blazing campfire. One by one, the few pieces of furniture that I own, including my easel, turn into monsters that strongly resemble those from Maurice Sendak's children's book, *Where the Wild Things Are*. The rain on the window is now drilling out a beat for the monsters to dance to around the fire. Chaos bolts from the room, but I'm sucked in by the good time the monsters seem to be having and join them in their quirky dance moves. Around and around the bonfire we go, laughing and shouting as we bob up and down like horses on a merry-go-round.

The fire glints off the faces of the monsters, and I notice they are beginning to sweat, an oily sheen on their fur. The sweat smells of gasoline and their once-joyful laughs turn into the screeching cries of a baby. I stop dancing at the first whiff of the gas, but the monsters sweep me up in their forward motion and urge me with forceful jostles to continue. I try once more to stop the dance. It doesn't feel right, and I feel desperate to find the baby that's crying. Just then, the largest monster, a creature with horns and giant teeth, picks me up and throws me into the fire.

At first, I can feel the burning heat knocking on the door, but then it throws etiquette to the wind and decides to barge right in. My clothing ignites. I begin to scream while the monsters continue to dance, resuming their playful laughter and banter.

The creature that looks like a mutant chicken yells, "Well done, old boy!" to the guy who tossed me into the inferno to burn alive.

"Yes," he responds, "well done, indeed. But I prefer medium

rare."

And with that he yanks me out of the fire and throws me into a lake to put out the flames.

My alarm blares loudly—disrupting the six o'clock in the morning silence—and I open my eyes to find that Chaos is sitting in front of my face staring at me.

"Oh hello, Butthead," I say breathlessly, which she takes as her cue to headbutt me forcefully. She twirls around my arm as I reach for my phone so I can turn off the obnoxious alarm—as if I even needed an alarm. I've been sleeping like crap since my nightmares and black holes have begun to escalate. Still reeling from the crazy yet utterly realistic nightmare, I look deep into Chaos' eyes, as if she might hold all the answers for me, and I ask her, "Am I unravelling?"

Surprisingly, she doesn't answer me.

"Oh, we're not talking, huh? Well, that's not very helpful of you."

Through my bedroom window I can hear that it's windy outside, which will make my run a little sucky, but there's no way, with the way I have been feeling lately, I'm going to skip it. I know I need my various forms of medicine now much more than I have in quite a while.

"C'mon, Chaos. Mama wants to chug a little coffee before she goes. Come sit with me, you little purr belly."

She jumps off the bed and runs ahead of me to the kitchen. While I wait for the coffee to brew, I feed the little monkey her favorite vittles and get my running clothes on. By the time I get back, both Chaos and the coffee are done. She sits on the floor and cleans herself daintily while I sit on the kitchen counter and stare at nothing. My usual morning fog is extra heavy today as I try to decide if I'm finally losing it.

It has been two weeks since the car crash that landed me on the nightly news, and I had thought that as time went by, things would get back to normal and my mind would begin to blur out the harshness of that night. Instead, it has been the exact opposite. Everyone around me thinks I'm doing fine, but I feel like a vase that has been glued back together and my cracks are beginning to show.

My first instinct is to rationalize a bit by telling myself I'm

just being overly dramatic, or maybe even a little hormon-
al. I'd be at peace with some good old-fashioned PMS right
about now, as opposed to slowly slipping into straight-up lunacy.

"I'm allowed to be human, right, Chaos?"

She looks up at me and answers with a sharp, "Mew" that
sounds to me like she said, "Meh."

"Thanks, dude. You always know how to feed a girl's
ego."

She stares at me blankly as I fire up my playlist, put on my
hat and gloves, and head out the door. I jog quietly down the
steps in the hallway and cast a glance over at Nathan's door,
like I always do. I can see through the window in the front
door that his car is parked out front, but that doesn't always
mean that he's home. I remind myself that it's not my business, and step out into the dark, windy morning.

I know better than anyone that runners should always vary
their routes—for safety reasons—especially women who run
alone in the dark. I often tell myself that I'll go at a different
time of the day, or run a different course, but when it comes
down to it, it's just easier to do the same six-mile route I always do. This is my time to go on autopilot and let my mind
either wander or to focus on, and work out, the things that I'm
extra anxious about. I often tell myself that working on my
anxiety is more important than coming up with a new route,
but this morning I'm questioning my own judgment...about
everything.

I can't shake the feeling that someone is following me. The
roads are empty, so I step off the sidewalk and run in the street.
I figure if someone jumps out of the bushes, or from behind a
building, it will take them longer to reach me and I'll have
time to decide if I want to respond with fight or flight.

I keep peering over my shoulder, but absolutely no one is
around, because everyone but me is inside where it's warm.
That's when it dawns on me that *I'm* the only crazy person on
the loose right now, and it's actually the rest of the world that
should be worried.

I cut my run a little short and tell myself that it's not because I'm scared; it's because I want to have plenty of time to

swing by Tarts & Vicars before my session with Dr. Sharee. I have texted Maya a couple of times, like she asked me to, but she hasn't responded. I can't wait to see her—I've replayed the way she hit on me over and over in my mind and thankfully memorized her phone number before the stupid squirrel stole it from me.

I'm actually pretty surprised she hasn't responded, so I wonder to myself if I should text her to let her know that the ink on the cup got smudged, and that I may have read the numbers wrong. If that's the case, the person receiving the texts would hopefully let me know that they weren't Maya, and I had the wrong number this whole time. I try not to overthink it. I know that I'll see her beautiful smile today, and that's all that matters.

When I get back to my street, I stop a couple doors down from my apartment to catch my breath and shake out my legs a little. Nathan's car seems like the perfect place to stretch my calves, so I stagger my feet—one in front of the other—and place both hands on his passenger-side window. My back knee is straight with my heel pressed into the ground, and I lean into the car for a good stretch as the sweat trickles down the back of my neck. While I wait to switch legs, I let my chin drop toward my chest to stretch my neck and think about Maya's smile (and her ass).

My nose starts to run like crazy, so I lift my head up quickly, and that's when something in Nathan's car catches my eye. It's not exactly broad daylight, but it's light enough for me to make out the outline of a bandana, or something in the middle console that looks familiar. I stand up and take a step away from the car like it's suddenly poisonous to touch.

I swipe at my nose with my sleeve and step back in a little closer, so I can shine my phone's flashlight into his car. The light catches and shines directly upon a silky little sugar skull. At first sight of it, I stumble backwards, incredulous; however, after closer inspection, there isn't a doubt in my mind that it is my scarf. Along with a chilling shudder of fear, I feel a sudden rush of blood flooding into my ears with a roar. My fear is quickly overtaken by a Molotov cocktail of confusion, adrenaline, and anger.

Why the fuck would he take my scarf? And what the hell would he be doing with it in his car?! I'm so pissed off I feel like I could easily head back out and run 100 miles into the wind and not even feel it. Instead I run into the house and bang on Nathan's door with a tightly clenched fist while I practically scream his name like a crazy banshee. Luckily for him—or me (I'm not sure which)—he isn't home.

I huff up the stairs, completely out of breath, and slam the door behind me, startling the shit out of Chaos. She jumps up and freezes in an arched position with eyes like headlights. Scaring her like that snaps me back into reality, and I feel bad that my extreme behavior made her feel even the slightest bit unsafe.

"Great, now I feel guilty about scaring the cat," I say out loud.

I scoop Chaos up and hug her into my chest while I tell her how sorry I am for frightening her. She forgives me immediately and assuages my shame and remorse by purring loudly in my ear, making me wish I could brush shit off that easily.

I can't stand to be with my thoughts in silence, so I ask Chaos, "Is it too quiet in here? How 'bout some tunes?"

She seems to be in full agreement, so I crank up a playlist that includes Middle Class Rut, Dead Sara, and Greta Van Fleet. They match my mood and shatter the suffocation of dead air in the space that surrounds me.

After I've calmed down a little bit, I tear my running clothes off and leave them in a heap on the bathroom floor. While I wait for the water to warm up, I send Nathan a text asking him if he has been going through my shit when he's in my apartment. The text is huffy and direct, and not at all like our usual playful banter, but I don't call him out yet about the scarf. I want to see what he says first, and for him to dig his own grave, so I can push him into it and bury him.

Of course, he doesn't answer, which just pisses me off more, even though I know damn well he isn't awake at this hour... no matter where he is. I put my phone down and step into the steamy, hot shower that feels like pins and needles on my cold skin. I don't bother adjusting the temperature, half hoping the hot water will melt the icy feeling I have in my heart for Nathan right now. I stand there so long I go numb to the prickles from the heat and my fingers begin to resemble little raisins. When I finally turn the water off and pull the shower curtain back, the entire bathroom is foggier than a scene from an Alfred Hitchcock movie.

I'm not sure if it's the ringing in my ears from the water pressure, or my blood pressure from nearly blowing a gasket over Nathan's bullshit, but I hear something that makes me freeze with one leg swung over the tub. I step all the way out, grab a towel, and stare down at my lobster-red feet while straining my ears to listen. Is it Chaos playing with her pineapple catnip toy? Is someone in my apartment? Is it all in my head?

I call out, "Nathan?" but there is no response. I wipe the steam off the mirror and tell myself to stop being absurd and delusional.

I push the door open and feel a gust of fresh air bereft of steam. It refreshes me and reminds me to take a few deep, cleansing breaths before I get dressed.

I look for Chaos in my bedroom, but I don't see her. Once I'm dressed and ready to get out the door, I take one more look around the apartment to be sure I was just hearing things, and that no one had been in my place while I was showering. I think to myself that I should have named my cat Paranoia instead of Chaos, and that's when I see the little booger in the kitchen sink. I rush over to find her sitting next to my toppled plant, looking quite proud and full of herself for knocking it over.

"Chaos, you little shit...are conspiring against me too? Give me a break, will ya, sweetie?"

I quickly attempt to clean the mess she created, give her a squeeze on both sides of her face, kiss her smack in the middle of her fuzzy nose, and then bolt out the door.

* * *

For such a crappy day outside, the line for hot coffee at Tarts & Vicars is surprisingly short. When I step inside, I look for Maya right away, but I don't see her behind the counter, and my heart sinks.

I check my phone, knowing full well that Nathan hasn't texted me back, but I check anyway. When I look up, I happily lock eyes with Maya just as she's stepping out from the back room behind the register. I smile at her instinctively, but she quickly looks away and intentionally busies herself by straightening the baked goods in the glass case, so she won't have to talk to me. I tell myself I'm reading her wrong or that I'm being too sensitive. She's at work...hence, she has work to do. *Get over yourself, Nora*, I say inside my head.

When I step up to the counter to place my order, she steps away to fill someone's gigantic YETI tumbler with drip coffee, allowing the other woman to ask me what I want and take my money. I feel like the walls are closing in a bit, and that maybe I have stepped into the *Twilight Zone*. I know for a fact that I didn't imagine the heat between us last time, but there's absolutely no mistaking the artic chill she's giving me today. As I stand and wait for her to make my latte, I feel like a puppy with my tail between my legs, which is really odd, since I have no clue what I could have done wrong.

Sheepishly, I say, "I texted you, but I think I got the number wrong."

She hands me my cup, sans smiley face, and simply says, "No, I got them."

"Oh, sorry. I'm sure you've been busy," I say in a cheerful voice. "Text me back when you get the chance, and maybe we can get together."

Without cracking a smile, she says, "I don't think so. Not after last time, and besides, I'm moving to New York City soon. So...yeah."

I stand there stiffly, holding my coffee and staring at her like a dumbfounded-looking mannequin. She walks away, which makes me realize I should probably do the same, but I keep hearing her voice over and over again in my head saying, "Not after last time."

Am I insane? Last time was amazing, and for all practical purposes, was a form of erotic foreplay. It was the shit that poetry and love songs are written about.

As I make my way to Dr. Sharee's office, I tell myself that I must have misinterpreted the signals and read too much into the last encounter, which isn't completely unheard of, but I still can't think of anything I could have done or said to have offended Maya. I try to put this new wackiness on the back burner, because my other problems, including the shit with Nathan, need to take precedence.

When I step into the calming surroundings of Dr. Sharee's office, she's already waiting for me with the door open and tells me it's good to see me. No matter how much I hate it when she says that, I still want to move into this place and be adopted by her.

I flop into the comfy chair and let out a deep sigh as I sink down into it.

"That doesn't sound good," she says.

"You have no idea."

Dr. Sharee gently closes the door and walks over to the coffee table that separates our two giant chairs and leans down to pick up the bowl of Swedish Fish that she always has freshly stocked and available for the taking. The mood I'm in at the moment makes me both appreciate and resent the ridiculous size and coziness of the chairs, but doesn't stop me from accepting the delicious, chewy red candy as it's offered to me.

She sets the bowl down and sits cross-legged in her chair without saying a word. She knows if she waits long enough, the silence will kill me, and I'll start spilling my guts, which is exactly what I do when I say, "Ya know how I'm always afraid that when something good happens to me, it will be taken away and something really bad will take its place?"

She nods with a close-mouthed smile, communicating to me without words that she understands and empathizes, but that I don't need to feel that way.

"Well, that's exactly what's happening to me—more so than I have felt in a long time, and I really feel like I'm losing it." A lump the size of a fist starts to well up in my throat, and I fear that I might need to use those stupid fucking tissues for the first time ever in one of my therapy sessions. I take great, albeit irrational, pride in the fact that I have never cried in front of her and fight the urge now with every cell of my existence.

"Okay, Nora, why don't you start with what you think is good—and then tell me why you feel it's being replaced by something bad."

"Well, you know all about the call I had with the baby, and how I was on the news being interviewed and given accolades and all that?"

"Yes, and to be honest, I'm extremely proud of you for that!"

"Well, I'm not! It sucks! I mean, of course I'm happy that the baby is okay, and her mom didn't lose a child that day, but that whole thing is an experience most people would think was amazing, and I feel like it's causing a chain reaction of shit that I don't want."

"Like what?"

"Like the fact that it's been a couple weeks now, and I still have nightmares about the baby screaming and hanging upside down like a bat or a vampire. And every day that I go into work, the guys still fuck with me and call me the celebrity and the superhero and ask for my autograph. I know they're just trying to be nice and they think it's funny, but I hate it."

"Nora, we both know that the car accident you have just dealt with is one that would have severely traumatized anyone, but that you are at a higher level of susceptibility to PTSD-like symptoms due to your childhood. Do you think seeing that baby in a horrific, unsafe state and one in which she wasn't able to receive help from her mother may have triggered you to feel this way?"

This time it's my turn to remain silent and let her continue. I chew on a Swedish Fish and then use my tongue to work its gooey remains from my teeth instead of formulating a response.

She takes my cue and says, "All you are experiencing can be explained by stress, lack of sleep, and the trauma of the car wreck. I don't think you are being punished by the Universe, let's say, for doing your job, and doing it well. Try to accept that you are worthy of—and be grateful for—the good in your life. How are things going with the young woman at the coffee shop that you met? That was something good, right?"

With a very satisfying final flick of the tongue, I dislodge the last bit of candy from my molar and say, "That's exactly where I'm going with this! It's not just at work. I have been texting Maya, like she asked me to, but she ignored them all, and today she was colder than Siberia when I went in for my latte. It's a good thing I don't have Bursitis, cuz she gave me the worst cold shoulder ever."

"Maybe she was busy, or she has her own issues to deal with right now. You never know what people have going on in their lives. I want you to concentrate on the positive things, and people, that fit your present, and eliminate those that fit your past."

"She did say she's moving to New York City, but honestly, that's the least of it. I only mentioned it because it happened just before I came in today, and it did kind of hurt my ego. Plus, I swear to God I thought she felt the same way I did when she gave me her number."

"Maybe she *did* feel the same way on that particular day. You of all people know how quickly moods and attractions can change. There most likely isn't any malicious intent on her part. Maybe she knows she's leaving town and doesn't want any complications, or maybe she puts her number on everyone's cup. You can't let your self-worth, or your sanity, be determined by the actions of others."

"True, but it's so much more than feeling rejected by someone that I wanted to play with—and God knows I *really* wanted to play with her—but I have some other concrete examples of why I think I might be losing my shit."

"Go on," she says while switching her position in her chair and writing a very brief note on her pad of paper, which drives me insane with curiosity as to what she's saying about me. I fucking hate when she jots her little notes, and that, presumably, my problems and feelings can be so easily summed up and outlined with single words and phrases scribbled in a margin.

"Well, for one thing, I have the most undeniable feeling that I'm being watched and followed, but as far as I can tell, no one is there. Clearly, we both know that one of my biggest issues is feeling like people are looking at me, or that I'm standing out too much, but this feels much different. Shit has been happening surrounding this new sensation which makes it more realistic and makes the usual stuff I worry about seem small in comparison."

"What are the examples?"

"Well, for one thing, this morning I was finishing up a run, and I saw one of my scarfs in Nathan's car. He has absolutely no reason to take anything out of my apartment when he goes up there to take care of Chaos, and it freaked me out to see it so boldly on display in the middle of his front seat!"

"Maybe you saw something else, or he borrowed it for a good reason, but didn't have the chance to tell you about it yet?"

"I suppose it's possible, but I am 99.9% positive that it was my sugar skull scarf, and besides, he knows how much my privacy means to me. And shit, given our past hookups, I didn't think he would ever mess with my stuff, regardless of the reason."

"Did you ask him about it?"

"I texted him. But he's probably still not even awake yet, so I haven't heard back. He's actually on the brink of becoming legit famous with his band and has been spending most of his time getting ready for a really important gig. It's hard to believe, but I think they're really going to make it."

"Wow! You have mentioned that they're talented and have a great fanbase, but I didn't know they were so close to making it big. That's really exciting; but do you think it might also play a major role in why you hold yourself back from him emotionally?"

I hate the fact that she's making me doubt myself on so many levels, but because she's always been able to make me see things more rationally and clearly, I do my best not to hold it against her.

"I don't know. Maybe. I'm not too worried about his band right now, but seeing my scarf where it shouldn't be, having the guys fuck with me at work, and witnessing Maya's Dr. Jekyll and Mr. Hyde routine, are really just the tip of my shit-brown iceberg."

She interjects with, "Go on."

"So, the other night I was at the Juice Box with Nathan and Ronnie. We haven't had a chance to all go out and actually have fun as friends—without any weirdness—for a while now, and we were having a great time together, laughing and doing a couple shots of Jägermeister, until someone decided to play 'Legs' by ZZ Top on the jukebox. It might seem stupid, but the song reminds me of Omzi, and I hate it, so I made a sarcastic remark about how I'm all for an eclectic mix of music, but the fucking jukebox hasn't been updated since 1984. They both laughed when I said it, but Ronnie kind of tilted her head and gave me a weird look, while Nathan said, 'If it bothers you so much, maybe you should stop letting other people pick the music. You're not a tree, rooted into the barstool, ya know. Get off your pretty little ass, cough up the dough, and choose your own damn songs.' At first, I thought it was funny, and he was right, so I started to get up to do just that, but Ronnie continued on with something that froze me in my tracks. She actually said to me, 'Hell yeah, and besides, you didn't seem to mind this old-school shit last week when you were in here before closing time, belting out Toto's 'Africa' with that old drunk everyone calls Chatty Cathy!' Nathan chimed in that he likes the Weezer version of that song better, and I just looked at Ronnie like I had no idea what she was saying...because I didn't!"

"How did you respond to Ronnie?"

"So, I answered her quizzically with my go-to response of 'Huh?' and she continued with, 'Girl, don't act like you don't remember putting your arm around ol' Cathy and using those pipes of yours like you were auditioning for *American Idol* or some shit.' She probably thought the look I was giving her was meant to be ironic, but I was truly confused. She freaked me out further by saying, 'If I hadn't seen it myself, I wouldn't have believed it was even you. Not just because of the stupid song you picked but—there you were—the center of attention and loving it! It was completely nuts!'

"Dr. Sharee, I don't at all like to admit this, but I truly don't remember doing any of that, and it seems like people are treating me poorly or looking at me like I'm crazy for things that I didn't do, and it's frankly scaring the shit out of me. I hate to be paranoid, but I wonder if someone is fucking with me. Maybe Nathan is upset about our relationship, or one of the guys from the firehouse is pissed that I was praised so much for saving Lilith? Or the worst one yet...what if—*somehow*—it's my mom?"

When I finish telling her all the things that have been going wrong, I can see from the look on her face that she truly empathizes with me. She jots down another little note, so quickly, I think it can only be one single word: *crazy.*

When she puts her pen down and speaks, it's in an authentic, kind, and even-toned manner. "Nora," she says, "I know how much your PTSD and anxiety play a role in your perception of the world and how you function in it, and that your profession can often amplify and exacerbate these emotions. I'm not ever going to downplay those facts.

"Now it's not my place to say, but you may want to cut back on the Jägermeister shots, and your drinking in general, especially while you're on medication. Your increased alcohol consumption, and the fact that you were retraumatized by the crash, would certainly increase your paranoia and episodes with black holes. That being said, we can certainly explore increasing the dosage of your anxiety meds, if that's something you would like to do, but first, I would like to point out how happy I am that you have taken it upon yourself to increase your weekly therapy sessions, and that you are actively asking personal questions that reflect an enthusiasm for personal growth and reflection. I'm really quite proud of you for that, and I agree with your decision to see me four times a week instead of two in order to aid in your journey of self-awareness and self-discovery. You have been opening up so well during the additional sessions. This is the first time you have mentioned feeling like you're being followed, however, so we need to keep an eye on those feelings."

My mouth immediately dries up like the Sahara Desert and I suppress the urge to hurl Swedish Fish and coconut latte all over her coffee table.

All I can manage to squeak out is, "The extra sessions?"

"Yes, they truly seem to be helping. Especially in that you're more actively participating in the therapy by questioning everything. I feel this will help you overcome your feelings of victimization, and that things are happening *to* you, instead of just happening. You have every right to feel that your life experiences have been unjust and unfair, and you have shown amazing progress with resilience, but doubling the sessions seems to be taking you even further."

Suddenly, it feels as if the beautiful Turkish carpet beneath my chair has been violently yanked out from underneath me, and I'm falling into a deep, dark hole that the carpet had artfully covered up without my noticing it until this exact moment.

The lethal combination of fear, anger, and confusion that I had originally come in here to get rid of is returning home like a wayward child. Dr. Sharee has never once given me reason not to believe what she says, and she has zero reasons to lie to me, but there is no way that what she's saying is true. It was a big enough deal for me to admit to her that I thought I saw something of mine in Nathan's car, that I grossly misinterpreted the signals from Maya, and that I didn't remember being in the bar with my new pal, Chatty Cathy, but not knowing that I have been seeing her two additional times per week is off the charts terrifying and off limits for me to disclose to her. Not at this time, anyway. Not until I can get a better handle on it all, and I no longer feel like I'm being choked by shock and surprise.

The hard realization that I'm not doing as well as I thought feels like a tropical storm has suddenly formed and hit my body. Enormous amounts of fear and uncertainty push against the already weakened dam that I have worked so hard to construct, and the entire structure begins to shake and collapse under the weight. The moment it breaks open, and my mind feels like a flash flood, I make the unequivocal decision to take a leave of absence from work so I can try to get my shit together.

When she sees the extremely overwhelmed look on my face, she says, "I know this is a lot, and perhaps the extra sessions might even be part of your added stress and current misinterpretations of various situations; however, I truly believe that with a little more time, it will all even out and the rough edges will become smooth. You *do* need to stop forgetting to bring your gratitude journal, though!"

She laughs and stands up when she says this, which signals the end of the session. I actually have my gratitude journal with me in my bag, but I don't tell her this. I don't tell her any of the thoughts in my head because, unlike what she seems to think, I'm toppling backward instead of moving forward, and none of this shit can really be happening. I wonder to myself if I will even remember the session we just had, the bullshit with my sugar skull scarf, or the embarrassing coffee shop fiasco? My intentionally small circles have somehow begun to clash, and the world I have created feels like it's shattering to pieces around my feet. Dr. Sharee is exactly right in that I have been triggered emotionally by the accident, but what she couldn't know, because I haven't shared with her, is the *extent* to which my black holes have resurfaced in full force as a result.

"Before you go, I'd like to share a quote with you that I think you'll like, and I feel is appropriate on *so many* levels. It's by a spiritual guide named Mama Indigo."

"Mama Indigo," I repeat flatly.

"Yes. She's an incredible woman who helps people find *their own* way on their journeys by offering mother-like support, instead of *telling* them which path they must take. Anyway, she said, 'The best thing you could do is master the chaos in you. You are not thrown into the fire; you *are* the fire.' I think this is the perfect way for us to end today."

I stand up to leave and thank her awkwardly for her kind words and sage advice as I grab my coat and bag and make a beeline for the exit. I'm petrified by the prospect of sinking so far down into my black holes—there's no other way I can explain losing time and messing so many things up—that I could very well lose my job, the little life I have built for myself, and everything I have worked so hard to overcome.

Now I'm back outside and thrilled to be in the cold air because it helps my head feel slightly less cloudy and polluted. At least I know that the biting cold on my face is real. Of course, this would be the time that Nathan sends me a text that simply says,

???

He's probably hung over and worn out from a gig, and I'm not sure of anything anymore, so I answer,

Nothing-I thought you might have knocked over the plant on my windowsill

Nah, wasn't me. But I do see Chaos batting away at that plant all the time

Yep. I actually caught her in the act right after I cleaned up the dirt and put it back

He sends an *LOL* and I return it with a hysterical emoji, which is exactly how I currently feel, just not in the laughing and joking way it is usually intended.

I'm suddenly overcome with gratitude that I have accrued about a week off from work and can have the time to go home and deal with this shit with a hefty dose of my self-prescribed medicine. For a split second I consider writing this in my gratitude journal, but the thought becomes comical enough to make me actually laugh out loud like the maniacal cuckoo bird I fear I am so obviously becoming.

When I get home, the first thing I do after hugging the crap out of poor little Chaos is pour a glass of Cabernet taller than the Jolly Green Giant.

"So much for cutting back on my alcohol consumption, huh, Chaos?"

For a brief moment I wonder if taking a leave of absence will result in more alcohol consumption, and therefore more problems, but I shake the thought away immediately. I crank up the playlist from earlier and take my trough of wine over to the easel. The beautiful white canvas I purchased a few weeks ago, but haven't had the time to work on, still sits where I left it, patiently waiting for me to fill its pristine surface with art. Geez Louise, I guess this is another thing I'm grateful for today, which really pisses me off. Haven't I already proven that anything good that happens to me will be immediately replaced by something equally as bad?

My need to control this fact overtakes me for a minute. I sit down in front of the canvas and feverishly begin working with a mix of oil pastels and paint, feeling a great desire to cover the entire surface, but not giving any thought to what I'm actually creating. The only thing I know for sure is that today will not be the day that I paint my self-portrait. The thoughts in my head are like an overstuffed washing machine, churning with great effort as I try to remember singing at the bar, or if I left my scarf in Nathan's car. Maybe some of the horribly dirty laundry in my mind was actually said out loud to Maya and that's why she hates me now.

Thoughts fly around my head like they're on a spin cycle, and my work with the paint keeps pace. I'm thoroughly entranced in the act of creation until there isn't an inch that isn't covered, and the thick layers of red, orange, and yellow grab my attention as they drip heavily onto the floor and on Chaos' head.

She seems to be getting a big kick out of the splashing droplets, but I quickly pull her off the floor (half expecting for the paint to actually be blood) and step away from the mess. Although it's abstract, there's no mistaking the fact that I have filled the canvas with a blazing inferno, and it steals my breath away.

I squeeze a meow out of Chaos, which makes me realize that I'm holding my breath, and that I should also loosen my grip on her. In a lame act of recovery from embarrassing myself in front of my own cat, I brush at the paint on her head with my fingers and all but "'tsk tsk" (like the sloppy mess was actually her fault) as I quickly bring her over to the kitchen sink.

"We'll just leave that there for now, girly. Let's get you cleaned up so mama can go out for a while."

Any fervor she may have felt for the paint droplets that playfully fell before her eyes a moment ago quickly evaporated as I swipe at the top of her head with a wet, bunched-up paper towel.

"You look kind of pathetic, butthead—but at least the paint came off."

I kiss her on the head, let go of her body, and watch her jump off the counter and tear out of the room without looking back.

I desperately need to go for a hunt, and after jamming my empty wine glass precariously into the sink, I rush out of the room even faster than Chaos just did. I head directly for my room to dig up my trusty bag of tricks and scan the pickings on the floor for something to wear that isn't covered in paint.

Once I'm changed, I pull out my bag and regard it like an old friend with big, dopey eyes and a wide grin. I'm in such a rush to get out (and get off) that I almost forgo my usual ritual of looking in the bag and surveying its contents before I leave. I turn it upside down and shake it like a kid at Christmas who is trying to figure out the contents of every wrapped box under the tree.

In the blink of an eye, what is once fast and furious becomes what seems like an excruciatingly slow-motion tumble of items onto my bed. What I see before me is simply unbelievable and makes me want to rip out my eyeballs. I feel like someone has just punched me repeatedly in the solar plexus, and my eyes become glued to my sugar skull scarf as it lays on top of all the other items, mocking me.

I try to calm my breathing, as well as unclench my jaw and newly balled up fists, but I can't comprehend what is happening to me. I rip the scarf away from the pile and stare at it, like it will tell me what I want to know if I look long and hard enough.

It's not talking.

I hold it off to the side in between my thumb and two fingers like it's a shit-filled diaper and look over at the rest of the stuff that fell out of the bag. Everything else seems to be the way I last remember it, except that my gum is gone. If someone was fucking with me by adding the scarf to my bag of tricks, why would they steal my gum? It makes no sense at all, and knowing how much fresh breath means to me, I wonder if it's at all possible that I have been hunting (and doing all the other shit) while in a black hole. But why would I put the scarf in my bag (which I never do) and not replace the gum (like I always do)?

I don't know what to think, and at this point, I begin to fear that I will *never* be able to decipher the difference between what's real and what isn't ever again. Since the accident, dreams of bugs on my skin have become more realistic every night and have begun to creep into my waking hours. I can feel them wriggling and crawling, and sometimes I even *see* them and desperately try to brush them off.

Now everything that has been happening has been compounded by this new, twisted grand finale, and it's enough to make me want to check myself into the looney bin. I drop the scarf and scoop everything else into the bag before I bolt out the door. I know exactly how to be sure, if only for a short time, that everything I'm doing is actually happening. I'm going to drive the extra twenty miles to that little bar called Hot Heads and find someone I can take into the bathroom where we'll both feel every bit of potent power that takes over our bodies. It's impossible to mistake the raw reality of what starts as a little ache and grows inordinately into a pulsating living thing until it gets too big to contain and spills out everywhere with no disguise and nowhere to hide. It's all too real when you make someone lose control in the heat of passion, and that's exactly how I'm going to achieve a moment of sanity and clarity.

Hot Heads isn't on a main street and is far enough away from the usual spots frequented by firefighters and cops in the city of Utica that I never run the risk of knowing anyone and feel at ease whenever I visit the bar.

By the time I get there, Happy Hour has just ended, and there's a small crowd of people standing around a table near the back, presumably feeling no pain by the way they're laughing and holding onto each other as they scream into each other's ears above the very loud, piped-in music.

The big wooden L-shaped bar has a few people around it sitting together in pairs, which does not bode well for me. Just before I grab a seat by myself, I notice the bartender chatting with a guy who is sandwiched between a woman and another guy. The fact that someone in this scenario is a third wheel works in my favor. I approach the trio and ask the dude on the far end, who hasn't just started making out with the woman on the other end, if I could sit in the empty spot next to him.

He rolls his eyes over at the two, who are really going at it now, and says, "Yes, please!"

I laugh as I take a seat on the barstool and plunk my bag of tricks onto the bar next to me.

He says his name is Gavin and asks me what I'm drinking. "The least I can do is buy you a drink for saving me from my friends."

I tell him I'll take a Manhattan if he's buying, but I don't bother offering him my name.

He gestures for the bartender, who comes over and makes a face at the two lovebirds before taking the order. Gavin tells him to put it on his tab, and then turns his attention back to me.

He's a nervous talker, which is great because I don't have to tell him anything personal about myself, and it gives me time to fully take him in. He has gorgeous hazel eyes with a light behind them like a Halloween cat that makes me wonder what kind of vitamins he takes. I wish my eyes were bright and shiny like that.

While Gavin blathers on about how his friend talked him into going out tonight with just himself and his girlfriend, I can't help but watch his beautiful lips move. My mind is wrapped in black leather and I can only half hear what he's saying. He doesn't need to talk so much, because his excruciatingly sexy lips are their own conversation. I'm not sure why, but I wish I could give him a slow, soapy hot bath so I could really take my time with him, but I'm done waiting and pretending to care what he's saying, and I need to get down to what I came here to do.

I take a large swig of my drink and lean into him. I feel heat coming off his arm that further ignites my already overtly forward behavior. In his ear I breathe the words, "Do you want to feel something real?"

He thinks we're still making small talk, as if I had at all been involved in his idle chatter and responds, "Well, yeah. I mean, I think we're all searching for something real."

In my head, I wonder if Gavin has the intuition of a sea sponge. I put my hand on his chiseled forearm and tell him I agree, and that he should follow me into the men's room. The look of confusion and apprehension on his face lasts for a couple seconds, but the heat between us never dissipates. He proves to be both clever and eager enough to take my direction almost immediately.

I grab my bag off the bar and stride toward the back of the large room, where it's almost dark and secluded enough to get to business, but I continue down the narrow hallway and around the corner to the men's room anyway. We push the door in, and he takes a quick look around to see if we're alone, while I pop into the stall furthest from the door. The walls are painted a deep red, and the ceiling and floor are black. The lighting is horrible, which I love, and we can just barely hear the music trickling in from the bar as the leaky faucets attempt to keep rhythm with the muffled, pounding bass.

Gavin practically falls into me and seems to take up every inch of the already tight space. I respond with a hoarse laugh, that doesn't feel like my own, as I press into him to feel every hard inch of his amazing body. The door to the stall is shut and nobody is getting in with our weight pressed against it. Our hands succumb to a bad case of wanderlust as they travel north and south in heated exploration of their uncharted territories. We're both breathing hard and I'm so wet I can barely stand it. His lips do not disappoint as he kisses my neck and my mouth with a feverish talent that, if I let him continue, might make me cum.

I grab him by the hips and rotate him around so that he's facing the door of the stall. He's heaving with excitement but lets me stand behind him and then watches me reach past him to slide the lock in place. From behind, I remove his belt and unzip his jeans, allowing them to sink low around his hips. I slowly place his hands one at a time up against the door, slide my own hands up into his T-shirt, and then down both sides of his torso. My hands are cupped so I can absorb and enjoy every inch of his smooth, gorgeous skin. I feel confident and in complete control of him, while simultaneously feeling personally out of control in all the best ways possible.

My fingertips enjoy an amazingly erotic voyage as they travel over perfect shoulders and taut muscles that call to mind magnificent mountaintops, and then dip into the sun-warmed valley beneath his ribcage before they arrive at the inviting destination of his open jeans. He's leaning back ever so slightly, and I love the way our bodies fit together (even with our clothes on) that makes it feel like we are one person.

It takes every bit of my willpower not to grab him where I can feel an energy that tells me he is pulsing and ready without even touching it. I slide my fingers along both sides of his lower abs and take in his sex lines. His obliques and lower abs make a V-line that is so perfect, you'd think he was an Olympic swimmer. The dude is killing me with this shit, and as if things couldn't be any better, he is more than happy to play my games. From his sex lines, I plunge my hands down a bit further to massage his inner thighs as I ask, "Do you want to establish a safe word?"

He gives me a sexy look over his shoulder and with a cocky smile says, "Are we going to need one?"

I skillfully pull his T-shirt over his head, but instead of letting it drop, I grab both ends of it and pull it firmly against his throat and say, "I don't know...you tell me."

He reaches back with one hand to stroke the wet heat between my legs, which I let him do while I pull the shirt the slightest bit tighter and whisper, "We can use 'Chaos.' It's my cat's name."

His voice is quite different now, sexier, deeper, but he can still talk (and even chuckles a bit) when he asks, "Your cat's name is Chaos?"

I grab his hand from between my legs and put it back where it was on the door of the stall and then press my foot against the door for leverage as I push back as far as we can lean without hitting the toilet. I hold him there choking a bit under his own T-shirt, and then I let go and say, "Yep. I like having a kitty known as Chaos."

He tries to tell me that he likes my style or some shit, but I interrupt him and say, "Get up against the door."

Gavin turns his head instinctively and presses his cheek against the gray metal door so he is as close to it as he can possibly get. I pull his pants all the way down and do the same with my own. His T-shirt has fallen away to the ground and I am stroking him from behind while I touch myself. His moaning is sexier than I thought it would be, and I like how into it he is, so I decide to bring in the big guns.

With a sexy little giggle, I kick his feet apart and tell him, "Assume the position."

He responds by widening his stance and leaning over as much as the space would allow. Gavin's perfect ass is now sticking out, and his arms are raised in front of him, with both palms pressed flat and firm against the door. His long, thick fingers are fanned out wide and his chest is heaving. This man's ass is so hot, it's criminal. In fact, I tell him he had better hope he never goes to jail because with an ass like that he would be screwed for real. I have to bite it. He knows the safe word, but he never uses it.

His body language tells me he loves what we're doing and he's dying for more, but he doesn't spoil any of it with words. I crouch down behind him and practically have to sit on the toilet as I use the palm of my hand to reach between his legs and pull his cock backwards so I can suck him from behind. Gavin goes out of his mind with ecstasy and can't help banging on the door with a fist as he says, "Oh fuck. Oh fuck. What is that? Everything you do is amazing. Oh fuck!"

I can tell he's going to blow, and I don't want him to, so I pull back, reach around the front and slip on a condom, and then tell him to turn around and fuck me from behind. I have already spun around and tilted my ass for him to do what I say, which he does…and he does it well.

It takes no time at all for us both to explode in the most agonizing waves of pleasure while we shake the bolts loose and break the stall. He lets his weight drop onto my back for a second, and then stands up so we can both get dressed. While he's zipping his jeans, he tells me I should go out first, but before he even has time to look up, I have already popped a piece of gum from a pack I picked up on the way to the bar, and I'm out the door.

13

I don't know what I expected, but when Omzi arrived in the hospital room, casting her fury in my direction, I started to second guess my decision to jump off the back porch and run. Although my head was turned away from her at the time, I knew exactly how she was looking at me, and what she was thinking, simply from the heat of rage I could actually feel emanating from her direction.

Even though she was no longer in the room, wave after wave of panic swept over me in the hospital bed as I thought about her and the fact that she now knew what I had done. One by one, the powerful swells crashed into my mind and violently disturbed what had been semi-calm waters. I was overtaken by a churning boil of 'what-if' and 'worst-case' scenarios, and I couldn't find the surface. Everything was spinning, and a froth of salty tears felt like tiny pin pricks as they tried to escape from behind my wide, frightened eyes. In that moment, I believed I was actually drowning and began to hyperventilate. That's when I heard a voice shouting, "Nora! It's okay. You're okay, Nora, calm down."

The waves began to dissipate, and somehow, I managed to raise my head above the surface to see Brad standing next to my bed.

"I told you I'd come back to see how you were doing. I guess I came at the perfect time!" he said.

I couldn't believe he'd actually come back, although I was slightly embarrassed that he has now seen me freak out for the second time. I pushed the embarrassment out of my head, because it was the least of my worries at this point. Firefighter Brad Graham has truly been a life preserver in the treacherous shit storm of my life.

"A couple more deep breaths, and you're good as new." He thought for a moment, and then as if suddenly remembering, said, "Hey, I brought you something! They didn't have any frogs, like the one in the picture I showed you, but I thought you might like this."

As if he knew, or the Universe was sending me some crazy cosmic message again, my favorite firefighter in the whole world had an adorable, bright purple lizard in his outstretched hand. I took it from him with a huge, dopey smile and managed to say thank you.

"You're so welcome! I thought you might like the company. I know it can be overwhelming in the hospital sometimes, but you're handling it all so well, Nora. I'm really proud of you."

"Really?" I said. "Why?"

He smiled and told me that everything I had been through was a lot for a ten-year-old.

I wanted to tell him that nobody had ever been proud of me in my whole life. I also wanted to tell him that he made me want to become a firefighter someday, but I decided to keep these things to myself. I didn't want to do anything to mess up the precious moment of goodness.

Brad told me to stay strong and that the doctors, nurses, and police officers were all doing a great job to make sure I was well taken care of. He said that a really nice social worker would be coming to see me soon too. He got up to leave, but before he stepped out of the room, I asked, "Would you mind if I named my lizard after you?"

He lowered his chin and looked at me in such a warm and caring way, it made me wonder if this was what other kids experienced all the time.

"I wouldn't mind at all! I would be honored. Thank you so much!"

He raised his hand, waved it at me slowly, and said, "Bye, Nora."

When he turned to leave, he almost bumped right into Detective DiMarco and a female nurse as they were coming in. The place was like a non-stop parade, but that's how it all worked, I guess.

The mood in the room became serious again, but at least I wasn't in panic mode anymore.

I sat up as straight as I could for the detective and the nurse, because it seemed like the right thing to do. The nurse who had examined me came back again as well, and I watched as they all awkwardly tried to make room for each other in that incredible shrinking space.

I kind of felt like I was in that scene at the end of *The Wizard of Oz* when everyone was standing around Dorothy's bed. In the movie, she explained, one at a time, what each of them had done in her dream. In my situation, it was basically reversed. I laid there and they all took turns telling me what each of them was going to do and what was going to happen next.

I knew exactly what they found when they examined me, yet here they were, seemingly stressed about how they would go about breaking it to me. I knew the situation was awkward in general, but it felt a bit weird that they seemed so tense and nervous to talk to me about it. I mean, I was already so used to it. It wasn't like they were springing some shocking news flash on me. I felt really bad for them, in an odd sort of way, and tried to make it easier by saying, "The rape kit you guys did probably shows you that I have been abused by Omzi and other people, right?"

"Um, well, yes, Nora, it did," the doctor said dryly. "We could see that it has been going on for quite some time."

"I told you," I said. "I'm not a liar."

He kindly, but firmly, answered me with, "No one here thinks you are a liar, Nora. We all believe you, and in fact, we would like to keep you here under observation until the morning, just to make sure you're completely healthy and ready to leave. Okay?" With that, he gently patted my foot, gave a few instructions to the nurse, and exited the room, sending me the message that his question was rhetorical.

Detective DiMarco cleared his throat, to let me know he

was next up at bat, and said, "Nora, can you tell me about any other family members you have?"

I looked at him blankly and said, "None."

"No brothers, sisters, aunts, uncles, or grandparents, maybe?"

"No. It's just me and Omzi. I don't know my dad, and he doesn't know I exist anyway. I don't have any other family. My grandma and grandpa are dead, and Omzi was an only child," I explained for what seemed like the millionth time.

He let out a sigh and scratched at the salt and pepper scruff on his chin and said, "Okay, hon, I don't know if anyone else already told you this, but I'm going to call someone to come in and talk to you. Since your mom has been taken into police custody, and you have no family members, you will need to have a social worker assigned to your case. Does that make sense?"

"Yes, I get it. I'm about to become a ward of the state."

Detective DiMarco gave me a look like I just sprouted giant elephant ears. He regarded me with his big, tired-looking eyes, slowly shook his head, and said, "You're truly unbelievable, kid! You're smarter than half the adults I come in contact with on a daily basis."

"I get that a lot," I responded.

Detective DiMarco told me he had to leave to get some work done on the case, and the nurse chimed in to let me know she was going to get me something for dinner. She asked if I had any food allergies, which made me want to laugh in her face. I told myself it wasn't her fault that I wasn't like all the normal kids she usually worked with but responded out loud that I didn't have any allergies that I was aware of. If only she had known what I was forced to eat on a regular basis—including rotten food—she would never have asked me such a ridiculous question.

The room was finally empty again, and I considered turning the TV on, but before I could even make the effort to pull the white cord attached to the remote control up and over the side of the bed, pure unadulterated exhaustion hit me like a Mack truck and I fell into a deep sleep. It felt like a heavy lead blanket or X-ray apron had been placed on top of me, and I found the weight quite comforting as I entered what I didn't know then was called a lucid dream state. I knew that I was dreaming, and I quite liked the active role, and the bit of control I had over the characters, narrative, and environment that played out in my mind like a private movie screening.

The dream was truly like a film that I was watching from a comfortable seat, holding a big tub of popcorn with warm, melted butter, the way people do in actual movies, TV shows, and commercials—I had watched a lot of people pretend to be at the movies, and always envied the experience. But now it was my turn, and no one but me was in the small, cozy theatre.

The large screen was flanked by heavy red velvet curtains and there was something sticky on the floor near my left foot. They must have done a poor job cleaning up after the last showing. The lights went down, and I sat back and watched the police cruiser bump up the badly potholed and cracked driveway of 621 Maple Street in the dark of night. The house glowed an eerie shade of yellow, like the eyes of a Halloween cat, but everything else on the screen was in black and white. Much to the chagrin of lead Detective DiMarco, officers Serdynski and Webb made remarks about the shabby condition of the home—which had obviously been in need of some serious TLC for years—with a little too much gusto.

In black and white, Webb looked like a policeman from a 1950s movie. His teeth seemed bigger than they ought to be, and for some reason he reminded me of Matt Damon. He said, "I'm already tired of this shithole. It makes me sick thinking about that bitch hurting her own kid in here."

Serdynski chimed in, "Yeah, and the piss yellow paint is probably the nicest thing about the fucking place. It's like a Stephen King novel fucked a Cohen Brothers movie and this fucking house was the evil offspring."

Webb started to say, "Just when I thought you couldn't get any weirder..." But DiMarco cut him off sternly.

"You two need to cut the shit with your stupid banter and focus. I didn't wake Judge Maxwell up twice tonight for you two knuckleheads to fuck up my whole case."

They both laughed and Serdynski said, "Geez, DiMarco, you

need to chill. When was the last time you got laid?"

"What?! Why am I even having this discussion with you?"

Serdynski answered sheepishly, "I don't know. Ask Nora; this is her dream. She's the one who read and watched all that horror and crime shit, like some kind of miniature adult."

DiMarco undid his seatbelt and let out a huge sigh. He scratched his beard with one hand as he reached into the glove compartment and searched for his bottled antacid with the other. After a hefty swig from the bottle, he wiped his mouth on his sleeve and just sat there, staring. Because it was my dream, I knew he was thinking that this was one of the most gnarly cases of abuse he had ever seen in his whole career; that these young guys were great, and they cared about the girl's well-being, but if they fucked up his case in any way, he would kill them himself.

He shoved the antacid back into the overstuffed glove compartment, slammed it shut, and exited the car. By the time he made his way up to the beat-up front porch, the young officers were already waiting for him.

"Okay, guys, I know tonight has been rough on all of us, but that fucking monster isn't going to get away with this shit on our watch. The first warrant we got gave us the opportunity to search the house, with the help of a forensic team, while that bitch was being held for obstruction. Since we found all the proof of abuse that has taken place here, not just tonight, but for many years, and we were able to corroborate Nora's story, we were able to make child abuse and child endangerment charges stick on top of obstruction. But now it's time to put the final nails in that crazy witch's coffin. It's time for a search of the entire house, and for that I've obtained an additional warrant.

"We have a case built on solid ground so far for this woman, but I want all the pieces of the puzzle to fit just right. No mistakes, you got it?! So, I see Garza and Varvaro have just joined us. Just in time, fellas. You two will maintain the perimeter. Don't let a soul in or out without my say so. I want this place—and this case—closed up tighter than a nun's cunt."

They both nodded and said, "Got it."

"Serdynski, you're going to search everything upstairs; I'll take the main floor; and, Webb, you take the basement. I want everything you find to be documented, bagged, and tagged. There's a good chance we'll find more than we bargained for buried under this steaming pile of dog shit disguised as a home."

When the officers stepped into the house, everything went from black and white to technicolor—kind of like *The Wizard of Oz* did when it switched locations from the farm to Oz. Everything reminded me of *The Wizard of Oz* that day, I guess. This was my lucid dream, so the officers didn't question it, but they weren't happy when they were attacked with stronger smells and brighter, more defined colors inside the house, as if it was trying to force its evil down their throats with its incredible affronts to their senses.

They squished up their faces and waved their hands in front of their noses as they split up and went to their assigned areas. Something in the house felt dark and sinister, which made the brightly lit colors seem even more psychedelic, as well as creepy as hell. Like the house was mocking them.

I decided to follow Webb first. I knew he wanted to do a good job, not just for DiMarco, but also for me, which is why he left no stone unturned in the musty, repellent basement. He wasn't down there for very long when he stubbed his foot on a bookcase up against the wall in one of the small maze-like hallways that comprised the lower level of the house of horror. At first, he didn't think much of it, because the house had shit everywhere and it was impossible not to step on or trip over something that didn't seem to belong where it was. But there was just something about the way the dust and grime looked different around the area at the base of the bookcase, as well as on the wall behind it, that I could tell nagged at him like a mosquito. Everything else down there was covered and buried in dirt that looked settled, but this particular area seemed cleaner, and in comparison, had a lot less dust and cobwebs.

For the hell of it, and to ease his curiosity, he pushed the bookcase down a few feet and pulled it away from the wall. When he stepped around to the back of it, he couldn't believe his eyes. It was really hard to see, but he was almost positive that the area behind the bookcase was actually a false wall with a door. In the middle of the door was some kind of rectangular opening or slot so that items, perhaps trays of food, could be slid in and out.

He radioed upstairs for DiMarco and then Serdynski and told them to get the hell downstairs as soon as possible—he'd found something.

The two men rushed down the stairs, shouting for Webb. They reached him at the same time, and froze in disbelief for a split second, before DiMarco said, "Jesus Christ, Webb, what are you waiting for, open that fucking door!"

Webb pried the door open and all three men stepped back in horror—like they had touched a blazing-hot surface.

"Jesus," said Webb.

"It's like a dungeon."

"It reeks like rotting flesh and shit," Serdynski added just before he bolted to find a safe place to puke. He managed to find an empty bucket in a far corner that he didn't think would get him into too much trouble for barfing in it. On his way back to the room, to join the others—who had stepped cautiously into the doorway—he took the time to stop and punch a wall in a fit of anger and rage.

Webb looked to DiMarco for guidance on how to handle the rancid, raw horror they were now faced with. When he saw that a veteran detective like DiMarco was both shaken and deeply disturbed by what they had found in the hidden room, his fear grew exponentially, because he knew that DiMarco had seen it all—and Webb had never seen the detective shocked by anything.

With great apprehension, DiMarco took the lead and stepped further into the dark space.

"Oh my God," somehow escaped from his lips. And then with a catch in his throat, he said, "I've never seen anything like this in my twenty years on the job. A *person* was actually living here or was being kept in here for a long period of time."

Webb suppressed the urge to run out of the house and cry, and Serdynski finally rejoined them, still heaving with anger and frustration.

"This is the most fucked-up thing I've ever witnessed, which is why we need to do everything right in order to nail this bitch to the wall for the shit she has done here," DiMarco said. "We need to keep our heads if we want to do our jobs and do them well. I'm talking to myself here too—not just to the two of you."

The officers silently nodded their heads in agreement as they carefully stepped into the room to join him.

The walls were made of concrete blocks that had been painted a dark shade of red, and a small, bare bulb hung awkwardly by a short, frayed wire from the middle of the stained, peeling ceiling.

In the far-left corner, they discovered a filthy old cotton throw on the floor that was really more rag than rug. Affixed to the wall above it hung a single pine board shelf. With gloved hands, DiMarco picked up a wide-mouthed glass container that was almost completely filled with crusty, dried-out centipedes. He put the jar back on the shelf next to some dust-covered coloring books and a small, naked baby doll that had no arms.

A terrifying bucket of murky sludge was tucked into a corner, and in the center of the room, beneath the lightbulb, was a tiny wooden table, like the ones you might find in a kindergarten classroom. Upon closer inspection, DiMarco saw that someone had scratched the word 'Ruby' into the table's beat up surface, and what seemed to be the remnants of a crayon wrapper, along with one worn-down nub of black wax, had been left behind.

Regardless of how small the room was, the negative energy that overflowed from it could have filled countless rooms. The impact it had on all three men was so great, that with each new heart-wrenching discovery, it became less like a single room and more like an entire house of horrors.

Of all the dreadful things they found, the worst by far was a six-foot-long chain made of mice that had been strung together by hand. Unlike the homemade chains that children often made to hang on Christmas trees, this one had been carefully crafted by tying little knots with the tail of one mouse around the neck of the next mouse, creating the most horrific garland imaginable. On the floor, next to the terrible rodent tinsel, was a stack of wrinkled papers—each depicting a child's scribblings and drawings done with heavy black wax—along with a sprinkling of small, shriveled orange peels.

I was shaken out of my dream, woken up by the sound of a food cart hitting my hospital-room door. My super-nice nurse pushed the wobbly-wheeled cart over to my bed and helped me sit up. She had a tray of breakfast food for me that included pudding, for some reason, along with a container of apple juice and a small plastic pitcher of water with an empty cup. I had no idea they let me sleep so long.

In a chipper voice I was quite unaccustomed to, the chubby nurse asked, "Did you get a good night's sleep? Without waiting for an answer, she said, "I want to make sure you stay hydrated, hon." While she straightened a few of the cords that hung like limp noodles off the side of my bed, she told me to be sure to eat all of my food, drink lots of fluids, and then she left the room.

I peeled the plastic film back from the plate and decided to eat the pudding first. I didn't care what time of the day it was, but glanced out the window anyway, and saw that it was still dark. For some reason, the tiny compartmentalized meal, and hushed early morning halls of the hospital, made me feel an even deeper level of sadness.

I had already shoveled a couple large spoons of thick chocolate pudding into my mouth when I heard the familiar echo of the detective's shoes coming down the hall. The door had been propped open, so Detective DiMarco stuck his head in and knocked on it lightly with a big, hairy knuckle.

"Hi, Nora! Mind if I come in? I have someone with me to see you too."

I told him I didn't mind (as if I really had a choice). But for real, I truly didn't mind seeing him. He really had grown on me already, and his large presence had become comforting in a stable and sturdy sort of way. He ambled in while I put down my spoon and wiped away the large glob of pudding that I could feel on my chin.

A few steps behind him was a short, dark-haired woman in

a long, red, well-worn winter coat. I liked her coat because it made me think of the little red caboose of a train, and I have always liked the color red. It was familiar. I wished to myself that I could have found a train, hopped on it, and rode it out of town, instead of getting caught up in all this crap.

I squeezed my stuffed lizard into my chest while the dark-haired lady introduced herself as Sherita Holmes from the New York State Office of Children and Family Services. She had kind, brown eyes and smelled like candy apples, which I liked. When she asked me about my lizard, I told her I just got him from the fireman.

"Wow," she said, "that was really nice of the fireman to give you a lizard to keep you company. What's his name?"

I simply said, "Brad."

"The firefighter's name is Brad...or the lizard's name is Brad?" she asked sweetly.

"Both," I answered.

She just smiled and said, "I see."

"Maybe you and Detective DiMarco should swap last names so he can be Sherlock Holmes. You know, because he's the detective."

The adults got a chuckle out of that one, but the laugher subsided more quickly than it erupted.

"Nora," Detective DiMarco said, "I know Ms. Holmes has a lot to talk about with you, and I don't want to overcrowd your room, so would you mind if I asked you some really important questions?"

"No," I said, "I don't mind."

"Thank you, I appreciate your help," he said, and then continued. "The other officers and I have been in your house a couple times already—both last night and early this morning—to look around, match everything up, and put the pieces together, kind of like a puzzle. Do you understand what I mean?"

"Yes, I do. I also understand that you have to have a warrant to do that, right?"

He laughed in a way that said he was more impressed than irritated with my remark and said, "You really are an intelligent young lady! Yes, you're correct, Nora, and based upon the condition of the house when we went over there the first time last night, and all the information you had given us, we called a judge and woke him up so we could get a warrant to search your whole house." He paused for a few heartbeats and then went on to say, "Nora, I have something important and very serious to ask you about, but I want you to know that if it makes you too uncomfortable to talk about—at any point in time—just let me know and we'll stop. Okay?"

I said, "Okay" and looked over at Ms. Holmes. She told me that she could leave the room, if I wanted her to, since I didn't know her yet, but I told her she could stay. When I looked back at Detective DiMarco, I could tell that he was upset and uncomfortable with whatever he was about to ask me.

"Nora, can you tell me anything about the basement in your house?" he asked.

"Like what about it?" I said, not sure where to begin.

"Did you or your mother spend a lot of time down in the basement, or can you tell me what some of the rooms were used for?" he said in a way that told me he must have found the playroom.

I answered him slowly and said, "Well, there are a lot of rooms down there. Some I am allowed in and some I'm not. There are two rooms that I spent the most time in. One is the laundry room and the other one is kind of a playroom; except I didn't exactly play in it. I was put in there when I was being punished."

"A playroom. Okay. Can you describe the playroom to me at all? Take your time; I know this isn't easy for you."

"It's just a small, yucky room with a bucket to use as a toilet."

"Was there anything else in the room? What did you do while you were in there?"

"Well, mostly I just screamed, or I cried. Sometimes I would fall asleep and mice would crawl on me and scratch me. That's it."

"If it was your playroom, did you have lots of toys to play with?"

"No. It was called the playroom because if I was put in there, I had to pay for things that I had fun doing. Omzi always said if you want to play you have to pay. She kept it pretty empty."

"What did the walls look like? Was there a window or anything on the walls?"

"No. The walls were just plain. I think they had a plaster or something on them, because chunks of white stuff would fall down when I banged on them."

He looked at me blankly and asked, "What was the door like?"

I said, "Locked, mostly."

"Sorry, hon, let me back up a little bit. It sounds like you're saying your mother..."

I interrupted him with, "Don't call her that. Please. She is Omzi."

"Okay, if I'm understanding you correctly, Omzi put you in a yucky, small room and locked you in there for long periods of time, right?"

"Well, she locked me in, and it felt like forever, but it was usually just overnight or maybe two nights at the most. Sometimes she gave me water and crackers, but the mice usually ate the Saltines before I did. Mice don't like orange peels, though, so once in a while I would eat those when I got them."

Ms. Holmes cleared her throat and looked at the floor as DiMarco said, "So, other than locked, can you tell me anything else about the door or the way it looked?"

"No. It was just a dirty, wooden door. I kicked it a lot, so there were cracks in it and stuff."

"Okay, thank you, Nora. You have been so helpful, and I'm extremely impressed with how incredibly smart and strong you are. I'm going to leave you and Ms. Holmes to talk about what will happen from here. She's really great, and I know you two will hit it off."

When he turned to leave, I could swear I saw a tear rolling down his cheek.

14

After an amazing dose of my medicine at Hot Heads, I'm on a natural high and can barely feel the chill in the night air. My car is another story, and it is absolutely freezing when I slide into it. I turn it on, crank up the heat (and the music), and pull out of the parking lot as fast as I can. I would prefer to just sit in the car for a minute, let it warm up a bit, and check my text messages, but I don't want to risk having Gavin come looking for me. I decide that my discomfort in this case is worth it, and that I can wait to bask in the afterglow of it all at the Fastrac Market a few miles away—I need gas, water, and maybe a new supply of gum. I'm still worried about my sanity, but at least the rough edge has been smoothed down a bit and I can breathe again. For now.

I see the bright lights of the Fastrac up ahead, and they somehow feel like a beacon in the night. I'm a sailor who has been tossed about by cold, cruel waves, but the warm glow of the lighthouse is now in sight and I feel saved. I pull right up next to an empty gas pump and just sit and stare at the dashboard for a moment. I think about how odd I am for wanting to be as healthy and unhealthy as I can possibly be at the same time. My desire to work out, drink water, and do all the right things to keep my mind and body healthy and full of vitality joins hands, fingers tightly entwined, with an ache in my core to run inside to buy cigarettes (even though I don't smoke), drink and fuck in excess, and not give a shit about tomorrow or the next day. Basically, I strive to feel as good, strong, and happy as I possibly can, and then become deathly afraid of it when I feel *too* good, strong, and happy. Maybe next week I'll try one of those cleanses where they shoot juice up my ass. Something like that just might cover a couple of my issues at once.

I make a mental note to bring up all of this duality shit again with Dr. Sharee when I see her next time. The sudden thought of her sends a little shiver across my neck that I literally shake away with a shimmy of my shoulders. I'm still reeling from the fact that she says I'm seeing her four times a week, and that I have absolutely no recollection of doubling the number of sessions. I also have no idea who is even paying for the extra sessions. I can't imagine the department is covering the additional therapy. Maybe they are taking it out of my pay? I mentally scold myself for not paying better attention to my bank statements and paystubs. I hate to admit it, but the thought of telling her the full extent of everything that's going on right now kind of scares the crap out of me. Not to mention, and I never thought I would say this, but for the first time ever, I wonder if I should even trust her.

I get out of my now-toasty warm car and go inside to grab a few essentials, as well as pay for the gas I'm about to get at pump number one. The guy behind the counter is high as hell and wishes me a good night at least four times from behind his long black bangs and perma-grin. God, I love convenient stores late at night.

While I'm waiting for my tank to fill up, I check my texts and see that Nathan has sent me three.

Hey

is the sum total of the first one, and—oh shit—in the midst of my solo journey to crazy town, I completely forgot about his gig! The second one says,

are you still coming to my show at Velvet Ministry tonight?

I know my head has been up my ass, and my brain is basically Swiss cheese, but it still seems impossible to me that his Velvet Ministry gig could have slipped through my black holes. I could tell myself that's what happens when your mind (and your cheese) is pure Emmentaler, but it's such an impressive venue, and way too huge a deal for even me to have flaked out on. The Velvet Ministry only books bands that are already famous, or are about to be, and Nathan has been excited about this happening for months. I would be a complete asshole, and no friend at all, if I blew it off—whether he was fucking with me or not.

I contemplate the dilemma of going vs. not going as I read the third text:

Dude, I know something is up with you, but we go on soon. I really hope you can be here.

At this point it feels like he has pulled my heart (if I even have one) out of my chest. I have to text Ronnie to see if she's there, and if she isn't, if she will go with me.

Hey Ron! Are you at Nathan's show?

While I wait for her to respond, I take the nozzle out of my now-full tank and put it back in the pump, spilling gas on my shoes. It's so cold that I don't care, and I hurry to get back inside my car. Before I can make it to the driver's side, I feel the old familiar horror of bugs crawling on my skin. I shake my head, thinking it will literally shake off the sensation, but it doesn't work. I know I'm hallucinating and, quite frankly, I'm getting fed up with myself at this point, so I slap at the itchy spots on my arms and neck and whip my car door wide open. I barely stifle a scream when the bright light from the gas station island bounces off the shiny backs of black beetles crawling and wriggling all over my seat.

I stumble backwards and look over at the window of the convenient store to see the high dude behind the register staring at his phone and eating licorice whips. My eyes frantically scan the parking lot—it's empty. I swear these little fuckers are real, because when I dump my entire bottle of water on them (and swipe them off my seat), I watch them fly in the air and land on the cold, hard concrete before I crunch them beneath my shoe. In an effort to sop up the remains of the beetle soup I have created, I use my sleeve to dry the seat off as best I can.

I pull away from the pump and park in a space in front of the convenience store so I can figure out what the hell is going on—and what I'm going to do—when I hear back from Ronnie.

I had to go into work. I took over for Snyder tonight. He's sick.

Oh shit...okay. I send back to her. *Have a good shift. Should I go to Nathan's show?*

What?! You're not there already? Of course you should...why would you ask me something so stupid? You kill me sometimes, girl...gotta go! Have fun.

I turn the music on my car radio up just a little bit louder and sit back to rest my crazy brain. She's right. *Why wouldn't I go?* In the big scheme of things, Nathan has always been there for me, and I'm already out for the night. My hunt went well... and I know that even if the bugs *were* real, which I'm almost sure they were this time, there's no way that Nathan could have been the one to put them there...so why the hell not? Besides, how much worse could things get?

I text Nathan back,

Sorry, dude, I've been painting and got caught up (not a full-on lie), *but I'm on my way now!*

When I get to Velvet Ministry, the parking lot is overflowing with cars and people. As I pull in, I look up at the marquee with Undressed Enema given top billing and it steals my breath away. I'm proud of Nathan and happy that he's doing so well. I can't get over how incredibly packed the show is, although it pisses me off that I can't find any place to park.

I pay the gigantic cover charge to get in and walk up a long, narrow staircase to the main level. The entire club is made up of three levels, each with its own bar, stage, seating, and dance floors. Every level has elevated areas to gather, get bottle service, and be seen—even in the dark. The sound system in this place is second to none, and the lighting effects are mind-blowing even for the biggest club-hopping snobs. The décor oozes a perfect combination of punk rock and leisure, and easily rivals the ambiance of the top clubs in Manhattan. Club owners from Tribeca, Chelsea, Midtown East, and SoHo come to Velvet Ministry to recruit DJs and bands, and maybe bartenders too, because they do serve a semi-deadly Moscow Mule.

I don't know where the crowd comes from, because you

never see all these hot-ass people at the library or the grocery store in Utica, but I love that the people-watching is always top-notch.

As I make my way to the bar, I bump elbows and try not to spill people's drinks. Nathan and his band are already on stage and are in between songs while I try to flag down a bartender's attention. From behind, I can hear Nathan start a very familiar guitar riff, and without looking I know he's stepping up to the microphone with that confident, sexy stance he takes just before blasting the lyrics from deep within his lungs and abdomen like an erotic rocket.

I finally succeed in screaming an order of Tito's and Red Bull into the bartender's ear, leaning over so far, I could make it myself. I leave the money on the wet bar, grab my drink, and try to push my way toward the huge, black stage. Nathan looks and sounds amazing. I stop for an instant and glance at my drink, as if it's trying to warn me about something, or could perhaps answer all my deep-seated questions about life and love like a cup of gypsy tea leaves. I tell myself that the damn drink isn't talking to me, it's the voices in my head. I should have ordered two.

The crowd is so dense I can only make it about halfway from the bar to the stage. Everything is swarming like a beehive and my shoulders are squeezed so tight I have no choice but to hold my drink in front of my face. I would like to put my arms down, but I can't.

Much like the way Kramer would burst into Jerry's apartment on *Seinfeld*, the Henry David Thoreau words, 'I would rather sit on a pumpkin and have it all to myself, than be crowded on a velvet cushion,' storm into my head uninvited, and for the moment, push the other voices out. A surprise, yet welcome, attack of distracting thoughts.

I let myself get lost in the music and the sound of Nathan's voice. I try to imagine having an ounce of his musical talent and close my eyes while the heavy sounds seem to penetrate me.

When I open my eyes, there is a small break in the crowd about ten feet in front of me, and a strobe light keeps catching on a person standing, motionless, in the middle of the opening. The entire club is packed, and every single person in it—except this woman—is facing the stage. Instead of watching the show like everyone else, her entire body is squared off and she's not only facing me, but I can feel her eyes staring at me with laser focus.

I squeeze my eyes shut and then open them again, thinking that I must be seeing something that isn't there. When I open them, she's still standing there, staring right back at me, and I'm so freaked out at the sight of her, I drop my cup. After all the elbow jostling and shoulder pushing, there was barely anything in it, but the little bit that remained spills onto my shoes, joining the gasoline from earlier.

Instinctively, my attention is pulled toward the floor and the fabulous, newly introduced cold, wet sensation that is seeping into my socks. As I look at my feet, I watch two people step on my empty cup, before lifting my head and realizing in shock and terror that I'm staring straight at...myself. I can't help but panic. The lights are making me dizzy, and the pushing and pulling of the crowd begins to feel like it's a living, breathing organism.

I look away to see if anyone has noticed that I'm a crazy person who should probably be feared, and when I look back again, I'm gone. She's gone. My *brain* is so fucking gone. I know she was there...but she was me...and that makes absolutely no sense at all.

When Nathan's show ends, and I make my way backstage through the druggies and groupies, I'm still shaking, but happy to see that he put me on 'the list' so I can get in to see him. This isn't Madison Square Garden, and my friend isn't Justin Bieber or a member of the Rolling Stones, but these dudes backstage take their jobs very seriously.

There's quite a party going on, and the longer it takes for me to find Nathan, the more I think about not wanting to be a downer on his big night. I decide not to tell him that I just saw myself—or that I *thought* I just saw myself in the middle of the crowd at his biggest show so far.

He sees me first and waves me over. He's propped up on the arm of a cool-looking loveseat and is surrounded by a couple of his bandmates and five hot girls who are wearing next to nothing. Everyone is laughing and having a great time celebrating the killer show that just ended, but Nathan steps away from the group to give me a huge hug. He's so genuinely happy to see me that it rattles me to my core. All hell has broken loose tonight already, so when he goes to pull away from me, I hold on, lean in, and kiss him. At first, he freezes up and tries to keep the kiss friendly, with closed lips. He quickly realizes, however, that I'm playing it tongue deep, and responds accordingly. Sufficiently out of breath, I stop to suck in some air and congratulate him on a great show.

He just closes his eyes and says thanks as he leans in to kiss me again, and it's my turn to respond to him. After a minute, I pull back one more time and tell him that I'm feeling really fucked-up and don't want to be alone tonight.

"Did you drink too much?" he whispers in between spit swaps.

"No, I hardly drank at all," I answer, "and I actually spilled more than I drank, I think. I just don't feel right. Everything is even further out of whack than it usually is and I'm kind of losing my mind."

"It's cool. I want to be with you too. I have to stay a while longer and pack up, but I can meet you at my place. You know where the key is if you want to get the bed warm."

"Yeah. That sounds perfect. I'll see you at your place in a little while. Thank you, Nathan," I say, and give him one last kiss before letting him get back to his friends and his fans.

15

My short time in the hospital came to an end, and I surprised myself by not wanting to leave. You would think, once given the chance, I would have high-tailed it out of there, but truthfully, it had been the only place where I had felt safe in ten years, and I was really worried about what foster care would be like.

Ms. Holmes had found an emergency placement for me until a more permanent foster home could be established. She came to get me when the doctors discharged me, and that's when it dawned on me that I didn't have clothes, or anything. That stupid lump moved its way up from my stomach, and into my throat again, but I fought the urge to break down and cry.

That's when I learned there was a special group of people who donated clothing to the hospital for people who were in my situation. I wasn't sure if I found this fact comforting or just sad. I was given white sweat socks, gray sweatpants, and a big navy-blue hoodie. The clothes were nicer than most of the stuff I had at home, anyway.

After we left the hospital, Ms. Holmes took me to Walmart for stuff she called incidentals, and then she drove me to a small apartment building where I would be staying for the night. We took our time as we walked through the tiny lobby and got in the elevator. It smelt like grilled cheese. I looked up at her and said, "Ms. Holmes, thanks for spending my birthday with me."

She looked at me with wide eyes and said, "Oh my goodness, Nora! Is today your birthday?! Somehow, I must have missed that bit of information, sweetheart."

"No, not officially, it's not my real birthday. I just feel like having a brand-new, scary start is like being a baby all over again. Like I'm reborn today, or something."

"Wow, Nora, that's a really great way to look at it. You are beyond your years; do you know that?"

"Yeah. I know."

The elevator doors made a short, weak ding as they opened on the fourth floor and we stepped into the narrow, dimly lit hallway. It had ugly wallpaper, and it still smelt like greasy, slightly burned grilled cheese. I was absolutely positive the smell was going to stick to my new clothes, but I tried not to let it bum me out too much.

We arrived at a door with a little green wreath hanging around the number 421, and Ms. Holmes knocked on it lightly. I couldn't tell, but it looked like there were either shamrocks or Christmas trees on the wreath, which may be why it was left up all year round.

A middle-aged woman in a bathrobe opened the door and told me right away that I could call her Nancy. She was obviously used to these encounters and was happy to dispense with the formalities of elaborate, lengthy introductions. We both knew I wouldn't be staying, but Nancy was very kind to me and made me feel welcome for the short time I was there. I only stayed at her place for one overnight, before Ms. Holmes picked me up to bring me to my 'permanent foster home.'

The new placement was with a couple named Rick and Katrina Parker. They had an okay house, since anything was better than where I lived with Omzi, except there were three other foster kids there besides me, and I hated living with so many people. I did what I could to get used to it, but I still spent the first couple nights at the Parkers' hiding upstairs while everyone else either played, ate meals, or watched TV.

I stayed with the Parkers for about a year, and they ended up being the very first of the six 'permanent' foster families that I had. Out of all the foster homes I lived in, the time I spent with the Parkers stands out the most in my mind. I have the sharpest memories of them, not just because they were my first placement, but also because Mr. Parker took great joy in telling me, before my case worker could tell me about it, that Omzi had been killed in her cell by another inmate in the state women's facility she had been sentenced to. I will never forget that day, or his face while he broke the news, in between long slugs of beer and an occasional belch. The news was made even worse by his mean-spirited smile, the stink of alcohol on his breath, and his unwanted touch.

After that day, I made it a habit to run away, which is why I kept getting moved from home to home. I was already an explosive kid with weird quirks and tendencies, so the fact that I often went AWOL just made things harder on my case worker when it was time to find a new placement.

This time in my life seemed to fly by so fast I can barely remember which bits actually happened to me, and which were scenarios taken from cliché movies and *Law and Order* episodes. My memories of all the different homes, family members, and experiences have blurred into one big brown, heavily smeared finger painting like the ones that bummed me out in kindergarten. Of course, I know there were different colors in the goopy mix, but I can no longer see them individually—each new placement came with the same exact shit, just different toilets. It was exhausting living like a classroom's paper doll who is taken out and played with by a new set of people over and over again. Sometimes the new people would change my outfit, or make up different names and situations, but then they'd stick me right back into the same old theatre that never, ever changed.

Over the years it got increasingly difficult, because I was getting older and had more and more issues to deal with. When I was sixteen, and in my last foster home, I snuck out one night and went to a nearby convenience store. I wandered the aisles for a while, before buying a frozen cherry slushy drink. While I was at the counter, a man came in and got behind me in line. He must have been a regular in the store, because he told the guy behind the counter to grab his cigarettes and he'd be right back to pay for them after he took a piss. I stepped out of the store, chugging my slushy, and the only car in the lot stood before me with its engine purring seductive-ly—simply beckoning me to steal it. I knew it had to belong to the guy in the pisser, and it may have been a bad case of brain freeze that made me do it, but I jumped in that car and took off.

It was the most exhilarating thing I have ever felt in my whole life. I had never really learned how to drive, officially, but I knew how to steer and work the pedals, so I figured it couldn't be too tough to figure out the rest. I tore out of the parking lot and sped down the street with no money, no plan, and absolutely no destination. I screamed with delight as I cranked down the window, cranked up the radio, and turned, probably too sharply, onto the entry to the highway.

My incredibly awesome adventure ended almost as soon as it started. I was pulled over by the cops not even ten miles from the store.

After several appearances in court, I was placed in a Residential Treatment Center. I didn't know it at the time—and in the beginning I was constantly being restrained by staff, as well as refusing group, meals, and therapy sessions—but being sent to RTC was probably the best thing that ever could have happened to me. Without it, I don't know that I would have made it on my own. They identified medications I need-ed, but more importantly, I learned actual coping strategies I could use that had nothing to do with meds. I started running in their gym, and the staff encouraged me to take art therapy as well. I hated to admit it at the time, but they provided me with tools to help me pursue my goals and lead as fulfilling and happy a life as possible. I had some great counselors and therapists there, and the other girls on my wing taught me a lot. Some of them taught me what I didn't want to be, and about drugs that I didn't want to get hooked on, while others showed me how to be a friend.

I'd never had friends before—and certainly not ones who truly understood the shit I had been through. Even if we didn't know each other's stories, which most of us shared, we knew damn well that each of us had one. Being in RTC was the first time I could see myself in other people, and actually let others see bits of me as well.

I kind of didn't have a choice, when it came to letting people see me, since we were forced to do everything together. We walked in straight lines through dingy hallways to all the things we did in groups on a daily basis. We got up, went to the bathroom for showers, attended our school classes, ate meals, did group therapy, exercised, and spent our free time... together. It was basically impossible to be in there and not develop a much closer bond with one particular girl than all the rest. Sometimes girls paired off as best friends, lovers, or both.

For Darcy and me, at that time, it was like we were the same person. Everyone called us sisters, but it went beyond that. It's hard to explain to anyone who hasn't lived in residential treatment, but when you're on the inside, you feel like it's you against the outside world and nobody gives a shit about you. You're basically living like you're in prison and made to feel like everything that has been done *to* you or stripped *from* you is because of something *you* did—you don't get put in a place like that because you were a 'good' kid.

I already felt very isolated and alone but being in there would have been the nail in my coffin if it weren't for Darcy. She made me feel worthwhile...like maybe I was a good person, and that I could show my true colors once in a while. Sometimes I felt like I learned more about overcoming my trauma from her than I did in group sessions.

One night at dinner I told her how scared I was that my life would never get any better, and I would always be a horrible mess of a person. She actually made me look at her, right into her eyes. I not only let her look at me, but I also let her *see* me. I had never let anyone do that before. In turn, she tried to help me see that my trauma and my wounds didn't make up who I was as a person. She said my 'mess' would someday turn into a message of courage, hope, and purpose. I just needed to wait and see.

We helped each other get through a lot in RTC and promised to always stay close no matter what, but one night, after we'd watched a movie, Darcy ran. At first, I was heartbroken and also enraged. I wanted to believe she was full of shit like everyone else, and I beat myself up for being stupid enough to think she ever actually cared about or understood me. She never returned, but once the anger passed and the smoke cleared, I saw that she'd meant everything she said, and that we were exactly what we needed to be for each other at that time in our lives. She wasn't full of horseshit; she was full of healing—for me, anyway. I don't think she should have run, but Darcy always felt that living in RTC wasn't living at all, and when she made up her mind about something, there was absolutely no changing it or holding her back.

It took a couple months for me to get back to some semblance of normal after she left, and I often drew upon thoughts of Darcy and our bond to keep me strong through the rest of my time in the program. It was really tough to sit in my own shit and attempt to heal from it (which is why I forgave Darcy for running) because it forced me to go back to the ugly places and see that my identity, and the things I had experienced, were not one and the same.

When you have an open wound, you put a bandage on it and trust that over time it will heal itself. When it comes to healing mentally and emotionally, it isn't that easy unless you have the right tools and resources, which is why, other than my friendship with Darcy, the best part about RTC was that I was able to take advantage of their academic programs in conjunction with my therapy. While I was there, I got my GED and even started taking some CPR and paramedic courses as well.

One night, we were back on our wing, hanging out before dinner, and the girls started talking about what they were going to do on the outs.

One at a time they chimed in:

"I'm gonna get high."

"I can't wait to see my mom and my dog."

"I can't wait to get fucked."

"I wanna get fucked and get fucked up."

"I just want some decent fucking food and a shower that doesn't run out of hot water."

"I want to see my daughter again."

"I can't wait to see my family."

"More than anything, I just want to be adopted."

Everyone had something to say, while I sat in confident, satisfied silence. When they realized I hadn't shared anything, they prodded me to spill it.

"Nora! What are you going to do when you get out of here?"

I answered them, "I'm going to age out of the system and become a firefighter."

The thunderous roar of laughter was deafening, but it didn't bother me in the least. I had the tools and I planned to use them.

16

The smell of gas and vodka mixed with the cold air permeates my car and it makes me want to puke—but that's the least of my worries. At least if I barfed, I would probably know it was really happening. Shit, at this point, I'm not even sure I could tell if a colonoscopy or a heart attack was real. I've certainly never been the damsel in distress kind of girl, but I'm grateful that I have Nathan's friendship to help me rest and regain some sense of calm. It will be nice to ease the heavy burden of my own brain's activity by letting him take a little of the weight for just one night.

Since Nathan is still at the show with his car, the driveway is empty, and I'm able to pull right in. He's left the front hallway light on for me, like he always does, but tonight it has an extra warm and fuzzy effect on me, which makes me feel suddenly even more idiotic than I did before. My hands are cold, so I fumble a little bit with the lock, before pushing the heavy old door open with my shoulder.

I barely set foot inside when I am face-to-face with the most ruthless and brutally savage thing that I have ever seen in my entire pathetic life. The viscous pain devastates me and steals my breath. It feels as though I have been punched directly in the stomach by the Incredible Hulk, causing me to fall to my knees.

I cover my eyes with both hands and wail for what could be a minute, or maybe an hour. The existence of time, space, and reality is gone, and I feel, as I kneel before a plate on the floor with a knife and fork placed neatly on each side, like I have left my body and I'm looking at myself from above. On the plate, in a torn-up little pile, is my Invictus poem, along with a white, folded place card that reads:

It would SERVE you well to remember: In order to be powerful, you can't be seen.

Above the plate hangs an all-too-familiar noose, wrapped horrifically around the broken little neck of Chaos.

Overcome with devastation, I try to stand up several times before I can get my legs to cooperate and hold my own weight. My heart has already been ripped out, so you would think I would be much lighter, but that isn't the case.

I get to my feet and desperately feel around the top of Nathan's door for his key. Tears burn my eyes as I fall inside his apartment and grab a blanket from his couch. I then stumble into his kitchen to get the largest knife I can find. The apartment is dark, but I know my way around it like it is my own, and I would rather not see anything at all right now, if given the choice.

I stand still as a statue for a brief moment, tilting the knife so that the moonlight glints off its edges, and for a split second I consider using it on myself. I shake the thought away and remind myself that I have not come this far to only come this far. I'm a weary warrior, but I will keep moving forward.

It takes every bit of courage, strength, and resolve I have in me to leave Nathan's apartment and climb the stairs so I can cut Chaos down from the banister and wrap her gently in the blanket. I don't recognize my own body, or any of its functions, as I make my way back downstairs and leave the knife on the floor next to the plate of unpalatable poetry. I bring Chaos back into Nathan's apartment and close the door on the ugliness in the hallway before placing her lovingly on the couch.

At this time, and without Nathan here to help me, I can't bear to think about doing anything else with her. My grief and anxiety have completely overcome every ounce of my being, and the only thing I can physically manage to do is crawl to the nearest dark corner and attempt to bury my face between the walls.

I have no idea how long I am there, pressing my body as far into the miniscule space between the walls as I possibly can, as if I'm trying to crawl into a nonexistent hole. Speaking of which, where the fuck are my black holes when I need them most?

Just then, I feel someone grab my left shoulder from behind. I am sobbing so uncontrollably; I don't even turn to see who or what is touching me. I hope it is an axe murder, or whoever just killed Chaos, returning to the scene to finish me off and put me out of my fucking misery.

I feel like a lifeless pile of shriveled-up beef jerky in drag.

I scream straight into the crease in the wall as if it were a megaphone in front of my lips instead of chipped-up Alabaster paint by Sherwin-Williams.

"You've already done the worst you can possibly do to me, whoever you are! And shit, you've got some *colossal fucking shoes* to fill if you came here to hurt me! You have no idea!"

The hand on my shoulder stays put, and it actually starts to feel more like I'm being hugged than grabbed.

"Nora, *what's wrong*?! Did something happen to you? It's Nathan! Please tell me *what's going on*!?"

The sound of Nathan's voice helps to slow down the NASCAR pace of my breathing. The lead foot of pain and anguish lighten up on the accelerator of my respiratory system, but my shoulders creep even higher up toward my ears. I'm more rigid than roadkill and can't seem to bring myself to turn around. It seems rigor mortis has set in.

I want to answer him, but no words come out, only uncontrollable sobs.

"Nora, you're scaring the shit out of me. What *happened*?"

The intense amount of heat being created by my distressed body is causing sweat, tears, snot—and whatever other bodily fluids that have decided to join the party—to mingle into one big, ugly, wet mess. I want to shrug my clothes off because they are sticking to my skin while whoever is behind me—presumably Nathan—is using his arms like the Jaws of Life to extricate me from the corner that I've tightly wedged myself into. When he finally gets me out and turns me around to face him, I wished to God that my red-rimmed, imploring eyes could do the talking for me.

"Why the fuck is there a huge knife out in the hallway? It's in the middle of the floor and I fucking stepped on it! If I wasn't wearing these boots, I could have really hurt myself."

At the mention of the knife, I squeeze my eyes shut as tight as I can and yell, "Chaos!"

"What about Chaos? Did someone break in? Did she get out?"

An irrational, momentary wave of calm sweeps through my body. I fill my lungs with air, close my eyes, and after a long exhalation, tell him to look on the couch.

"Okay, are you going to be alright here? I'm letting go of you," he says, like I am a fragile, dying animal myself, which I suppose I am.

He backs up slowly to traverse the three or four feet to the couch, most likely because he is afraid to turn his back on the crazy banshee on his floor—but returns in a heartbeat holding the blanket up above his head with one long, outstretched arm.

"It's my old blanket. What about it? What does this have to do with Chaos and the knife?"

The way he shakes the blanket at me makes everything feel worse, and even more confusing, like roaring waves inside my head. I become an even deeper, more pathetic puddle on the hardwood floor, looking up at him in shock and horror like he is Michael Jackson dangling his baby over a hotel balcony. Michael Jackson had his Blanket in total chaos, while the blanket I have is completely without Chaos, unless you count the immense amounts being created in my mind and soul. I look at the empty blanket and my hand instinctively darts to my mouth as I shake my head back and forth in tiny, fast movements.

"No, no, no, no, no! Didn't you see the rope and the plate and the ripped-up poem in the hallway? I got home and Chaos was *dead*, Nathan! She was hanging from the banister! I don't know who, but someone is out to hurt me, they've been fucking with me, and they *killed* her! Please tell me you had nothing to do with it!"

"What?! What are you even saying? Stay right here; I'll be right back. Don't move!"

I do what I'm told—as if I had the ability to get up and go anywhere—and he bolts out of the door and into the hallway. I can hear the distinct click of a light switch followed by the loud thudding of heavy boots on the wooden stairs as he bounds up, two at a time, to my apartment. When he returns, in what seems like no time at all, I become filled with a sickening and heavy combination of joy and dismay, because in his arms, Nathan holds my Chaos...alive and well, and she is her happy, purring self.

I finally understand what those goofy scenes in movies are meant to convey when a kid is missing in a shopping mall. When the kid turns up again, the teary-eyed mom is simply beside herself with happiness mixed with streaks of anger at the child for scaring the bejesus out of her in the first place, and for forcing the poignant reminder on her that bad things could indeed happen to her child.

The joy I feel stems from knowing that Chaos is okay after all. The dread comes from the realization that I am not well. I clearly have had some sort of episode where I hallucinated the murder of my own beloved pet. I am so confused and defeated; I don't know how to react.

Nathan is trying his best to act like he is at least somewhat calm, and I can feel the compassion and empathy emanating from him. He gently hands Chaos to me and I take her in my arms. Holding her and pressing my face into her head makes me choke up a little and I begin to shiver uncontrollably. The snot from my nose mats her fur and creates tiny spikes that look like mini mohawks on the top of her head, but she just purrs loudly and nuzzles into my neck.

"She's fine, Nora. It's all going to be okay. I'm not sure what we should do. Maybe I should take you to the emergency room. You might be in shock or something."

I feel like a zombie as he helps me stand up and begins to guide me gently toward the door.

"Let's leave Chaos here. Wrap the blanket around you and we'll get you in my car."

I don't remember the walk from inside his apartment to the car, but somehow, I make it down the driveway, and I'm in the passenger seat of Nathan's car. He tucks the blanket in around me, shuts the door, and runs around the back of the car to the driver's side. Before his ass even hits the seat, I begin hyperventilating and sobbing again.

There is a long, rectangular shaped Taco Bell wrapper in the center console, and I realize that Nathan hasn't been fucking with me. How could I mistake an old burrito wrapper for my favorite scarf? I am overcome with the realization that the only one fucking with me is me.

"I'm not going to the hospital!" I yell as I jump out of the car.

"Nora! Stop! You need some help. Should I call Ronnie?"

"No!!"

"Well, we need to call someone, right?"

"Call Ruby or Darcy."

"Who the hell are they?"

"I don't even know what I'm saying anymore. I'm going inside."

He closes the car door softly, but I know he's scared and frustrated. I am too. We go back into his apartment and I scoop up my baby. Nathan comes in right behind me, exhales loudly, and runs his hand through his hair.

We both take a seat on the couch and just stare at each other.

"Nora, you have to tell me what the hell is going on. This is so messed up. I'm worried about you; even more than usual, dude."

"I know," is all I can manage to say.

I have never been able to fully trust anyone, and right now I can't even trust myself, but in this moment, I become all too aware of the undisputable need to put my complete trust in Nathan. I stuff all my doubts and fears into my brain's garbage disposal, turn it on, and completely succumb to that need.

For the next few hours, we sit on his old, brown couch and I unravel, much like the seams around each cushion. I tell him that he needs to call Dr. Sharee for me, if he doesn't mind, because I clearly haven't been doing as well as we all seemed to think. Then I tell him—everything. We talk, and even manage to laugh a little, until warm sun rays filter through the window, strongly piercing the space between us, and rudely interrupting the conversation.

17
MOVING ON

It feels like forever since I last stepped into Tarts & Vicars, or had spent any quality time with Ronnie, and I will miss her more than she could ever know—so much has been uncovered and discovered in such a short period of time, that, for me, it feels like an entire lifetime ago. This will be the last time I get to see her, and we can sit face-to-face and catch up on everything, before I move next week.

While I wait for my turmeric latte (and the green tea latte I order for Ronnie), I chat with the new barista, who introduces himself as Edwin. He's got amazing tattoos, long dreads, and a huge, toothy smile that could light up Times Square.

I ask him how long he's been working here, and he tells me it's been about a month or so and that he kind of took over for a girl who went to NYC to audition for a reality show in Fiji—and got it.

"Wow! That's incredible," I say. "Good for her!" And I mean it.

"Who needs Fiji when it's so nice right here, yeah?" he says in a way that could even cheer up that donkey named Eeyore from the *Winnie-the-Pooh* books.

He reaches over and hands me both drinks, as I respond, "You got that right. It's a beautiful day today. Have a good one."

"You too, mon chéri," he quips, and I decide he's going to do well here.

I'm scanning the place for a good, secluded spot for us to sit, when the door flies open and Ronnie rushes in with the wind.

"Shit, am I late?"

"No," I laugh. "You're just in time. Here, I got this for you."

"You're a rock star, Nora! She takes the hot drink from me and we make our way over to a table in the back that is almost completely surrounded by several philodendron and fiddle leaf fig floor plants. We take our seats directly across from each other and settle into the bistro-styled two top table. Maybe it's the tranquil setting, or the bright sun, but I feel at peace with myself and with Ronnie. She already knows just about everything that went down but being able to talk about it with her today brings me a sense of calm instead of anxiety, which wouldn't have been the case only a short time ago. I realize Ronnie isn't just someone. She's my best friend—but I allow myself to recognize the fact that no matter *who* it is, I have made some truly significant progress.

She takes a sip from the painted, ceramic cup and says, "Yum! I'm so glad we're able to do this. Are you sure you have time? Once we get going, we might not stop."

"Yeah, I'm good. I'm making a quick stop to say goodbye to Dr. Sharee after this, but I have a couple hours before our appointment. Are you good on time?"

"Yep! I'm working out later, but I'm good. I just can't believe you're actually doing it! You're moving! Shit, we have so much to cover, I feel like our conversation is going to be like my laptop when I have too many tabs open."

"I know, it's pretty crazy, right?!"

"What's *really* crazy is how much I'm gonna miss you. And it's certainly not going to be the same without you at work. I can't believe how emotional the guys were at your goodbye party."

"It was nice. Who knew they even cared?" I say with a laugh. "It blew me away when Mike told me everyone got together and decided that I could take Roger with me if I wanted to. I wasn't expecting that at all, and it meant a lot to me. Just the offer spoke volumes, ya know?"

"That was all Mike's idea. We all love Roger to death, and will take good care of him, but if you wanted to bring him with you, it just seemed like the right thing to offer because of how close you two are. I'm actually kind of surprised you declined."

"Believe me, it was a really tough call. I wanted to say yes because I love him so much, but that would have been a selfish move on my part, I think."

"Why?"

"Because he belongs to the whole house. He's part of the family. If I took him, everyone but me would have suffered in the end—especially Chaos. She's a sweetheart, but I don't think she would be crazy about the idea of Roger as a travelling companion and new member of the family." Suddenly I get the impression Ronnie isn't giving me her full attention. "Dude, are you drifting off? You ask me a question and then start looking all over the room. Rude!"

"Hilarious," she says while we both lean back in our chairs and laugh. "Girl, I was admiring all the awesome paintings in this place with the cute little SOLD stickers attached to them."

"Stop it, you goof," I say sheepishly.

"Don't act all modest on me now. I told you a million times how talented you are. I guess it takes actually making money from the art in your apartment for you to finally believe me."

"If I haven't said thank you enough times for talking me into asking the owners to display and sell my art, please know how much I appreciate it. The money is going to help make the move a lot easier, that's for sure, and the confidence boost has inspired me to sell my work when I get out there. Oh my gosh, speaking of extra money, are you happy with the extra hours at the Juice Box? How is that all working out?"

"That depends how you look at it."

"What do you mean?"

"Well, the hours and extra cash are great, but..."

"But what? There's never a but with you—unless it's attached to a hot woman."

"Exactly! I'm moving in with Sophie."

"Ahhh! You *are*?! What happened to not shitting where you eat? And she's the bar manager too, so she's the big boss lady."

"We'll see how it works out, I guess. You never know unless you try, right?"

"Well, at least it's not Chatty Cathy."

"Very funny! What about you and Nathan? Is he taking your move okay? Shit, what about your lease? Oh, and did you look into that art therapy program out there? Holy crap, there I go opening too many tabs at once."

"Speaking of tabs, we're going to need another round of lattes if I'm going to cover all that before I go see Dr. Sharee."

"Let me get them. I don't want you going out to California and telling your new friends I never gave you anything."

"You gave me a lot, dude, and I'm not going to California after all. I thought it would be the perfect place because, hell, everyone goes there to soak up the sun and to be seen, right? But Dr. Sharee has a really good referral for a therapist who is the perfect fit for me in Taos, New Mexico, and I'm looking into the possibility of working at an animal shelter or maybe the Ghost Ranch in Abiquiu. I just need to be surrounded by what makes me happy, working in less stressful conditions, and seeing a good therapist. New Mexico has all that and more, I think."

"What the hell is the Ghost Ranch?"

"It's kind of like my idea of heaven on Earth, really. It figures I thought I wanted to go to California, only to have Dr. Sharee help guide me and realize what I truly want and need. Anyway, it's where Georgia O'Keeffe lived and had a studio. You've probably seen it many times without realizing, because it was actually the subject of many of her paintings. It's surrounded by these magnificent multilayered cliffs and red hills, and it has both a retreat and an education center. You and Sophie can stay there when you come to visit me."

I make sure to accompany the last sentence with an ultra-exaggerated double wink and nod.

"Fuck you!" she says kiddingly as she stands, grabs our mugs, turns on her heel, and heads for the counter to get our second round of coffee drinks, though not before adding, "Quit playing! When I get back, we still need to cover all the serious stuff. And by the way, I tend to favor O'Keefe's floral paintings, but I'm sure her landscape stuff is great too."

I watch her as she places our order and I think about how all the things in my life, both good and bad, have led me to this exact moment in time. To be honest, if I died right now, I would die happily, with a heart full of love, a head full of Frida Kahlo and Georgia O'Keefe, and a bladder full of turmeric latte.

Ronnie rushes back to the table like she's going to miss out on something—the commercials are over and it's back to our regularly scheduled programming.

"Slow your roll, goofy! You're gonna spill!" I say with a big smile as she plops my steamy mug of frothy goodness in front of me.

"Umm, nope, girl, you're the one that's gonna spill. Let's hear it. What is up with you and your little boy toy? Is he heartbroken that you're moving? Did he write a song about it? Are you going to lose a ton of money for breaking your lease?"

"Dude, I hope you got decaf this time. I think you could have been one of those soap opera voiceover people back in the day that listed all the cliffhanger questions at the end of the show so people would tune in again the following week. You missed your calling: 'Will Derrick escape from the alligator?' 'Is the alligator Rachel's secret Bolivian love child?' 'Tune in next week to find out! Same bat channel, same bat time'."

"What are you, eighty years old? You watch too much old crap on YouTube."

"You might be right about that, but would an eighty-year-old spend four extremely hot days in bed with Nathan saying goodbye?"

"I hope not...for Nathan's sake. No, seriously, that sounds like a great way to say goodbye. I'm glad he was there for you when you needed him most and that you let him in."

"I'm glad too. Oh, and I'm glad I'm not going to be fucked for breaking my lease because the drummer from Undressed

Enema is taking it over for me. Mr. and Mrs. Stavropoulos were super cool about it. I'm pretty sure they were more upset about the fact that Nathan and I weren't moving away together to live happily ever after."

"Your story isn't done yet, my friend, and crazier things have happened, as we both know."

"No shit, dude. Speaking of which, Undressed Enema has a kickass agent now, who booked them for a bunch of summer music festivals out West, so Nathan and I will be seeing each other again really soon."

"Damn, that's what's up, girl! I have an idea! Let's make it a goal to run a marathon out there this summer, go see him play at a festival, and you can show me around the Ghost Ranch."

"A marathon? Are we ready for all that?"

"Nora! You of all people have taught me that we can use all the tough shit we've been through in our lives to overcome any obstacle...even 26.2 miles in the freakin' desert. Plus, we've put in the miles. We've got this."

I look at the bottom of my empty cup, wondering again how time flies by so quickly.

"It's a plan, Stan."

We get up to leave, but before she can get too far, I wrap my arms around her and squeeze her as I say, "Thanks for being real."

She squeezes back and said, "Bitch, I'm as real as it gets."

* * *

I step inside the familiar waiting room of Dr. Sharee's office, and her door is wide open, so I can see her sitting behind her desk. The second I walk in, she pops up and comes to greet me with a hug. She's barefoot, of course, and is wearing black leggings with a long, sleeveless Led Zeppelin T-shirt, and I am instantly reminded, once again, of all the many reasons I love this woman. As we pull away from each other, she tells me it's good to see me. I don't even cringe this time and instead, I answer, "It's good to be seen."

We take our seats, like we would in a regular therapy appointment, but we both know that's not what this will be. She's letting me say my goodbyes in a way that will benefit me the most, and I'm grateful for her immense amounts of care and compassion. If I were to analyze myself, this session will probably serve as a summation of sorts, and maybe even the closure I never felt I was able to attain with my long-ago art teacher, Miss Vega.

I look out the window for a second and turn my attention back to her and say, "I feel a little awkward and nervous for some dumb reason, so I'm going to dive right into it. I want to thank you for, well, absolutely everything. It's truly because of you and all of our sessions that I get to be reborn. It's kind of like you have given me a new birthday. I have said these exact words to only two people on Earth: you and the social worker who helped me on that first night I ran from Omzi. I said it to her then, and I'm saying it to you now because I feel like you have both quite literally saved me with new beginnings."

"Thank you, Nora. That means a lot to me. Everything you have been through—and that you're still processing and healing from—is a heavy burden and a lot of pressure to endure." She shifts in her chair. "I feel honored that you trusted me enough to help you sort through your repressed memories. I'm not saying I'm glad you were retraumatized by the car crash or saving a baby's life in such a stressful way, but the incident certainly expedited your journey to discovering why your black holes were becoming so much more prevalent and extreme. Truthfully, because of that, it may have saved you many years of destructive and, to you, inexplicable self-sabotaging behaviors."

"I've basically centered my entire identity and existence around trying to hide who I am. What if I never completely heal or overcome my past?"

"Nora, I'm not sure anyone is ever *completely,* one hundred percent healed. I look at it like we're all at different levels of handling our shit in the healthiest ways we possibly can. What speaks volumes to me is the mere fact that you're making the conscious choice to learn and grow, which ultimately lends to a continuous state or process of healing."

"Well, I'm not going to lie, I'm not exactly psyched about the dissociative disorder diagnosis, but I'm both ecstatic and grateful that you helped me understand I'm not crazy, but instead, that my brain found Ruby and Darcy to be necessary companions during the times I was locked up in either the playroom or RTC."

"People with dissociative disorders often escape reality in involuntary and unhealthy ways that cause major problems in their everyday life, but just like bipolar disorder, it's treatable and certainly not anything that will hold you back from living a great life. You have chosen to fight for what's good and to overcome obstacles that most people couldn't ever imagine. I don't think you need to get caught up in any of the labels or stigma that may or may not be attached with a diagnosis, but instead, embrace it and keep fighting the good fight."

She stops short, and I can see she's fighting back tears by pressing her lips together as she slowly nods her head twice in my direction. This is my opportunity to get it all out and I take it. I'm in the need to purge and she's my willing receptacle.

"It may have been a necessary evil, and if I had to get my repressed memories kicked up by that horrendous car accident, I'm just glad that Lilith and her mom are okay, and that it was what ended up sending me on a journey of healing. You are my flesh and blood version of Ruby and Darcy because you are what has kept my head above water. You have allowed me the ability to cope. Because of you, I can not only face the reality that they were not real, but I can also actually point to the main reasons I needed them in the first place. My mother had been literally holding my hands over the stove for so long—an inch away from the glowing red coils so that I didn't have scars—that the hair on my hands and arms never grew back. It was the perfect way to torture me without creating any major red flags, so to speak. She used to wear oven mitts so she wouldn't burn herself."

I stop to catch my breath and look to her for a nonverbal cue that will hopefully tell me she is okay with having to hear all of this again. Of course, we have covered it in previous sessions, but as I study the look she conveys on her beautiful face, I am able to determine she agrees it all needs to be said again, and I am overcome with an immense sense of relief and gratitude. Without saying it aloud, she confirms the need to draw it out of the shadows one last time, into the light where it can no longer hide and destroy like a cancer.

Her shoulders relax about an inch, and she considers me with a look that I take to be reserved for actual mothers and daughters.

And so, I continue.

"That day she came home cranked up on meth. I knew something really bad was going to happen if she came in and caught my grandma and I baking a cake together. Omzi had been out all day getting high, she didn't want me to wear clothes in the house, or to feel like we did something as horrible as baking a cake behind her back, so it really set her off when she got home and saw me wearing a long-sleeved shirt and sweatpants...not to mention how happy I was.

"I saw her go for the oven mitts and turn on the stove. She was trying to recite one of her catch phrases at me, but she was so jacked up, it just came out as gibberish. Usually when she held my hand above the burner it only *felt* like my skin was on fire. This time, the excruciating pain was amplified by intense terror as I watched my sleeve catch fire and begin to burn like an out of control roasted marshmallow at a campfire.

"Omzi let go of my arm and jumped back like I had suddenly transformed into a three-headed cobra. I took off running and frantically flew down the stairs to the basement, where I flung myself into the water bucket that I usually hated to be near. Cake, fire, water, fear, and sadness competed to see who could drown me first. I suffered no real damage to my skin, but the emotional scars were far deeper and uglier than any she had given me before."

In my effort to fight back some big fat tears, I decide to wrap things up quickly.

"I've lived my entire life feeling anxious and worried about being seen, and I guess I never thought about it before, but we're all chameleons in our own ways. We all have our shit, we just have to learn how to face, embrace, understand, and deal with it. I guess now, it's time for me to be a snake by shedding all this ugliness and moving on. And I just couldn't have possibly done any of it without you."

She regards me with such authentic kindness and respect it almost hurts. She says, "It sounds like you finally feel a true sense of freedom and control, and although I appreciate and am truly grateful that you attribute it to me, it's all because of you, Nora, your strength and your desire to want to be the amazing person you are. It doesn't matter that you have a mental illness or that you take medication for that illness. None of that changes the fact that you're amazing. If anything, it's an incredible example of how amazing people take care of their mind, body, and soul so they can go out into the world and slay—no matter what."

"Thank you for saying that. Being on meds...real meds... has always bothered me, but I suppose it bothers me much more to see things that aren't really there." I say this with a laugh as I swipe a rogue tear from my cheekbone.

She stands up and walks toward the window as she says, "I'm positive that you are going to love the referral I gave you in Taos. She's the absolute best, and you will be in great hands out there, but I really hope you don't forget about me and that you stay in touch. To be sure that happens, I have a present for you."

"What? A present? No, you don't need to give me anything...I will never forget you and will always stay in touch! And speaking of presents, guess what? Well, this isn't a present exactly, but I threw away my bag of tricks! I also gifted my self-portrait to Nathan. It turned out so perfectly, it would have actually hurt my heart if I had kept it for myself. I'm not great at goodbyes, or having things come to an end, so if he has it, I'll always be with him."

"Wait, back it up. No more bag of tricks? Wow, that's great!" she says as she beams brighter than the sun spilling in from the window.

"I don't think I need it anymore, so I want to see how I do without it."

"You never really did, hon, but I'm glad you figured it out in your own time. Good for you. Now tell me about what Nathan thought of your self-portrait! I'm thrilled that you finally finished it, and that it has found its perfect home."

"I worked on it for so long, and made so many failed attempts at expressing myself the way I wanted to, I can hardly believe I finally created something that not only makes a powerful statement of who I am, but is also a piece that I'm really happy with! I guess it's understandable that over the years, it felt like I could never get it right. I mean, how could I when I never had a clear vision of who I was? But I did it, and he made me blush with his response to it! When I gave it to him, he said it was the most beautiful botanical painting he'd ever seen. He really and truly thought it was simply a gorgeous and vibrant Frida-esque painting of mingling flowers, jungle plants, branches, and birds. I had to tell him to take a step or two back from it so he could take a closer look and see that all the leaves, brush, branches, and petals were actually created to depict a fairly accurate likeness to myself."

"A fairly accurate likeness? Nice try. I know it was Louvre-worthy. Who are you kidding?"

"Okay, let's be honest, I will never forget how good it felt to watch him as he studied the painting. I could actually *see*, little by little, as he began to discern leaves and petals as eyes, nose, and mouth and then, eventually, my entire face. He actually said out loud, 'Oh my God, this is your *self-portrait*! Nora, I can't believe I didn't see you in it right away, but now that I have, it's impossible *not* to see you—and it's absolutely breath-taking.' He also said he was blown away by how I captured my raw, natural beauty without being too in your face and obvious. 'Like a chameleon.' I hugged him and simply said, 'Thank you. That was kind of the point'."

Dr. Sharee says, "I'm pretty sure that story is the best going away present or thank you gift you could have ever given me. Now *I* get to give you *my* gift!"

She takes the beautifully framed Invictus poem from her bookshelf and holds it out to me. As a I take it from her, speechless with gratitude, she says, "You earned it, warrior. You are truly the captain of your soul."

* * *

New Mexico is called the Land of Enchantment, and now that I'm finally here after the crazy-long drive cross country, I can definitely understand why. I pull up to the Ghost Ranch because I want to see it before I go to Taos. I know it will be the perfect beginning point for our new journey.

I step out of the car and stretch, taking in a few deep breaths of the magical desert mountain air. I whip open the door to my backseat so Chaos can feel the air on her whiskers.

She peers out at me through the little openings in her cat carrier. I smile at her dopily until my attention turns to two hawks as they float over my head with wingspans that could rival my running strides. They drift in the wide open, never-ending sky like miniature hang gliders in slow motion. I tell myself that I've seen hawks before, but I'm simply enamored by their particular beauty and the fact that the sight of them has moved me to tears.

I am exactly where I need to be.

ACKNOWLEDGEMENTS

There are so many people I need to thank for their time, help, and support. Without all of your kindness and invaluable input, this book would have never come together the way it did. It's impossible to thank everyone, but let me start with my publisher, Usher Morgan of Library Tales Publishing, for giving my first work of fiction a shot, and for always being such a pleasure to work with.

Many thanks and much gratitude to 21-year veteran officer, Sergeant Michael Eder, for taking the time to go over police procedure with me, and for kindly giving me the input and ideas I needed to get the story rolling.

Many thanks to Nikki Schnupp for the amazing advice and constructive criticism I needed along the way! I appreciate your expertise in both writing and editing, and that you were kind enough to lend your time to this book, and for helping me put forth my best effort. You, as well as my friend, Jacqui Fleming, both gave me incredible advice, and told me more than once to step away from the writing for a bit, so I could come back to it later with fresh eyes. The rewrites I did later proved to bring out the best story, and I can't thank you both enough for making me realize I needed to get my head out of my ass and stop being lazy. It's worth it in the end to take the time needed to unfold the story that truly needs to be told. You have really inspired me in so many ways, Nikki! Thank you for that.

For the many words of support and encouragement when I became frustrated, thank you to my husband Frank and both my kids. Jake and Morgan – you are my heart!

Last, but certainly not least, huge amounts of gratitude go out to my editor, Gary Dalkin, for always being incredibly kind, talented, and professional. Your input was invaluable and so greatly appreciated.

CPSIA information can be obtained
at www.ICGtesting.com
Printed in the USA
FSHW021649100521
81268FS

9 781736 241837